英国文学经典选读

Selected Classical Readings of British Literature

主　编　蒙雪梅　张　扬
副主编　秦　怡　董艳焱
主　审　张　瑾　王　洋
编　者　金晓玲　王化玲　王　旸
　　　　王雪松　周　洁　徐卓睿

哈尔滨工业大学出版社
HARBIN INSTITUTE OF TECHNOLOGY PRESS

内容简介

《英国文学经典选读》是"史""选"结合的教材,各个部分按照英国文学史的时间顺序划时期,简明介绍了英国文学从古代到 20 世纪的历史文化背景、文学史特点,选择代表作家和经典作品。每章包括作家生平简介、作品介绍、注释、名词解释、思考题等。本书线索清晰,旨在为学生搭建英国文学框架,引导学生阅读经典原著,感受英国文学的人文精神和丰富的思想内涵,帮助学生开阔视野、丰富想象、体悟人性、品味人生。

本书适合我国高等院校学生作为通识课程教材。

图书在版编目(CIP)数据

英国文学经典选读:英文/蒙雪梅,张扬主编.—哈尔滨:哈尔滨工业大学出版社,2016.9(2019.1 重印)
ISBN 978-7-5603-6167-3

Ⅰ.①英… Ⅱ.①蒙… ②张… Ⅲ.①英语-语言读物 ②英国文学-作品综合集 Ⅳ.①H319.4:I

中国版本图书馆 CIP 数据核字(2016)第 191472 号

策划编辑	常 雨
责任编辑	李长波
出版发行	哈尔滨工业大学出版社
社　　址	哈尔滨市南岗区复华四道街 10 号 邮编 150006
传　　真	0451-86414749
网　　址	http://hitpress.hit.edu.cn
印　　刷	黑龙江艺德印刷有限责任公司
开　　本	787mm×960mm 1/16 印张 13 字数 230 千字
版　　次	2016 年 9 月第 1 版 2019 年 1 月第 2 次印刷
书　　号	ISBN 978-7-5603-6167-3
定　　价	28.00 元

(如因印装质量问题影响阅读,我社负责调换)

前　言

　　进入21世纪以来,我国高校大学英语改革迅速,而大学英语教材建设工作相对滞后,教学内容单一,不能满足学生对高质量英语教育的需求。教育部颁布的《大学英语课程教学要求》(2007)指出:大学英语课程不仅是一门语言基础知识课程,也是拓宽知识、了解世界文化的素质教育课程。不断深入的大学英语改革越加注重培养学生的实际应用能力与综合文化素养。一些有创造性的教材及课程也随之应运而生,"博雅"理念根植于古希腊的Liberal education,以期实现培广博之才,育雅正之人的目的。因此,设计大学英语课程时也应当充分考虑对学生文化素质的培养和国际文化知识的传授,以适应我国社会新世纪发展和国际交流的需要。

　　近年来,我国对英美文学的介绍和研究日益重视,为适应新世纪人才培养需要,哈工大在2012年开设了大学英语教改拓展课程"英美文学史与选读"。我国很多优秀的英美文学类教材的使用对象是英语专业学生,但不适合大学英语教改通识课程使用,我们自编了教材,这门课程和教材得到理工科大学生的肯定和欢迎。为优化课程体系我们更新教学内容,今年再次修订本套教材,本书为《英国文学经典选读》,这是一套适合我国高等院校大学非英语专业使用的通识课程教材。

　　《英国文学经典选读》内容包括英国文学七章,各章按照文学史的时间顺序划分时期,简明介绍各时期历史背景和文学史特点,精选了每个时期主要的作家及代表作品,突出人文教育的特点,传承西方社会正统主流文化。本书主要介绍作家在文学史上的地位、人生经历、创作经历、代表作品。在博雅教育理念下,我们着重选择经典作品,根据理工科学生的学科特点和复合型人才培养的特点,加入注释、思考题等,力求深入浅出,通俗易懂。

　　本拓展课程教材是一本集历史、文化、文本于一体的文学选读教材,引领大学英语教改方向,首次打破了长期以来只有精读与听力单一的传统大学英语教学模式，是大学英语教学有益的、必要的补充。我们希望在培养学生欣赏英美文学的同时，让他们领略英美文学的魅力，把握文化的精髓和人文精神的脉动，提高学生的英语认知水平和人文素养。

《英国文学经典选读》不仅仅是一本教材，而是结合了多种形式的独特授课方式的一个蓝本。

第一：《英国文学经典选读》是原哈工大大学英语教改新课型中自编教材，是针对非英语专业学生量身制作的第一本语言文学类教材，适合复合型人才培养方案。

第二：《英国文学经典选读》首次结合了独特的翻转课堂授课方式，如针对早期英国文学精品所选的《贝奥武夫》等作品，课前布置和组织学生观看根据同名小说改编的电影，然后展开相关的课堂讨论。

第三：《英国文学经典选读》首次针对诗歌选读部分采用录制视频的作业方式，课堂报告，学生展示自己创作和制作的诗歌视频作品。有配乐，有画面，有学生自己声情并茂的朗读，有学生的专业评论。

第四：《英国文学经典选读》针对文艺复兴时期的莎士比亚戏剧作品选读部分，策划推出了"哈工大首届莎士比亚戏剧表演大赛"。学生分组选剧本片段，背台词，借服装，准备道具，利用教室布置舞台，多媒体屏幕做舞台布景，配乐和英文字幕，表演十分精彩震撼。傍晚的校园里，正值丁香花盛开，暮色里花香袭人，教室里时光穿越，莎士比亚的世界海市蜃楼般地出现在眼前，流利的英语和投入的表演使《奥赛罗》组获一等奖，《哈姆雷特》获二等奖，《仲夏夜之梦》获三等奖。这是理工科学生奉献给哈工大的一次充满人文情怀的盛宴。

《英国文学经典选读》教材与教学设计是不可分割的一个完美的整体。它从酝酿到诞生凝聚了文学组教师们的心血和对学生无比赤诚的热爱，以及对教育事业的热情，像山谷里的野百合，在全国大学英语教改的春风里，轻柔地、静静地绽放，也有自己独特的春天。

特别感谢朱勤一老师给我们提供的大力帮助。

本书适合大学英语通识课程使用，书中不足之处恳请读者批评与指正，以便进一步修订与完善。

蒙雪梅　王化玲
2016 年 8 月

Contents

Chapter 1	**Early and Medieval English Literature**	....	1
Unit	Geoffrey Chaucer	....	5
	The Canterbury Tales	....	7
Chapter 2	**English Literature in the Renaissance**	....	12
Unit 1	Edmund Spenser	....	16
	The Faerie Queene	....	18
Unit 2	William Shakespeare	....	21
	Hamlet	....	22
	Sonnet 18	....	25
Chapter 3	**Literature of the English Revolution and Restoration**	....	27
Unit 1	John Milton	....	30
	Paradise Lost	....	32
Unit 2	John Bunyan	....	37
	The Pilgrim's Progress	....	39
Unit 3	John Donne	....	43
	A Valediction: Forbidding Mourning	....	44
Chapter 4	**18th-Century English Literature**	....	48
Unit 1	Daniel Defoe	....	52
	Robinson Crusoe	....	54
Unit 2	Jonathan Swift	....	63
	Gulliver's Travels	....	64
Unit 3	William Blake	....	72
	London	....	73
Unit 4	Robert Burns	....	75
	A Red, Red Rose	....	76
Chapter 5	**Romanticism in English Literature**	....	78
Unit 1	William Wordsworth	....	80

      I Wandered Lonely as a Cloud ·················· 81
  Unit 2 Samuel Taylor Coleridge ···························· 83
      The Rime of the Ancient Mariner ················ 84
  Unit 3 George Gordon Byron ······························· 89
      The Isles of Greece ································· 91
  Unit 4 John Keats ·· 98
      Ode to a Nightingale ······························· 100
  Unit 5 Percy Bysshe Shelley ································ 105
      Ode to the West Wind ······························ 106
  Unit 6 Jane Austen ··· 110
      Pride and Prejudice ·································· 112

Chapter 6 **19th-Century English Literature** ······················ 117
  Unit 1 Charles Dickens ······································· 119
      Great Expectations ··································· 120
  Unit 2 The Brontë Sisters ··································· 126
      Jane Eyre ··· 128
  Unit 3 Thomas Hardy ··· 142
      Tess of the D'Urbervilles ·························· 144

Chapter 7 **20th-Century English Literature** ······················ 154
  Unit 1 Joseph Conrad ··· 157
      Heart of Darkness ···································· 158
  Unit 2 William Butler Yeats ································ 161
      When You Are Old ·································· 162
      The Second Coming ································· 163
  Unit 3 James Joyce ··· 165
      Ulysses ·· 167
  Unit 4 Virginia Woolf ··· 175
      Mrs. Dalloway ··· 176
  Unit 5 David Herbert Lawrence ·························· 178
      Sons and Lovers ······································ 180
  Unit 6 Doris May Lessing ··································· 185
      A Woman on a Roof ································ 187

参考文献 ··· 200

Chapter 1

Early and Medieval English Literature

I. Historical Background

1. The Making of England

More than 7,000 years ago, when the Ice Age ended, melting ice flooded low-lying lands in continental Europe, creating the English Channel and the North Sea and turning Britain into an island. Around 3000BC, the first known settlers of Britain were the Iberians. More dramatic monuments were the henges, the most important of which was Stonehenge in Wiltshire.

1.1　The Native Celts 凯尔特人

The Celts may originally have come from eastern and central Europe (now called France, Belgium and southern Germany); they came to Britain in three main waves: Gaels, Britons and the Belgae. Celts, also called the Britons, are regarded as the natives of Great Britain. Celts began to move into Great Britain in about 700BC, and they are believed to be ancestors of the Highland Scots, the Irish and the Welsh people. Some of the Celtic words or sounds were later assimilated into the English language. Their languages, the Celtic languages, are the basis of Gaelic, Irish and Welsh.

1.2　Roman Britain

In 55BC, Julius Caesar sailed across the English Channel after he had conquered Gaul. In 43AD, the Romans occupied England by driving the native Celts into mountainous Scotland and Wales, and completely conquered the southern part of the island of Great Britain, including England and Wales. But they were never able to completely defeat or control what is now Scotland. For nearly 400 years, Britain was under Roman occupation. The Romans built many towns, roads, baths, temples and buildings. They made good use of Britain's natural resources. They also brought the new religion, Christianity, to Britain.

2. The Anglo-Saxon Period

In the mid-5th century, Jutes, Saxons, and Angles came to Britain. A Jutish chief became the King of Kent in 449. Then the Saxons established their kingdom in Essex, Sussex and Wessex from the end of the 5th century to the beginning of the 6th century. In the second half of the 6th century, the Angles, who also came from northern Germany and were to give their name to the English people, settled in East Anglia, Mercia and Northumbria. These seven principal kingdoms of Kent, Essex, Sussex, Wessex, East Anglia, Mercia and Northumbria have been given the name of Heptarchy. The early Anglo-Saxons converted to Christianity.

Viking and Danish Invasions

The Norwegians and the Danes, the invaders, attacked various parts of England from the end of the 8th century. They even managed to capture York, an important center of Christianity in 867. By the middle of the 9th century, the Vikings and the Danes were posing a threat to the Saxon kingdom of Wessex.

Alfred (849 – 899), a king of Wessex, defeated the Danes and reached a friendly agreement with them in 879. He founded a strong fleet and is known as "the father of the British navy". All this earns him the title "Alfred the Great".

3. The Anglo-Norman Period

3.1 The Norman Conquest

It was said that King Edward had promised the English throne to William, the Duke of Normandy but the Witan chose Harold. In 1066, William defeated Harold and killed him during the important battle of Hastings. William was crowned king of England, thus beginning the Norman Conquest of England. The Norman Conquest is perhaps the best-known event in English history. The feudal system was completely established in England. Norman-French culture, language, manners and architecture were introduced. The Church was brought into closer connection with Rome. The English is a mixture of nationalities of different origins. The ancestors of many English people were the ancient

Chapter 1 Early and Medieval English Literature

Angles and Saxons. Some English people are of the Norman-French origin.

3.2 The Hundred Years' War

The Hundred Years' War was a series of conflicts from 1337 to 1453 between the Kingdom of England and the Kingdom of France.

It was due to a dynastic disagreement to William the Conqueror, while remaining Duke of Normandy. As dukes of Normandy and other lands on the continent, the English kings owed homage to the King of France. The question of legal succession to the French crown was central to the war. Although primarily a dynastic conflict, the war gave impetus to ideas of French and English nationalism.

During the Hundred Years' War, Joan of Arc believed she could rescue the French people. She rallied the demoralized French troops, leading them in battle. Ultimately captured and imprisoned by the English, Joan was condemned as a heretic and a witch and stood trial before the Inquisition in 1431. She eventually became a martyr and was then burnt at the stake and became a national hero.

3.3 Wars of Roses

The Wars of the Roses in the 15th century were fought by the noble families of York and Lancaster between 1455 and 1485. They are called the Wars of the Roses because each family used a rose as its symbol—a red rose for York and a white rose for Lancaster. These wars were very bloody, full of battles, betrayals and murders. Finally the last Yorkist king, Richard III, was beaten by a Welsh noble, Henry Tudor in England who became King Henry VII, the first Tudor monarch. He made a Tudor rose— a red rose with a white rose in the middle. This came to symbolize the peace that had come after all the fighting. The House of Tudor subsequently ruled England and Wales for 117 years.

II. Literature Background

1. Anglo-Saxon Literature

Anglo-Saxon literature, that is, the Old English literature is almost exclusively a verse literature in oral form. It could be passed down by word of mouth from generation to generation. Its creators for the most part are unknown. It was only given a written form long after its composition.

Beowulf is the oldest poem in the English language, commonly cited as one of the most important works of Anglo-Saxon literature; and also the surviving heroic epic poem consisting of 3182 alliterative long lines. Alliteration is used for poetic effect, a repetition of the initial sounds of several words in a group. e. g. a. To his kin the kindest, keenest for praise; b. Sing a song of southern singer.

Beowulf, king of the Geats who live in Juteland, Denmark, comes to the help of Hrothgar, the king of the Danes, whose mead hall (Heorot) has been under attack by a monster known as Grendel. After Beowulf slays him, Grendel's mother attacks the hall and is also defeated. Beowulf goes home to Geatland in Sweden and later becomes king of the Geats. After a period of fifty years, Beowulf defeats a fire-spewing dragon, but Beowulf is severely wounded during the fight. He dies a heroic death. The poem ends with the funeral of the hero.

A lot of metaphors and understatements are used in the poem. For example, the sea is called "the whale-road" or "the swan road"; the soldiers are called "shield-men"; human-body is referred to as "the bone-house"; God is called "wonder-wielder"; monster is referred to as "soul-destroyer".

2. Medieval English Literature

Medieval literature covers about four century, which encompasses essentially all written works available in Europe and beyond during the Middle Ages. In the early part of the period (1066 up to the mid-14th century), there was not much about literature in English. The works of this time were composed of religious writings. In the second half (the 14th century), English literature started to flourish. Middle English literature deals with wider subjects and various styles, tones and genres.

2.1 The Romance

The most prevailing kind of literature in feudal England was the romance, which was a long composition, sometimes in verse, sometimes in prose, describing the life and adventures of a noble hero, often in the form of allegory. The knight was the central character of romances.

The romance of King Arthur (adventures of King Arthur and his Knights of the Round Table) is comparatively the most important for the history of English literature.

King Arthur is a legendary British leader of the late 5th and early 6th centuries, who led the defense of Britain against Saxon invaders in the early 6th century. Some Welsh and Briton tales and poems relating the story of Arthur date from earlier than this work. In these works, Arthur appears either as a great warrior defending Britain from human and supernatural enemies or as a magical figure of folklore, sometimes associated with the Welsh Otherworld, Annwn.

2.2 English Ballads

The most important department of English folk literature is the ballad. A ballad is a story told in song, usually in 4-line stanzas, with the second and fourth lines rhymed.

Popular folk literature occupies an important place in this period. The Middle English literature strongly reflects the principles of the medieval Christian doctrine, which are primarily concerned with the issue of personal salvation. An emphasis has also been placed on the humanity of Christ and the imagery of human passion. Love has largely superseded fear; and explorations into undiscovered regions of the heart offer fresh possibilities for introspection.

The most famous cycle of English ballads centers on the stories about a legendary outlaw called Robin Hood. In English history, Robin Hood is partly a real and partly a legendary figure. The ballads tell us that he lived during the reign of Richard Ⅰ. The dominant key in his character is his hatred for the cruel oppressors and his love for the poor and downtrodden. He was the leader of a band of outlaws, and they lived in the deep forest. They often attacked the rich, waged war against the bishops and archbishops, and helped the poor people. Therefore, Robin Hood and his followers were constantly hunted by the sheriffs.

Unit Geoffrey Chaucer (1340? – 1400)

Appreciation

When in April the sweet showers fall 春雨给大地带来了喜悦,
And pierce the drought of March to the root, and all 送走了土壤干裂的三月,
The veins are bathed in liquor of such power 沐浴着草木的丝丝经络,
As brings about the engendering of the flower 顿时百花盛开, 生机勃勃。

Geoffrey Chaucer is widely considered the greatest English poet of the medieval Ages. Chaucer rose in royal employment and became a knight of the shire for Kent. As a member of the king's household, Chaucer was sent on diplomatic errands throughout Europe. From all these activities, he gained the knowledge of society that made it possible to write *The Canterbury Tales*.

Although he wrote many works, which include *The Book of the Duchess*, *The House of Fame*, *The Legend of Good Women* and *Troilus and Criseyde*, and he is best remembered for his immortal *The Canterbury Tales*. Chaucer died in October 1400 and he was the first poet to have been buried in Poets' Corner of Westminster Abbey.

Chaucer is the first to use the rhymed couplet of iambic pentameter, which is to be called the heroic couplet. Iambic pentameter is the basic rhythmical pattern in English verse, with five feet in a line, usually an unaccented syllable followed by an accented syllable. Thus, he lays the foundation of the English tonic-syllabic verse.

He uses London dialect in his writings and he contributes to making it the foundation for modern English speech. Though drawing influence from French, Italian and Latin models, he is the first great poet who wrote in the English language. His production of so much excellent poetry was an important factor in establishing English as the literary language of the country. The spoken English of the time consisted of several dialects, and Chaucer did much in making the dialect of London the standard for the moden English speech. Chaucer is considered the source of the English vernacular tradition and "the father of modern English literature".

Brief Introduction

The Canterbury Tales is a collection of stories written in Middle English by Geoffrey Chaucer between 1387 and 1400. It is composed of humorous, bawdy, and poignant stories told by a group of fictional pilgrims, who travel together on a journey from Southwark to the shrine of Saint Thomas Becket at Canterbury Cathedral. They come from all layers of society, and tell stories to each other to kill time while travelling to Canterbury. Many of the stories seem to fit their individual characters and social standing: the innkeeper shares the name of a contemporary keeper of an inn in Southwark, and real-life identities for the Wife of Bath, the Merchant, the Man of Law and the Student have been suggested.

Incomplete as they are, these tales cover practically all the major types of medieval literature; courtly romance, folk tale, beast fable, story of travel and adventure, saint's life, allegorical tale, sermon, alchemical account, and others. Taking the stand of the rising bourgeoisie, Chaucer affirms men and women's right to pursue their happiness on earth and opposes the dogma of asceticism preached by the church. As a forerunner of humanism, he praises man's energy, intellect, quick wit and love of life. His tales expose and satirize the evils of the time. *The Canterbury Tales* is considered to be among the masterpieces of literature.

The Prologue provides a framework for the tales. It contains a group of vivid sketches of typical medieval figures. It supplies a miniature of the English society of Chaucer's time. Looking at his word-pictures, we know at once how people lived in that era. That is why Chaucer has been called "the founder of English realism".

Selected Reading

The Canterbury Tales
The Prologue①

When in April the sweet showers fall
And pierce the drought of March to the root②, and all
The veins are bathed in liquor of such power③
As brings about the engendering of the flower④,
When also Zephyrus⑤ with his sweet breath

---

①prologue：序言
②pierce ... to the root：The gentle spring rain penetrates the very roots of the plants
③bathed in liquor of such power：liquor，甘霖。The water of the spring rain moistening every rib of the leaves and endowing the plants with its power
④As brings about the engendering of the flower：engendering，生长；发芽。With the power of the water, flowers begin to blossom
⑤Zephyrus：the west wind，西风（在英国，春天里西风从大西洋上吹来，是温暖和煦的。）

Exhales① an air in every grove and heath②
Upon the tender shoots③, and the young sun④
His half-course in the sign of the Ram has run,
And the small fowl⑤ are making melody
That sleep away the night with open eye
(So nature pricks them and their heart engages⑥)
Then people long to go on pilgrimages
And palmers⑦ long to seek the stranger strands⑧
Of far-off saints, hallowed⑨ in sundry⑩ lands,
And specially, from every shire's end⑪
Of England, down to Canterbury⑫ they wend⑬
To seek the holy blissful martyr⑭, quick
To give his help to them when they were sick,
It happened in that season that one day
In Southwark⑮, at The Tabard, as I lay
Ready to go on pilgrimages and start

---

①exhale：呼出；吐出

②grove and heath：树林和荒地

③shoots：新芽

④the young sun/ His half-course in the sign of the Ram has run：Ram, 白羊宫, 古代用于解释天体运行的黄道带十二宫中的一个。太阳经过白羊宫时正是春天, 所以称太阳为 the young sun

⑤fowl：[复数] 鸟

⑥So nature ... engages：So nature stimulates them and attracts their hearts

⑦palmers：朝圣者；香客

⑧the strange strands：异乡的海岸

⑨hallowed：被奉为神圣的

⑩sundry：各种各样的

⑪from every shire's end：from the farthest limit of every county

⑫Canterbury：坎特伯雷。a town southeast of London, in the county of Kent

⑬wend：行；走

⑭the holy blissful martyr：martyr, 殉道者, 指坎特伯雷大主教 St. Thomas Becket, 他死后被葬于坎特伯雷

⑮Southwark：当时伦敦的一个郊区

For Canterbury, most devout at heart,
At night there came into that hostelry①
Some nine and twenty in a company
Of sundry folk happening then to fall
In fellowship, and they were pilgrims all
That towards Canterbury meant to ride,
The rooms and stables of the inn were wide;
They made us easy; all was of the best,
And, briefly, when the sun had gone to rest,
I'd spoken to them all upon the trip
And was soon one with them in fellowship,
Pledged② to rise early and to take the way
To Canterbury, as you heard me say.
But none the less, while I have time and space,
Before my story takes a further pace,
It seems a reasonable thing to say
What their condition was, the full array
Of each of them, as it appeared to me,
According to profession and degree③,
And what apparel④ they were riding in;
And at a Knight I therefore will begin.

---

①hostelry: inn, 旅店;客栈。这里指 Tabard
②pledged: 发誓
③degree: 社会地位
④apparel: 服饰

Questions for Discussion

1. What is the importance of "The General Prologue" in *The Canterbury Tales*?
2. What are Chaucer's contributions to English literature and the English language?
3. Give a brief analysis of the quotation.

> When in April the sweet showers fall
> And pierce the drought of March to the root, and all
> The veins are bathed in liquor of such power
> As brings about the engendering of the flower,
> When also Zephyrus with his sweet breath
> Exhales an air in every grove and heath
> Upon the tender shoots, and the young sun
> His half-course in the sign of the Ram has run,
> And the small fowl are making melody
> That sleep away the night with open eye
> (So nature pricks them and their heart engages)
> Then people long to go on pilgrimages
> And palmers long to seek the stranger strands
> Of far-off saints, hallowed in sundry lands,
> And specially, from every shire's end
> Of England, down to Canterbury they wend
> To seek the holy blissful martyr, quick
> To give his help to them when they were sick.

※ Chapter 1 Early and Medieval English Literature ※

Terms

1. Epic
2. Lambic pentameter
3. Heroic couplet
4. Alliteration
5. English Ballads
6. Middle Ages
7. Romance

Chapter 2

English Literature in the Renaissance

I. Historical Background

In 1485, the Wars of Roses came to an end, and in 1492, Christopher Columbus's voyage to the America opened European eyes to the existence of the New World. New Worlds, both geographical and spiritual, are the key to the Renaissance, the rebirth of learning and culture, which reached the peak in Italy in the early sixteenth century and in Britain during the reign of Queen Elizabeth from 1558 to 1603.

1. The Reformation

England emerged from the Wars of Roses with a new dynasty in power, the Tudors 都铎王朝. The greatest of the Tudor monarchs was Henry Ⅷ (1509 – 1547) who established himself as both the head of Church and the head of state. England became Protestant 新教, and the nation's political and religious identity had to be redefined.

2. The Reign of Queen Elizabeth Ⅰ

Elizabeth Tudor, 7 September, 1533 – 24 March, 1603, the last Tudor monarch, was the daughter of Henry Ⅷ and Anne Boleyn, his second wife, who was executed two and a half years after Elizabeth's birth. During Mary's reign, Elizabeth was imprisoned for nearly a year on suspicion of supporting Protestant rebels. In 1558, Elizabeth succeeded her half-sister to the throne and set out to rule by good counsel. Elizabeth's 45-year reign, known as the Elizabethan era, is generally considered one of the most glorious in English history.

Elizabeth was very well-educated and inherited intelligence, determination and shrewdness from both parents. She used her notoriously sharp tongue to settle any

❀ **Chapter 2　English Literature in the Renaissance** ❀

argument, usually in her favour. Her indecisiveness often infuriated her ministers; when faced with a difficult decision, she would busy herself with other matters for months on end. It could be argued that her legendary indecision helped to delay the inevitable and expensive war with Spain for many years, but history regards her as a wise ruler.

Elizabeth established an English church that helped shape a national identity and remains in place today but there were constant threats, plots and potential rebellions agaist her. Many Protestant extremists left the country for religious reasons to set up the first colony in Virginia and Pennsylvania, the beginnings of another New World. Elizabeth's reign did give the nation some sense of stability, national and religious triumph when the Spanish Armada, the fleet of the Catholic King Philip of Spain, was defeated in 1588.

Elizabeth followed a largely defensive foreign policy, and her reign raised England's status abroad. She believed that God was protecting her. Elizabeth chose never to marry. Elizabeth herself refused to make windows into men's souls. There is only one Jesus Christ and all the rest is a dispute over trifles. Elizabeth used her marriage prospects as a political tool in foreign and domestic policies. However, the Virgin Queen was presented as a selfless woman who sacrificed personal happiness for the good of the nation. The image of Elizabeth's reign is one of triumph and success.

She died at Richmond Palace on 24 March, 1603, having become a legend in her lifetime. The date of her accession was a national holiday for two hundred years. The arts flourished during Elizabeth's reign. The Elizabethan era is recorded in history as a time of great poets and writers such as Edmund Spenser, William Shakespeare and Christopher Marlowe; great adventurers like Sir Francis Drake and Sir Walter Raleigh; and also as an era of great statesmen.

3. Economic Movements

With this growth in wealth and political importance of the nation, London developed as the capital, and from the foundation of the first public theatre in London, the stage became the forum of debate, spectacle, and entertainment. The writer took his work to an audience, including the Queen herself and the lowliest of the subjects. With the growth in theatrical expression, the growth of Modern English went as a national language. Country houses such as Longleat and Hardwick Hall were built, miniature painting reached its high point, theatres thrived—the Queen attended the first performance of Shakespeare's *A Midsummer Night's Dream*.

The political and religious confusion of the age were the reflection of the changes of the national economy in England which developed at a slow but steady pace. With the Enclosure Movement from the 15th century on, England developed from a mere producer of wool to a manufacturer of cloth, which stimulated the development of the clothing industry on a capitalist line; also it produced helpless, dispossessed peasants who became hired labour for merchants.

4. The Renaissance

Renaissance refers to the period between the 14th and mid-17th century in western civilization and the movement marks the transition from the medieval to the modern world. It first started in Florence and Venice of Italy and went to embrace the rest of Europe, with the flowering of painting, sculpture and architecture.

The word "Renaissance", which means rebirth or revival, is usually regarded as the result of an emphasis upon the discovered Greek and Roman classics and the combination or compromise of a newly interpreted Christian tradition and an admired tradition of pagan classical culture, which was stimulated by a series of historical events, such as the rediscovery of ancient Roman and Greek culture, the new discoveries in geography and astronomy, the religious reformation and the economic expansion. Two striking features of Renaissance: People had a thirsting curiosity for the classical literature; the keen interest in the activities of humanity arose.

II. Literature Background

1. The Beginning of the English Renaissance

Renaissance was a cultural and artistic movement but its style and ideas were slow in penetrating England. In the days of Henry VIII, a group of scholars called Oxford Reformers introduced the classical literature to England and strove to reform education on a humanistic line. These English humanists were all churchmen, and the greatest was Thomas More, the author of *Utopia*, which may be thought of as the first literary masterpiece of the English Renaissance.

During the reign of Elizabeth Ⅰ and then James Ⅰ (1603 – 1625), a London-centred culture, both courtly and popular, produced great poetry and drama. The greatest and most distinctive achievement of Elizabethan literature is the drama. Christopher Marlowe was the greatest playwright before Shakespeare and the most gifted of the "University Wits".

2. The height of the English Renaissance—the Elizabethan era

English literature in the Renaissance Period is usually regarded as the highlight in the history of English literature. After 1588, the flourishing period of English drama arrived, and the summit was Shakespeare's works. Other important figures in Elizabethan theatre include Christopher Marlowe, Ben Jonson, Thomas Dekker, John Fletcher and Francis Beaumont.

English literature developed with a great speed and made a magnificent achievement. Marlowe's subject focuses on the moral drama of the Renaissance man. He introduced the story of *Faust* to England in his play *Doctor Faustus*, which is about a scientist and magician who, obsessed by the thirst of knowledge and the desire to push man's technological power to its limits, sells his soul to the Devil. *Faustus* makes use of "the dramatic framework of the morality plays the story of temptation, fall, and damnation, and its free use of morality figures such as the good angel and the bad angel and the seven deadly sins, along with the devils Lucifer and Mephistopheles." Marlowe first made blank verse (unrhymed iambic pentameter) the principal instrument of English drama.

Elizabethan lyrical poetry is remarkable for its variety, its freshness, its youthfulness and its romantic feeling. A group of great poets appeared, and a large number of noble poetry was produced. In that period, writing poetry became a fashion. England then became "a nest of singing birds".

Edmund Spenser is often referred to as "the poets' poet", who is the author of *The Faerie Queene*, an epic poem and fantastical allegory celebrating the Tudor dynasty and Elizabeth I. He is generally acknowledged to be the greatest non-dramatic poet of the Elizabethan Age. Spenser employs the archaic language of Chaucer but the modern pronunciation of the Renaissance and the biblical allegory poem to tell his story, whose purpose is to educate, to turn a young man into a gentleman. Spenser influenced many of the poets who followed him, including John Milton, Percy Shelley, John Keats, Lord Byron, and Lord Tennyson.

Francis Bacon wrote more than fifty excellent essays, which make him one of the best essayists in English.

Unit 1 Edmund Spenser
(1552/1553 – 1599)

Edmund Spenser ranks as the foremost English poet of the 16th century in the Elizabethan age. He is recognized as one of the premier craftsmen of Modern English verse, and one of the greatest poets in the English language, and his work reflects the religious and humanistic ideals as well as the intense but critical patriotism of Elizabethan England. His contributions to English literature—in the form of a heightened and enlarged poetic vocabulary, a charming and flexible verse style, and a rich fusing of the philosophic and literary currents of the English Renaissance—entitle him to a rank not far removed from that of William Shakespeare and John Milton.

Spenser was the son of a London tailor, but his family seems to have had its origins in Lancashire. The poet was admitted to the newly founded Merchant Taylors' School in about 1561 as a "poor scholar". The curriculum at Mulcaster's school included Latin, Greek, and Hebrew; music and drama were stressed; the English language was also a subject of study—then a novelty. In 1569 he went to Cambridge, where he entered Pembroke College as a sizar (a student who earns his tuition by acting as a servant to wealthy students). Spenser's health was poor but he had an excellent reputation as a student. He studied Italian, French, Latin, and Greek; read widely in classical literature and in the poetry of the modern languages; and authored some Latin verse. He read Plato and Aristotle and was influenced by Puritan moral beliefs. Though Spenser strove to emulate such ancient Roman poets as Virgil and Ovid, many of his best-known works are notably divergent from those of his predecessors. The language of his poetry is purposely archaic, reminiscent of earlier works such as *The Canterbury Tales* of Geoffrey Chaucer and Ⅱ *Canzoniere* of Francesco Petrarca. His works includes *The Shepheardes Calender*, *The Faerie Queene*, *Amoretti*.

Famous as the author of the unfinished epic poem, he is the poet of an ordered yet passionate Elizabethan world. *The Faerie Queene* is a masterpiece of English literature written in the Spenserian stanza. The Elizabethans hailed him as their "Prince of

Poets". Edmund Spenser is the most outstanding poet who lived between the age of Chaucer and that of Shakespeare.

★ **The Spenserian stanza and sonnet**

Spenser used a distinctive verse form, called the Spenserian stanza, in several works including *The Faerie Queene*. The stanza's main meter is iambic pentameter with a final line in iambic hexameter (having six feet or stresses, known as an Alexandrine), and the rhyme scheme is ababbcbcc. He also used his own rhyme scheme for the sonnet.

The chief qualities of Spenser's poetry: a perfect melody, a rare sense of beauty, a splendid imagination, a lofty moral purity and seriousness, and a dedicated idealism. In addition, Spenser uses strange forms of speech and obsolete words in order to increase the rustic effect.

Brief Introduction

The Faerie Queene is an English epic and fantastical allegory celebrating the Tudor dynasty and Elizabeth Ⅰ, which is a vast patriotic celebration of English culture set in a mystical fairy tale world.

Spenser gives the allegorical presentation of virtues through Arthurian knights in the mythical "Faerieland". Arthur represents the virtue of Magnificence and the Faerie Queene herself represents Glory (hence her name Gloriana). At last spenser only managed to cover six of the virtues: Holiness, Temperament, Chastity, Friendship, Justice, and Courtesy. The incomplete seventh book appears to represent the virtue of Consistency.

The selection from Book Ⅰ of *The Faerie Queene* illustrates the virtue of Holiness, telling the tale of Red Cross Knight of Holiness, and reveals his virtue through adventures to protect the Virgin Una, and relieve her kingdom from a menacing dragon. He sets out on the orders of the Glorious Queen of Faerie to kill the dragon who has imprisoned Una's parents. Una accompanies him, concealing her face behind a veil to keep her dazzling beauty. She mounts on a donkey and leads by a cord a milk-white lamb. They are made victims by the subtle tricks of the devil himself. The Red Cross Knight kills Sansfoy (without faith), but is deceived by false Fidessa, whose real name is Dussa, symbol of sin. The Knight manages to escape her seduction. However, Una is taken prisoner by Sansloy and left for a moment at mercy of his rage and lust. At the mansion of Lucifer, a daughter of Pluto and Porserpina, he fights a fierce battle with Sansjoy and is tricked by Duessa into a luckless combat with the giant Orgoglio, who represents fleshly and irrational presumption and diabolical vainglory. King Arthur comes and rescues him from the dragon's place at this crucial moment. Book Ⅰ ends with the happy marriage between Una and the Red Cross Knight.

Spenser's aim was to "fashion a gentleman or noble person in virtuous and gentle discipline", including elements of the romance of chivalry, the handbook of manners and morals, and the national epic.

Canto 1

Archimago has escaped from his imprisonment and is intent on revenge upon Redcrosse. When he meets the knight Guyon and his squire, Palmer, Archimago tells that a wicked knight who bears the cross of Christ on his shield has just recently attacked a virgin and is intent on despoiling her. During the journey, they meet the alleged virgin who is actually Duessa in disguise. She confirms Archimago's story, inflaming Guyon to righteous anger, finally they encounter Redcrosse. Guyon balks at attacking a knight bearing a red cross. The two knights become friends.

Later, they meet Amavia who stabs herself in the chest as they approach but find the woman holding a newborn baby and lying next to the body of a dead man, and her husband Mordant who was seduced by Acrasia. The enchantress lures men to her Bower of Bliss with the promise of sex and magically turns them into beasts. Mordant is able to free himself of the enchantment, but Acrasia exerts revenge upon him by poisoning him, and finally she dies in Guyon's arms.

Selected Reading

The Faerie Queene

1
A Gentle Knight was pricking① on the plain,

---

①prick：鞭策，策马

Clad in mighty arms and sliver shield,
Wherein old dints① of deep wounds did remain,
The cruel marks of many a bloody field;
Yet arms② till that time did he never wield③.
His angry steed④ did chide⑤ his foaming bitt⑥,
As much disdaining to the curb⑦ to yield:
Full jolly⑧ knight he seemed, and fair did sit,
As one for knightly joust⑨ and fierce encounters fit.

2
But on his breast a bloody Cross he bore,
The dear remembrance of his dying Lord,
For whose sweet sake that glorious badge⑩ he wore,
And dead as living ever him adored⑪:
Upon his shield the like was also scored,
For soveraine⑫ hope, which in his help he had:
Right faithful true he was in deed and word,
But of his cheer did seem too solemn⑬ sad;
Yet nothing did he dread, but ever was dreaded⑭.

3
Upon a great adventure he was bond,

---

①dints：凹痕
②arms：武器，兵种
③wield：挥舞（剑等）
④steed：[诗]马，战马
⑤chide：斥责，责骂
⑥bitt：缆柱，系于缆柱
⑦curb：抑制
⑧jolly：欢乐的，高兴的，快活的
⑨joust：骑马用长矛打斗；持矛比武
⑩badge：徽章，证章
⑪adored：爱慕者，崇拜者
⑫soveraine：sovereign，至高无上的，君主的，独立自主的，完全的
⑬solemn：庄严的，隆重的，严肃的
⑭dread：恐惧，恐怖，可怕的人（或物），畏惧；惧怕，担心

That greatest Gloriana to him gave,
That greatest Glorious① Queen of Faerie Land,
To win him worship②, and her grace to have,
Which of all earthly things he most did crave③;
And ever as he rode, his heart did yearn
To prove his puissance④ in battle brave
Upon his foe⑤, and his new force to learn
Upon his foe, a Dragon horrible and stern⑥.

Questions for Discussion

1. What's the knight's name in this part?
   What does the knight stand for?
   The knight set out on his quest to rescue the parents of Una, a beautiful lady.
   What does she symbolize?
   Analyze the writing features of the poem.
2. What more than anything else on earth does the knight want?
3. What do we learn about the Lady?
4. Please briefly analyze Edmund Spenser's *The Faerie Queen*.
5. What was Spenser's primary purpose in writing *The Faerie Queene*?
6. How is the virtue of Holiness depicted in *The Faerie Queene*?

---

①Glorious：光荣的，显赫的
②worship：崇拜，礼拜，尊敬；*vi.* 敬神，拜神；*vt.* 崇拜，尊敬
③crave：恳求，渴望
④puissance：（马的）越障能力测试，<古>权力，权势，力量，影响
⑤foe：反对者，敌人，危害物
⑥stern：严厉的，苛刻的

Unit 2 William Shakespeare (1564 – 1616)

Appreciation

To be, or not to be; that is the question:生存还是毁灭,这是一个值得考虑的问题;
Whether 'tis nobler in the mind to suffer 这两种行为,哪一种更高贵?
The slings and arrows of outrageous fortune,默然忍受命运的暴虐的毒箭,
Or to take arms against a sea of troubles,或是挺身反抗人世的无涯的苦难,
And by opposing end them? 通过斗争把它们扫清

William Shakespeare is the greatest of all English authors and one of the greatest authors in world literature. He is generally considered the greatest dramatist in human history and the supreme poet of the English language.

Shakespeare was born in Stratford-on-Avon in 1564. He got education in a local grammar school for a few years. There he picked up "small Latin and less Greek". In 1582 Shakespeare married Anne Hathaway, the daughter of a peasant family, eight years older than her husband. A few years later, Shakespeare went to London and became an actor and a writer. During the twenty-two years of his literary career, he produced 37 plays, 154 sonnets and some long poems. Shakespeare wrote 11 tragedies: *Hamlet*, *Othello*, *King Lear*, and *Macbeth* and etc. All of these plays express a profound dissatisfaction with life. They show the struggle and conflicts between good and evil of the tune, between justice and injustice. In these plays, Shakespeare condemns the dark and evil society. Comedies are, *As You like It*, *The Merchants of Venice*, *Much Ado About Nothing*, *A Midsummer Night's Dream*. Histories are *Henry IV*, *Henry V*, *Richard II*, *Richard III*, *Henry VIII*.

In the 20th century, his works were repeatedly adopted and rediscovered by new movements in scholarship and performance. His plays remain highly popular today and are constantly studied, performed, and reinterpreted in diverse cultural and political contexts throughout the world.

Brief Introduction

Hamlet is Shakespeare's longest play and among the most powerful and influential tragedies in English literature. The protagonist of *Hamlet* is Prince Hamlet of Denmark, son of deceased King Hamlet and Queen Gertrude. The play dramatizes how Hamlet exerts revenge on his uncle Claudius, who has murdered Hamlet's father—the King, and then taken the throne and married Hamlet's mother.

Hamlet's character is one of virtue and integrity at the beginning of the play, fearing the consequences of his actions. As the play unfolds, Hamlet becomes more and more confused and his inner struggle seems to be getting worse. Hamlet finally wins the battle within himself, causing him to act against his own inhibitions to dutifully avenge the murder of his father. This speech connects many of the play's main themes, including the idea of suicide and death, the difficulty of knowing the truth in a spiritually ambiguous universe, and the connection between thought and action. In addition, this speech reveals the quality of Hamlet's mind. His deeply passionate nature is complemented by a relentlessly logical intellect, which works furiously to find a solution to his misery.

Selected Reading

Hamlet

Act Ⅲ   Scene Ⅰ

To be, or not to be[①]**; that is the question:**
Whether 'tis nobler in the mind to suffer
The slings and arrows of outrageous fortune,
Or to take arms against a sea of troubles,
And by opposing end them? To die: to sleep;

---

①To be, or not to be：生还是死，生存还是死亡；是反抗还是屈从；是耐心地忍受这样的痛苦和折磨更显得高尚，还是奋起反抗，去终结给人带来痛苦和折磨的原因？

Chapter 2 English Literature in the Renaissance

No more; and by a sleep to say we end
The heart-ache and the thousand natural shocks
That flesh is heir to①, 'tis a consummation②
Devoutly to be wish'd. To die, to sleep;
To sleep: perchance③ to dream: ay, there's the rub④;
For in that sleep of death what dreams may come
When we have shuffled off this mortal coil⑤,
Must give us pause: there's the respect⑥
That makes calamity of so long life;
For who would bear the whips and scorns of time,
The oppressor's wrong, the proud man's contumely,
The pangs of despised love, the law's delay,
The insolence of office and the spurns
That patient merit of the unworthy takes,
When he himself might his quietus make
With a bare bodkin⑦? who would fardels⑧ bear,
To grunt and sweat under a weary life,
But that the dread of something after death,
The undiscover'd country from whose bourn
No traveler returns, puzzles the will
And makes us rather bear those ills we have
Than fly to others that we know not of⑨?
Thus conscience does make cowards of us all;

---

①That flesh is heir to: 人类注定要承受的苦难
②consummation: 事件、生命的完成, 终结
③perchance: 也许
④rub: obstacle, 阻拦、麻烦
⑤When we have shuffled off this mortal coil: 当我们摈弃了这一切的人生烦恼
⑥respect: 考虑
⑦With a bare bodkin: 出鞘的匕首
⑧fardels: 重负
⑨fly to others that we know not of: 进入了我们不知道的地域(暗指死亡)

· 23 ·

And thus the native hue of resolution①
Is sicklied② o'er with the pale cast of thought,
And enterprises of great pith③ and moment
With this regard their currents turn awry,
And lose the name of action. Soft you now!
The fair Ophelia! Nymph, in thy orisons
Be all my sins remember'd.

Questions for Discussion

1. What's the essence of Hamlet's most exhaustively discussed soliloquy "To be or not to be"? Write an essay with any topic of your choice.
2. Is Hamlet a frail and weak-minded youth? A thought-sick dreamer? A man active in thought but passive and slow in action? Why does he delay taking revenge for his father?
3. Examine Hamlet's passionate enumeration of life's calamity: "the whips and scorns of time" is parallel structure and antithecal structure: "To be or not to be". How does the language help present the sense of pain of life? Why would people rather bear suffering of the world instead of ending their life according to *Hamlet*?
4. Analyze Hamlet's character through this soliloquy and list the possible reasons for his melancholy and dely.
5. What is the theme of *Hamlet*?
6. Please ananlyze the image of *Hamlet*.
7. Suppose you were Hamlet, what would you do?

---

①the native hue of resolution：hue, *n.* 色调，样子，颜色。resolution，坚定，决心，决定。西方通常认为脸色泛红表示人的坚强决心。这句话指人脸上表示决心的天然色晕

②sicklied：受到损害；露出病态（指失去了表示决心的红晕）

③enterprises of great pith：enterprise，事业心，进取心。pith，（植物的）木髓，骨髓，重要部分。对崇高事业的追求

Appreciation

So long as men can breathe or eyes can see, 只要人类还在呼吸、眼睛还在欣赏，
So long lives this and this gives life to thee. 这诗就将不朽，令你生命绽放。

Brief Introduction

Sonnet 18 deserves its classic because it is one of the most well-known out of all Shakespeare's 154 sonnets. In the sonnet, the speaker compares his beloved to the summer season, and argues that his beloved is better. He also states that his beloved will live on forever through the words of the poem. There is great use of imagery within the sonnet. The chosen subject matter, describing the theme of love, has created a remarkable longevity for this poem until these days.

Selected Reading

Sonnet 18

Shall I compare thee to a summer's day?
Thou art more lovely and more temperate[①]:
Rough winds do shake the darling buds of May,
And summer's lease[②] hath all too short a date:
Sometime too hot the eye of heaven shines,
And often is his gold complexion dimm'd;
And every fair from fair sometime declines[③],
By chance or nature's changing course untrimm'd;
But thy eternal summer shall not fade
Nor lose possession of that fair thou owest;

---

①temperate：温和，柔和
②lease：租赁期。这里指夏天延续的时间
③every fair from fair sometime declines：第一个 fair 指"美貌之人"，第二个 fair 广指"美貌"或"美丽"

Nor shall Death brag thou wander'st in his shade[①],
When in eternal lines to time thou growe'st[②]:
So long as men can breathe or eyes can see,
So long lives this and this[③] gives life to thee.

Questions for Discussion

1. Give a brief analysis of *Sonnet 18*.
2. What is the theme of *Sonnet 18*?

Terms

1. Renaissance
2. Spenserian stanza and sonnet
3. Soliloquy
4. Stanza
5. Meter
6. Sonnet

---

①Nor shall Death brag thou wander'st in his shade: 死亡也无法夸口，无法把你纳入自己的阴影之下
②When in eternal lines to time thou growe'st: lines, 诗人的诗行
③this: "这"，指"诗歌"

Chapter 3

Literature of the English Revolution and Restoration

I. Historical Background

The earlier 17th century, and especially the period of the English Revolution (1640 – 1660), was a time of intense ferment in all areas of life—religion, science, politics, domestic relations, and culture.

1. The House of Stuart

After the death of Elizabeth in 1603, James Ⅵ of Scotland succeeded the throne known as James Ⅰ. With the belief of "Divine Right of Kings", James Ⅰ never allowed the Parliament to interfere in his rule. His succession brought a temporary union of England and Scotland, but his reign was troubled by religious controversy.

The Puritans became very powerful in the Parliament. They demanded further religious reformation away with the elaborate ceremonies, calling a purer form of worship, and demanded a simple religious belief. The refusal of their proposals in purifying the Church, and the pro-Spanish foreign policy made many Puritans flee England for Holland. The most famous sailing was made by 102 puritans in 1620, which landed America from Plymouth with a ship named Mayflower.

2. The Civil War

King Charles Ⅰ succeeded the throne after his father James Ⅰ's death. Without enough money, Charles Ⅰ was not capable to handle the severe religious dispute and the clash between the king and the parliament, and dissolved the parliament for not granting import duties for life. His efforts to obtain money without the aid of the Parliament by all kinds of extraordinary levies became notorious. Conflicts between the King and the Parliament finally brought about a civil war in 1642.

The various classes in England soon split up into two camps. The parliament was supported by the merchants, the workers and the peasants; while the king was supported by the conservative gentry, the big landlords and the monopolists. The king's men were called "Cavaliers" because they were skillful at riding and shooting, and the soldiers of the parliament were called "Roundheads" because they wore their hair short. At last, the royalists were defeated by the parliament army led by Oliver Cromwell. In 1649 Charles Ⅰ was sentenced to death, and England was declared to be a commonwealth 君主立宪制 and Cromwell became the Lord Protector.

In 1658, Cromwell died and his son Richard succeeded him as the new Lord Protector, who was too weak-minded. In 1660, Charles Ⅱ was welcomed back and became the new king. That was known as the Restoration. Charles Ⅱ carried on reprisals on the revolutionaries and persecuted the puritans.

3. The Glorious Revolution

A white terror was introduced to the country during the reign of Charles Ⅱ and James Ⅱ, brother of Charles Ⅱ. In 1688, James Ⅱ was forced to flee to France. His Protestant daughter Mary Stuart and her husband William, Duke of Orange, were invited to come and rule over England. This was the so-called "Glorious Revolution"— "glorious" because it was bloodless and there was no revival of the revolutionary demands. After a century of disputes and battles, modern England was firmly established and capitalism would develop freely within the state structure of modern England constitutional monarchy. In 1688, William signed "The Bill of Rights" presented to him by the Parliament, which greatly restricted the power of the English king and henceforth England has become a country of constitutional monarchy.

The Revolution of 1688 meant three things: the supremacy of Parliament, the beginning of modern England, and the final triumph of the principle of political liberty for which the Puritan had fought and suffered hardship for a hundred years.

II. Literature Background

The 17th century literature is closely related to politics. English literature of the revolution and restoration was very much concerned with the tremendous social upheavals of the time. Literature in the 17th century mainly includes baroque literature, puritan literature and classicist literature, roughly according to the sequence of time. John Milton and John Bunyan stood firmly with the English Revolution. The Cavalier poets sided with the king. The Metaphysical poets wrote in their unique way, paying

Chapter 3 Literature of the English Revolution and Restoration

more attention to religion than politics.

Literature 4 Johns: John Milton, John Bunyan—two representatives of the puritan writers; John Donne, the greatest metaphysical poet; John Dryden, noted for his literary criticism and forerunner of the English classicism.

1. Baroque literature

It is the transition from Renaissance to classicism. Classicism is the main literary school in Europe esp. in France in 17th century and a little later in England, which praises the leadership of the king and combines closely literature with reality and politics and demands the restraint of personal wishes and expresses the subjects that emotion is submissive to responsibility and individual to the country.

2. Puritan literature

Puritanism was the religious doctrine of the revolutionary bourgeoisie during this period which preached thrift, sobriety 清醒, hard work, but with very little extravagant enjoyment of the fruits of labor. Worldly pleasures were condemned as harmful. The Puritans believed in simplicity of life. In the triumph of Puritanism under Cromwell, severe laws were passed, many simple pleasures were forbidden and an austere standard of living was forced upon unwilling people. The London theaters were closed in 1642. *The Bible* became the one book of the people.

The Revolution Period was one of confusion in literature due to the breaking up of the old ideals. Puritanism disapproved of the sonnets and the love poetry written in the previous period. Literature was as divided in spirit as were the struggling parties.

The Revolution period produced one of the most important poets in English literature, John Milton, whose work would glorify any age and people, and in his work the indomitable revolutionary spirit found its noblest expression. This period is also called the Age of Milton. The main literary form of the period was poetry. In the field of prose writing of the Puritan Age, John Bunyan occupies the most important position. They both represented the extremes of English life in the 17th century and wrote the two remarkable works that have imbued with the mighty Puritan spirit.

3. Metaphysical Poets 玄学派—Neo-Platonism

The early 17th century was an age of transition, of conscious change. In literature, there is also a tendency to investigate novelties, just as in the spirit of science. The term "metaphysical poetry" is commonly used to designate the works of the 17th century writers under the influence of John Donne, the founder of this school. The metaphysical works are characterized by mysticism in content and fantasticality in form.

They tended to logically reason the things, esp. emotions; psychologically analyze the emotions of love and religion; love the novelty and the shocking; use the metaphysical conceits, and ignore the conventional devices. In literature, a conceit is an extended metaphor with a complex logic that governs a poetic passage or entire poem.

The group was to have a significant influence on 20th century poetry, especially through T. S. Eliot, whose essay *The Metaphysical Poets* (1921) helped bring their poetry back into favor with audience. T. S. Eliot is an example of modern poets who have been mostly affected by the metaphysical influence.

"When the evening is spread out against the sky
   Like a patient etherized upon a table" (T. S. Eliot)

4. Cavalier Poets

Another school of poets prevailing in the period was the Cavalier Poets. Most of these poets were courtiers and soldiers who sided with the king to fight against the revolution. They mostly wrote short songs on the flitting joys of the day, but underneath their light-heartedness lies some forbidding and impending doom. Their poetry expresses the spirit of pessimism. The representatives of this school are Sir John Suckling (1609 – 1642), Richard Lovelace (1618 – 1657), Thomas Carew (1595 – 1639) and Robert Herrick (1591 – 1674). Cavalier poets wrote some best known poems in English literary history, though they were conservative in politics. A case in point is Herrick's "Gather Your Rose Buds While You May".

Unit 1   John Milton (1608 – 1674)

Appreciation

What though the field be lost? 我们损失了什么？
All is not lost; the unconquerable Will, 并不是一无所剩；
And study of revenge, immortal hate, 坚定的意志、热切的复仇心、不灭的憎恨；
And courage never to submit or yield, 以及永不屈服、永不退让的勇气，
And what is else not to be overcome? 难道还有比这些更难战胜的吗？

John Milton was born in London in December 1608. In 1625, Milton went to Christ's College, Cambridge University and spent seven years there, earning his B. A.

Chapter 3 Literature of the English Revolution and Restoration

and M. A. then retired to the family homes in London and Horton, for years of private study and literary composition. He began his traveling around Europe, mostly in Italy, and then returned to England in 1639.

The phases of Milton's life parallel the major historical and political divisions in Stuart Britain. Under the rule of Charles Ⅰ and its breakdown, he launched a career as pamphleteer and publicist. Under the Commonwealth of England, he acted as an official spokesman in certain of his publications. During the Restoration of 1660, Milton, now completely blind, completed most of his major works of poetry. Three great poems: *Paradise Lost* 失乐园, *Paradise Regained* 复乐园, *Samson Agonistes* 力士参孙。

William Hayley's 1796 biography called Milton the "greatest English author" and he remains generally regarded as "one of the preeminent writers in the English language". Samuel Johnson praised *Paradise Lost* as "a poem which... with respect to design may claim the first place, and with respect to performance, the second, among the productions of the human mind". His book *Paradise Lost* is called Three Western poetry with *Homer* 荷马史诗 and *The Divine Comedy* 神曲.

Brief Introduction

Paradise Lost is Milton's masterpiece. Before its composition, he had had the subject in his mind for a quarter of a century, and made some drafts about the characters and plot. It is a long epic, published first in 1667 in 12 books, written in blank verse, which is written in regular metrical but unrhymed lines, almost always iambic pentameters. It is also a quintessential epic poem, following the conventions originating from the works of Homer and Virgil and the Anglo-Saxon epic *Beowulf*.

The poem concerns the Judeo-Christian story of the Fall of Man: the temptation of Adam and Eve by Satan and their expulsion from the Garden of Eden. The story of the epic goes as follows: Satan and his followers rose against God, but they were defeated and cast out of Heaven into Hell before Adam and Eve were created. Even in Hell, Satan and his adherents are planning another plot. Having managed to escape from Hell, Satan goes to the newly created world to corrupt man. Satan chooses for his battlefield the most perfect of spots ever created by God—the Garden of Eden, where live the first man and woman, Adam and Eve, who are allowed by God to enjoy the superme beauties of Paradise. Having over-heard the secret of the Tree of Knowledge of Good and Evil in the Garden of Eden, Satan enters the body of the serpent and convinces Eve that he has eaten the fruit of the *Tree of Knowledge* and gained wisdom and speech. She eats the fruit from the forbidden tree, and then persuades Adam to eat the fruit too. God sees all this and both Adam and Eve are deprived of immortality. They are expelled from the Paradise to live an earthly life of hardships and suffering. Satan is punished by God and turned into a serpent.

Selected Reading

Paradise Lost

Book I

What though the field① be lost?
All is not lost②; the unconquerable Will,
And study③ of revenge, immortal hate,
And courage never to submit or yield,
And what is else not to be overcome④?
That Glory⑤ never shall his wrath or might
Extort⑥ from me. To bow and sue for grace⑦
With suppliant knee, and deifie his power,
Who⑧ from the terrour⑨ of this Arm so late

---

①field: the battle 战役;斗争
②all is not lost: not all is lost 并非所有的方面都失败了
③study: earnest intention 强烈的愿望
④what is else not to be overcome: what else is not to be overcome? 还有什么是比这更难以战胜的吗?
⑤that glory: the glory of not being overcome
⑥extort: obtain 侵占,强求
⑦sue for grace: beg for mercy 乞求怜悯
⑧Who: the God 此处指上帝
⑨terrour: terror

Chapter 3 Literature of the English Revolution and Restoration

Doubted his Empire①, that were low indeed,
That were an ignominy② and shame beneath③
This downfall④; since by Fate⑤ the strength of Gods⑥
And this Empyreal substance⑦ cannot fail⑧,
Since through experience of this great event⑨
In Arms not worse, in foresight much advanc't,
We may with more successful hope resolve
To wage by force or guile eternal Warr
Irreconcileable, to our grand Foe⑩,
Who now triumphs, and in th'excess of joy
Sole reigning holds the Tyranny of Heav'n⑪.
So spake⑫ th'Apostate Angel⑬, though in pain,
Vaunting⑭ aloud, but rackt⑮ with deep despare:

---

①Who from the terrour of this Arm so late/ Doubted his Empire:God, fearing the strength of our power which he lately confronted became uncertain of his authority and rule. Arm:battle 战争; so late:lately; Empire:imperium (Lat.), power 权威统治

②ignominy:dishonor 耻辱

③beneath:worse than 有过之而无不及

④this downfall:the defeat of Satan 撒旦的失败

⑤by fate:命中注定

⑥Gods:gods (Satan still believes himself gods.) 神

⑦Empyreal substance:heavenly being, angels 天使

⑧fail:perish 毁灭

⑨this great event:the rebellion of Satan from God and the battle against God

⑩our grand Foe:God 上帝

⑪Who now triumphs, and in th'excess of joy/ Sole reigning holds the Tyranny of Heav'n:who (God) now wins and in too much of joy holds the merciless control of heaven with monopoly. 他现在正沉湎于成功, 得意忘形, 独揽大权, 在天上掌握暴政呢

⑫spake:speak 的过去式

⑬th'Apostate Angel:here refers to Satan 变节的天使, 撒旦

⑭vaunt:boast 吹嘘

⑮rackt:racked 被折磨

And him thus answer'd soon his bold Compeer①.
O Prince, O Chief of many Throned Powers,
That led th'imbattelld② Seraphim③ to Warr
Under thy conduct④, and in dreadful deeds
Fearless, endanger'd Heav'ns perpetual King;
And put to proof his high Supremacy,
Whether upheld by strength, or Chance, or Fate,
Too well I see and rue⑤ the dire⑥ event,
That with sad overthrow and foul⑦ defeat
Hath lost us Heav'n, and all this mighty Host⑧
In horrible destruction laid thus low,
As far as⑨ Gods and Heav'nly Essences⑩
Can perish: for the mind and spirit remains
Invincible, and vigour soon returns,
Though all our Glory extinct, and happy state
Here swallow'd up in endless misery.
But what if he our Conquerour, (whom I now
Of force⑪ believe Almighty, since no less

---

①his bold Compeer：Beelzebub。Beelzebub（比尔泽布）又名 Baal-Zebul、Baal-Zebub,"豪宅之主""苍蝇王"。在希腊神话中也有这个魔王的痕迹,因为万神之父,Zeus 又名"避讳苍蝇者"。（失乐园中的）堕落天使

②imbattled：embattled 严阵以待的

③Seraphim：pl. of seraph, 六翼天使,"六翼天使"是来自《圣经》中以赛亚书第六章第二节,六翼天使即 Seraphim,在《圣经》中译作撒拉弗,是所有天使九阶中的最高位,即赞美上帝的天使,共有三对翅膀

④conduct：command 指挥

⑤rue：regret 后悔

⑥dire：dreadful or terrible 可怕的

⑦foul：shameful 可耻的

⑧mighty Host：strong army, the rebel angels 反对派的天使

⑨As far as：与前文的 thus 相搭配,意为"如此……以至于"

⑩Heav'nly Essences：the angels；essence：being

⑪of force：necessarily 必定地

Chapter 3　Literature of the English Revolution and Restoration

Than such could have orepow'rd such force as ours)
Have left us this our spirit and strength intire[①]
Strongly to suffer and support[②] our pains,
That we may so suffice[③] his vengeful ire[④],
Or do him mightier service as his thralls
By right of[⑤] Warr, what e're his business be
Here in the heart of Hell to work in Fire,
Or do his Errands in the gloomy Deep;
What can it then avail though yet we feel
Strength undiminisht, or eternal being
To undergo eternal punishment?[⑥]
Whereto with speedy words th'Arch-fiend[⑦] reply'd.

Fall'n Cherube, to be weak is miserable
Doing or Suffering[⑧]: but of this be sure,
To do aught[⑨] good never will be our task,
But ever to do ill our sole delight,
As being the contrary to his high will
Whom we resist. If then his Providence[⑩]
Out of our evil seek to bring forth good,
Our labour[⑪] must be to pervert that end,

---

①intire：entire 完整的
②support：endure 忍受
③suffice：satisfy 满足
④ire：anger 愤怒
⑤by right of：through 通过……的方式
⑥or eternal being / To undergo eternal punishment?：or being eternal, so as to undergo eternal punishment?
⑦Arch-fiend：Satan 大恶魔
⑧Doing or Suffering：Taking action or enduring 无论是采取行动还是在这里忍耐
⑨aught：anything 任何东西
⑩his Providence：God 上帝，天公
⑪labour：effort 努力

And out of good still① to find means of evil;
Which oft times may succeed, so as perhaps
Shall grieve him, if I fail not, and disturb
His inmost counsels from thir② destind aim.
But see the angry Victor hath recall'd
His Ministers③ of vengeance and pursuit
Back to the Gates of Heav'n: The Sulphurous Hail
Shot after us in storm, oreblown④ hath laid
The fiery Surge, that from the Precipice
Of Heav'n receiv'd us falling, and the Thunder,
Wing'd with red Lightning and impetuous rage,
Perhaps hath spent his shafts, and ceases now
To bellow through the vast and boundless Deep.
Let us not slip⑤ th'occasion, whether scorn,
Or satiate⑥ fury yield it from our Foe.
Seest thou yon⑦ dreary Plain, forlorn⑧ and wilde⑨,
The seat of desolation⑩, voyd of light⑪,
Save⑫ what the glimmering of these livid flames
Casts pale and dreadful? Thither⑬ let us tend
From off the tossing of these fiery waves,

---

①still: always 总是；常常
②thir: their
③His Ministers: the cherubs (天使 < cherub 复数 >) at God's disposal
④oreblown: blown over 被吹倒
⑤slip: miss 错过
⑥satiate: satiated, satisfied 满足了的
⑦yon: distant 远方的
⑧forlorn: desolate 人迹罕至的
⑨wilde: wild 荒凉的
⑩desolation: wilderness 荒芜
⑪voyd of light: void of light 没有光
⑫Save: except 除了
⑬Thither: to there 向那边

There rest, if any rest can harbour① there,
And reassembling our afflicted Powers,
Consult how we may henceforth most offend②
Our Enemy, our own loss how repair③,
How overcome this dire Calamity,
What reinforcement we may gain from Hope,
If not what resolution from despare④.

Questions for Discussion

1. Briefly summarize this excerpt.
2. Analyze Satan in *Paradise Lost*.

Unit 2 John Bunyan (1628–1688)

Appreciation

So the men were brought to examination; and they that sat upon them asked them whence they came, whither they went, and what they did there in such an unusual Garb? The men told them that they were Pilgrims and Strangers in the World, and that they were going to their own Country, which was the Heavenly Jerusalem; and that they had given no occasion to the men of the Town, nor yet to the Merchandizers, thus to abuse them, and to let them in their Journey, except it was for that, when one asked them what they would buy, they said they would buy the Truth. 于是那两个人被带去受审讯；审问他们的人问他们，从哪儿来，往哪儿去，穿着这种稀奇古怪的衣服在那儿干什么。那两个人说，他们是旅

---

①harbour: dwell 存在于
②offend: hurt 冒犯
③our own loss how repair: how we may repair our loss 我们如何修复我们的损失
④what resolution from despare: what resolution we may gain from despair 我们可能从绝望中获得什么决策

客,在世上是寄居的,他们到自己的家乡去,也就是到天上的耶路撒冷去;而且还说他们认为市民和商人没有理由这样辱骂他们,妨碍他们路,除非当有个人问他们要买什么时,他们说要买真理这件事可以算作一个理由。

John Bunyan was born in 1628 to Thomas and Margaret Bunyan in Bunyan's End in the parish of Elstow, Bedfordshire, England. Although he is regarded as a literary genius today, he had little formal education. His varied spiritual experience furnished his sensitive imagination with profound impression and vivid images. He wrote them down. The result is his book, *The Pilgrim's Progress*.

Brief Introduction

The Pilgrim's Progress, published in 1678, was written in the old fashioned medieval form of allegory and dream. It is a Christian allegory, which is regarded as one of the most significant works of English literature, and has been translated into more than 200 languages. Protestant missionaries commonly translated it as the first thing after the Bible. It tells of the spiritual pilgrimage of Christian.

The Pilgrim's Progress tells of a religious man's search for salvation, and gives a truthful picture of English society. The basis of the allegorical narrative is the idea of a journey. The traveler's name is Christian, and he represents every Christian in human world. The figures and places he encounters on his journey stand for the various experiences every Christian must go through in the quest for salvation.

The whole book falls into two parts. Part 1 tells of the religious conversion of Christian and his religious life in this world. Part 2 describes the subsequent conversion of his wife and their children. Christian, with a book in his hand and a burden on his back, flees from the City of Destruction and meets the perils and temptations of the Slough of Despond, Vanity Fair, and Doubting Castle. He faces and overcomes the demon Appollyon, journeys through the Interpreter's House, the Palace Beautiful, the Valley of the Shadow of Death, and the Delectable Mountains and finally reaches the Celestial City. The "pioneer pilgrims"—Christian and his associates—belong to the Puritan sect, who was undergoing persecution in the reign of Charles II, especially during the earlier years of Restoration. Bunyan uses simple, strong, masculine and direct style and language of the common people, which all readers can understand. He links the religious allegory with realistic character sketches.

One of the most remarkable passages is Vanity Fair in which the persecution of Christian and his friend Faithful are described. Christian, the hero, and his companion, Faithful, are passing through a town called Vanity during the season of the local fair. On the Vanity Fair, honors, titles, kingdoms, lusts, pleasures and lives can be sold or bought, and cheating, roguery, murder and adultery are normal phenomena. In the descriptions of the Vanity Fair, Bunyan not only gives us a symbolic picture of London at the time of the Restoration but of the whole bourgeois society.

"Vanity Fair" is a remarkable passage. It is an epitome 缩影 of the English society after the Restoration.

Selected Reading

The Pilgrim's Progress
Vanity Fair

Then I saw in my Dream, that when they① were got② out of the Wilderness, they presently saw a Town before them, and the name of that Town is Vanity; and at the Town there is a Fair kept, called Vanity Fair: it is kept all the year long; it beareth③ the name of Vanity Fair, because the Town where 'tis④ kept is lighter than Vanity; and also because all that is there sold, or that cometh thither, is Vanity. As is the saying of the wise, all that cometh is Vanity.

This Fair is no new-erected business, but a thing of ancient standing; I will shew you the original⑤ of it.

Almost five thousand years agone⑥, there were Pilgrims walking to the

---

①they: Christian and Faithful
②were got: had got
③beareth: bears 承受
④tis: it is
⑤original: origin 原点
⑥agone: ago

Celestial City, as these two honest persons are; and Beelzebub①, Apollyon②, and Legion③, with their Companions, perceiving by the path that the Pilgrims made, that their way to the City lay through this Town of Vanity, they contrived here to set up a Fair; a Fair wherein should be sold all sorts of Vanity, and that it should last all the year long: therefore at this Fair are all such Merchandize sold, as Houses, Lands, Trades, Places, Honours, Preferments④, Titles, Countries, Kingdoms, Lusts, Pleasures, and Delights of all sorts, as Whores, Bawds, Wives, Husbands, Children, Masters, Servants, Lives, Blood, Bodies, Souls, Silver, Gold, Pearls, Precious Stones, and what not⑤?

And moreover, at this Fair there is at all times to be seen Jugglings, Cheats, Games, Plays, Fools, Apes, Knaves, and Rogues, and that of every kind.

Here are to be seen too, and that for nothing, Thefts, Murders, Adulteries, false-swearers, and that of a blood-red colour.

And as in other Fairs of less moment⑥, there are the several Rows and Streets under their proper⑦ names, where such and such Wares are vended; so here likewise you have the proper places, Rows, Streets, (viz.⑧ Countries and Kingdoms) where the Wares of this Fair are soonest to be found: Here is the Britain Row, the French Row, the Italian Row, the Spanish Row, the German Row, where several sorts of Vanities are to be sold. But as in other Fairs, some one commodity is as the chief of all the Fair, so the ware of Rome and her Merchandize is greatly promoted in this Fair; only our English nation, with some

---

①Beelzebub: price of the devils（圣经中的）魔王，恶魔

②Apollyon: the Destroyer, "the Angel of the bottomless pit", 亚波伦，基督教的圣经启示录里，说是一位来自无底坑的使者，也就是来自地狱的魔鬼，也就是撒旦、恶魔的意思

③Legion: the "unclean spirit" sent by Jesus into the Gadarene swine 基督再临

④Preferments: appointments and promotions to political or ecclesiastical positions（尤指教会中的）美差，肥缺

⑤and what not: and so on

⑥moment: importance 重要，契机

⑦proper: own 本身的

⑧viz.: videlicet, namely

Chapter 3 Literature of the English Revolution and Restoration

others, have taken a dislike① thereat②.

Now, as I said, the way to the Celestial City lies just through this Town where this lusty③ Fair is kept; and he that will go to City, and yet not go through this Town, must needs go out of the world. The Prince of Princes④ himself, when here, went through this Town to his own Country, and that upon a Fair-day too; yea, and as I think, it was Beelzebub, the chief Lord of this Fair, that invited him to buy of his Vanities: yea, would have made him Lord of the Fair, would he but⑤ have done him reverence as he went through the Town. Yea, because he was such a person of honour, Beelzebub had him from Street to Street, and shewed him all the Kingdoms of the World in a little time, that he might, (if possible) allure that Blessed One⑥ to cheapen⑦ and buy some of his Vanities; but he had no mind to the Merchandize, and therefore left the Town, without laying out so much as one Farthing upon these Vanities. This Fair therefore is an antient thing, of long standing, and a very great Fair.

Now these Pilgrims, as I said, must needs go through this Fair. Well, so they did; but behold, even as they entered into the Fair, all the people in the Fair were moved, and the Town itself as it were in a hubbub about them; and that for several reasons: for

First, the Pilgrims were clothed with such kind of Raiment as was diverse from the Raiment of any that traded in that Fair. The people therefore of the Fair made a great gazing upon them: some said they were Fools, some they were Bedlams, and some they are Outlandish men.

Secondly, and as they wondered at their Apparel, so they did likewise at their Speech; for few could understand what they said: they naturally spoke the language of Canaan, but they that kept the Fair were the men of this World; so

---

①dislike: disapproval 反感
②thereat: at it, at Rome
③lusty: merry, cheerful 精力充沛的
④Prince of Princes: Christ 耶稣
⑤would he but: if only he would
⑥that Blessed One: Christ
⑦cheapen: barter for, to trade for, 贬低

that, from one end of the Fair to the other, they seemed Barbarians① each to the other.

Thirdly, but that which did not a little amuse② the Merchandizers was, that these Pilgrims set very light by all their Wares, they cared not so much as to look upon them; and if they called upon them to buy, they would put their fingers in their ears, and cry, turn away mine eyes from beholding Vanity, and look upwards, signifying that their trade and traffic③ was in Heaven.

One chanced mockingly, beholding the carriages④ of the men, to say unto them, What will ye buy? But they, looking gravely upon him, answered, We buy the Truth. At that there was an occasion taken to despise the men the more; some mocking, some taunting, some speaking reproachfully, and some calling upon others to smite them. At last things came to a hubbub and great stir in the Fair, insomuch that all order was confounded. Now was word presently brought to the Great One of the Fair, who quickly came down and deputed some of his most trusty friends to take those men into examination, about whom the Fair was almost overturned. So the men were brought to examination; and they that sat upon them asked them whence they came, whither they went, and what they did there in such an unusual Garb? The men told them that they were Pilgrims and Strangers in the World, and that they were going to their own Country, which was the Heavenly Jerusalem; and that they had given no occasion to the men of the Town, nor yet to the Merchandizers, thus to abuse them, and to let⑤ them in their Journey, except it was for that, when one asked them what they would buy, they said they would buy the Truth. But they that were appointed to examine them did not believe them to be any other than Bedlams and Mad, or else such as came to put all things into a confusion in the Fair. Therefore they took them and beat them, and besmeared them with dirt,

---

①Barbarians: foreigners, 外国人，外来人
②amuse: cause to gaze in astonishment, wonder, 消遣
③trade and traffic: business 贸易和交通
④carriage: behaviour 举止
⑤let: hinder, 障碍

and then put them into the Cage, that they might be made a spectacle to all the men of the Fair.

Questions for Discussion

1. How is satire used in *Vanity Fair*?
2. What does Bunyan want to express in *The Pilgrim's Progress*?

Unit 3　John Donne（1572－1631）

Appreciation

Such wilt thou be to me, who must, 这就是你和我的关系,我必须,
Like the other foot, obliquely run; 像另一只脚,斜走侧踱,
Thy firmness makes my circle just, 你的坚定能使我的圆圈圆得完美,
And makes me end where I begun. 让我的游离结束在我开始的地点。

John Donne was born in 1572 in London, England. Born into a Roman Catholic family, Donne's personal relationship with religion can be seen in his poetry. John Donne is known as the founder of the Metaphysical Poets, a term created by Samuel Johnson, an eighteenth-century English essayist, poet, and philosopher. Donne reached beyond the rational and hierarchical structures of the seventeenth century with his exacting and ingenious conceits, advancing the exploratory spirit of his time.

Brief Introduction

In *A Valediction*: *Forbidding Mourning*, the speaker explains that he is forced to spend time apart from his lover, but before he leaves, he tells her that their farewell should not be the occasion for mourning and sorrow. In the same way that virtuous men die mildly and without complaint, they should leave without "tear-flood" and "sigh-tempests", for to publicly announce their feelings in such a way would profane their love. The speaker says that when the earth moves, it brings "harm and fears", but when the spheres experience "trepidation", though the impact is greater, it is also innocent. The lover of "dull sublunary lovers" cannot survive separation, but it removes that which constitutes the love itself; but the love he shares with his beloved is so refined and "inter-assured of the mind" that they need not worry about missing "eyes, lips and hands".

Though he must go, their souls are still one, and therefore, they are not enduring a breach, they are experiencing an "expansion"; in the same way that gold can be stretched by beating it "to airy thinness", the soul they share will simply stretch to take in all the space between them. If their souls are separate, he says, they are like the feet of a compass: His lover's soul is the fixed foot in the center, and his is the foot that moves around it. The firmness of the center foot makes the circle that the outer foot draws perfect.

Selected Reading

A Valediction: Forbidding Mourning[①]

As virtuous men pass mildly away[②],
And whisper to their souls to go[③],
Whilst some of their sad friends do say,
"The breath goes now," and some say, "No,"

So let us melt[④], and make no noise,
No tear-floods, nor sigh-tempests move[⑤];
'Twere profanation of our joys

---

① A Valediction: Forbidding Mourning: A farewell. Don't grieve over my leaving. 再见，节哀
② pass mildly away: die peacefully 安祥地去世
③ Whisper to their souls to go: 向他们的灵魂说，走
④ So let us melt: 让我们融化，合二为一
⑤ No tear-floods, nor sigh-tempests move: 不再叹如风暴，泪如洪波。诗人把泪水比作洪水，把叹息比作风暴。move: stir up 激起，搅起

Chapter 3   Literature of the English Revolution and Restoration

To tell the laity our love.①

Moving of the earth② brings harms and fears,
Men reckon what it did and meant;③
But trepidation of the spheres④,
Though greater far, is innocent.⑤

Dull sublunary lovers' love⑥
(Whose soul is sense⑦) cannot admit⑧
Absence⑨, because it doth⑩ remove
Those things which elemented it.

But we, by a love so much refined⑪
That our selves know not what it is,

---

①'Twere profanation of our joys / To tell the laity our love: 如果向俗人诉说我们的爱情,就是对我们欢乐的亵渎。'Twere: It were, 诗人在这里使用了虚拟语气,说明事实上他不可能把自己的爱情向俗人诉说。profanation: blasphemy 亵渎。laity: one who is not a clergyman 非教会圣职人员。这两个词的选用充分显示了本诗浓重的宗教色彩

②Moving of the earth: earthquake 地震

③Men reckon what it did and meant: 人们猜测着,它(地震)的运动和意图

④trepidation of the spheres: trembling of the spheres 诸天体的震荡。根据托勒密的天文学(地心说),trepidation 指的是天体运行轨道中的第九重天(水晶圈)或第八重天(众恒星的轨道)的震荡或移动

⑤Though greater far, is innocent: 尽管诸天体震荡(与地震相比)更为巨大,然而,这种震荡却是无害的。innocent: harmless。根据托勒密的学说,诸天体运动有序和谐,虽然更加强烈巨大,却不会对人们构成伤害。然而,地震却能引起人们的恐慌。这里,诗人把爱人的别离比作巨大的天体运动,高尚而神秘,因此不能为凡人所理解

⑥Dull sublunary lovers' love: 乏味的凡夫俗子的爱情

⑦Whose soul is sense: 他们所注重的是感官。凡夫俗子的爱情重视感官上的满足,而不是精神上的追求。这和多恩本人所持的柏拉图式的爱情观形成鲜明的对照

⑧admit: suffer, stand 可容纳

⑨absence: being away 没有

⑩doth: does

⑪refined: purified 精练的

Inter-assured of the mind,
Careless, eyes, lips, and hands to miss.

Our two souls therefore, which are one,
Though I must go, endure not yet
A breach, but an expansion.
Like gold to airy thinness beat.

If they be two, they are two so
As stiff twin compasses are two①:
Thy soul, the fixed foot, makes no show
To move, but doth, if the other do;

And though it in the center sit,
Yet when the other far doth roam,
It leans, and hearkens after it②,
And grows erect, as that comes home.

Such wilt thou be to me, who must,
Like the other foot, obliquely run;③
Thy firmness makes my circle just,④
And makes me end where I begun.

---

①As stiff twin compasses are two: as stiff as the two legs of compass 如同圆规的双脚那样坚定
②It leans, and hearkens after it: 它(圆周角)也随之倾斜,并且侧耳倾听。hearken: listen to
③who must / like the other foot, obliquely run: (我)必将像那另一只脚,即动脚,倾斜着身子转圈。这里诗人着意指他即将启程的欧洲之旅。obliquely: slantingly 斜的
④Thy firmness makes my circle just: 你的坚定使我把圆画得完整

✤ Chapter 3 Literature of the English Revolution and Restoration ✤

Questions for Discussion

1. What are the writing features of *A Valediction: Forbidding Mourning*?
2. How is conceit used in *A Valediction: Forbidding Mourning*?

Terms

1. Allegory
2. Blank Verse
3. Conceit
4. Metaphysical poets
5. Cavalier poets

Chapter 4

18th-Century English Literature

I. Historical Background

1. The Augustan Age

After the tempestuous 17th century, England entered a period of comparatively peace and unity. In the middle of the 18th century, England had become the first powerful capitalist country in the world. The Tory and the Whig joined hands against tyranny and restoration of Catholicism, establishing a constitutional monarchy. The Puritan spirit of wisdom, diligence, honesty, and thriftiness contributed greatly to the development of the country.

Abroad, a vast expansion of British colonies in Asia, Africa and North America, and a continuous increase of colonial wealth and trade provided England with a market for which the small-scale, manual production methods of the home industry were hardly adequate. Besides, there were large-scale and long-drawn-out wars by professional armies and the station of large regiments in the colonies. The peaceful change of occupants of the throne entitled this period with the name Augustan Age or the Golden Age, chosen by those neoclassicists because of their admiration for the ancient culture of Roman Emperor Augustus Caesar (27BC – 14AD) and the belief that the greatest height of all proceeding civilizations had now found a worthy and comparable successor in the 18th century England.

2. The Industrial Revolution

The 18th century England witnessed unprecedented technical innovations which equipped industry with stream, the new moving force, and new tool, and rapid growth of industry and commerce, which influenced the way of social life as a whole. This is called the Industrial Revolution.

The Industrial Revolution widely developed in Britain and the English bourgeoisie accumulated more wealth and money and their social status was raised. The Enclosure Movement forced the peasants to seek new employment for their daily bread with a cheap price. The Industrial Revolution in Britain first began in the textile industry. And with the invention of large machines, new power had to be found. The increased production and trade promoted the transportation revolution. As a result, "workshop of the world" became another name for Britain by 1830.

With the fast development of industry in Britain, many big cities turned into "Black Country" with countless chimneys. More and more impoverished people herded into labour market and tended to work more time with less payment.

3. Great Changes in Social Life

The Industrial Revolution simplified class structure of Britain. The noble class could no longer compete with the middle class both in political influence and social influence. The biggest social problem in Britain at that time was the contradiction between the capitalist class and the proletariat class. The former was composed of the industrial and commercial classes and their appendices, and the latter was composed of expropriated small peasantry, victimized small craftsmen and small traders.

4. The Enlightenment

The 18th century marked the beginning of an intellectual movement, known as the Enlightenment, an expression of struggle of bourgeoisie against feudalism. The Enlightenment was a furtherance of the Renaissance of the 15th and 16th centuries.

The English enlighteners were bourgeois democratic thinkers. The purpose was to enlighten the whole world with the light of modern philosophical and artistic ideas. They celebrated reason or rationality, equality and science and advocated universal education. They stressed the importance of knowledge and reason, and they longed for a country of freedom, equality and love.

People were encouraged to cultivate a sound sense of rationality and a witty intellectuality. More schools were set up. Besides the popular forms of poetry, novel and drama, the period also saw the appearance of such popular press as pamphlets, newspapers and periodicals.

In the meantime of the Industrial Revolution, social life developed rapidly. Coffeehouses became the most striking feature of London life because people from many different walks of life could have enjoyable social lives and discuss intriguing and thought-provoking matters, especially those regarding philosophy to politics in a unique environment. The first English coffeehouse opened in Oxford in 1650. Nearly all writers frequented the coffeehouses and thus such manners as politics and fashion became subjects of literature.

II. Literature Background

In the later part of the 18th century, people began to feel discontented with the rigidity of rationality. A demand for a release of one's spontaneous feeling, a relaxation from the cold and rigid logic of rationality and an escape from the inhuman Industrial Revolution gradually took shape in the form of sentimental and pre-romantic novel and poetry. Novel, sentimental and pre-romantic poetry and fiction appeared in the last few decades of the 18th century.

1. Neoclassicism

In the early decades of the 18th century, the Enlightenment Movement brought about a revival of interest in the old classical works. This tendency is known as neoclassicism.

In England, neoclassicism was initiated by John Dryden, culminated in Alexander Pope and continued by Samuel Johnson. It was a reaction against the fire of passions that blazed in the late Renaissance, whose literary artistic model was the classical literature of ancient Greek and Latin authors, such as Homer, Virgil, Horace. They believed that the artistic ideals should be order, logic, restrained emotion and accuracy, and that literature should be judged in terms of its service to humanity. Neoclassicism made a rapid growth and prevailed in the 18th century. In drama, they follow the Three Unities 三一律 closely which were called respectively unity of action, unity of place, and unity of time.

Alexander Pope (1688 – 1744) is the early representative poet of neoclassical school, best known for his satirical verse and for his translation of Homer, who introduced Enlightenment and popularized the neoclassical literary tradition from

France. Pope was a master in the art of poetry whose style also depended upon his great patience in elaborating his art. By frequently writing in the form of heroic couplet, he became so perfect that no one has been able to approach him. He was singularly direct and compact. He represented the highest glory and authority in matters of literary art and made great contributions to the theory and practice of prosody 诗学. His Major Works: *An Essay on Criticism* (a manifesto of English neo-classicism)论批评, *Essay on Man* 人论, *The Dunciad* 愚人志, *The Rape of the Lock* 卷发遭劫记.

He was a great satirist and a literary critic who occupied a prominent place in his time. The early period of the 18th century has often been named after him as "The Age of Pope".

2. The Rise of the Novel

The novel emerged in England at the beginning of the 18th century in the form of a fictional imitation of the diaries, autobiographies, travelers' tales and biographies of criminals. The rise and growth of the realistic novel is the most prominent achievement. Realism plays a leading role in the 18th century literature, readers of novel were enlarging, and novel writing became colorful.

The summit of 18th century English literature is the novel. Excellent novelists emerged and told about ordinary people's thoughts, feelings and struggles. By combining the allegorical tradition of the moral fables with the picaresque 流浪汉的 tradition of the lower-caste stories, they achieved in their works both realism and moral teaching. The realist novelists of the 18th century are Daniel Defoe, Jonathan Swift, Henry Fielding and Tobias George Smollett.

3. Sentimentalism

One of the significant and popular trends in the second half of the 18th century is sentimentalism, which is a mild kind of protest against the social crisis. It could be defined to be overindulgence in one's emotion for the sake of his overwhelming discontent towards the social reality, and pessimistic belief and emphasis upon the virtues of man. Along with a new vision of love, sentimentalism presented a new view of human nature which prized feeling over thinking, passion over reason, and personal instincts of "pity, tenderness and benevolence" over social duties. Literary work of the sentimentalism marked by a sincere sympathy for the poverty-stricken, expropriated 征用

peasants, wrote the "simple annals of the poor". Sentimentalists appealed to sentiment, to the human heart and turned to the countryside for its material.

Thomas Gray, Oliver Goldsmith, Laurence Sterne, Samuel Richardson are representatives of Sentimentalism who criticized the viciousness of the social reality, and dreamed in vain for the return of the patriarchal mode of life. The obvious hopelessness of their dream brought about a pessimistic outlook. They blamed reason and the Industrial Revolution for the miseries and injustices in the aristocratic-bourgeois society and indulged in sentiment. Generally speaking, sentimentalism found fine expression in poetry and novel. They attacked the progressive aspect of this great social change in order to eliminate it and sighed for the return of the patriarchal times which they idealized. Writing still in a classical style, sentimentalism marks the midway in the transition from neoclassicism to its opposite, Romanticism in English poetry.

4. Pre-Romanticism

Pre-Romanticism originated among the conservative groups of men and letters as a reaction against the Enlightenment. In the second half of the 18th century, a new literary movement arose in Europe, called the Romantic Revival. It was marked by a strong protest against Classicism, by a recognition of the claims of passion and emotion, and by a renewed interest in medieval literature. In England, this movement showed itself in the trend of Pre-Romanticism in poetry. William Blake and Robert Burns are the representatives. Their writings provide a new code of social morality for the rising bourgeoisie and give a true picture of the social life of England in the 18th century.

Unit 1　Daniel Defoe (1660 – 1731)

Appreciation

It might be truly said, that now I worked for my bread. I believe few people have thought much upon the strange multitude of little things necessary in the providing, producing, curing, dressing, making, and finishing this one article of bread. 人们常说"为面包而工作", 其意思是"为生存而工作"。为了制成面包这样小小的不起眼的东西, 你首先得做好播种准备, 生产出粮食, 再要经过晒、筛、制、烤等种种奇怪而繁杂的

必不可少的过程，真不能不令人惊叹。我也想，很少人会想到，我们天天吃的面包要真的自己动手从头做起是多么不容易啊！

The son of a London butcher, and educated at a Dissenters' academy, Defoe was typical of the new kind of man reaching prominence in England in the 18th century.

Defoe has been called the father of modern journalism; during his lifetime he was associated with 26 periodicals. In 1719 he published his famous *Life and Strange Surprising Adventures of Robinson Crusoe*, followed by two less engrossing sequels. Based in part on the experiences of Alexander Selkirk, *Robinson Crusoe* is considered by some critics to be the first true novel in English. From 1719 to 1724, Defoe published the novels for which he is famous.

Daniel Defoe died on April 24, 1731, probably while in hiding from his creditors. He was interred in Bunhill Fields, London, where his grave can still be visited.

Brief Introduction

At the head of Defoe's works stands his most important work *The Life and Strange Surprising Adventures of Robinson Crusoe* and held its popularity for more than two centuries.

The story was based upon the experiences of a Scotch sailor called Alexander Selkirk, who had been marooned on a desert island off the coast of Chile and lived there in solitude for four or five years. After his return to Europe in 1709, his experiences became known. Defoe got inspiration from this real story and with many incidents of his own imagination, he successfully produced the famous novel *Robinson Crusoe*.

The story is told in the first person singular as if it was told by some sailor-adventurer himself. In this novel, Defoe created the image of a true empire-builder, a colonizer and a foreign trader, who has the courage and will to face hardships and the determination to preserve himself and improve his livelihood by struggling against nature. Crusoe represents the English bourgeoisie at the earlier stage of its development. Being a bourgeois writer, Defoe glorifies the hero and defends the policy of colonialism of British government.

Selected Reading

Robinson Crusoe
Chapter 3

I was now, in the months of November and December, expecting my crop of barley and rice. The ground I had manured and dug up for them was not great; for, as I observed, my seed of each was not above the quantity of half a peck, for I had lost one whole crop by sowing in the dry season. But now my crop promised very well, when on a sudden I found I was in danger of losing it all again by enemies of several sorts, which it was scarcely possible to keep from it; as, first, the goats, and wild creatures which I called hares, who, tasting the sweetness of the blade, lay in it night and day, as soon as it came up, and eat it so close, that it could get no time to shoot up into stalk.

This I saw no remedy for but by making an enclosure about it with a hedge; which I did with a great deal of toil, and the more, because it required speed. However, as my arable land was but small, suited to my crop, I got it totally well fenced in about three weeks'time; and shooting some of the creatures in the daytime, I set my dog to guard it in the night, tying him up to a stake at the gate, where he would stand and bark all night long; so in a little time the enemies forsook the place, and the corn grew very strong and well, and began to ripen apace.

But as the beasts ruined me before, while my corn was in the blade, so the birds were as likely to ruin me now, when it was in the ear; for, going along by the place to see how it throve, I saw my little crop surrounded with fowls, of I know not how many sorts, who stood, as it were, watching till I should be gone. I immediately let fly among them, for I always had my gun with me. I had no sooner shot, but there rose up a little cloud of fowls, which I had not seen at all, from among the corn itself.

This touched me sensibly, for I foresaw that in a few days they would devour all my hopes; that I should be starved, and never be able to raise a crop at all; and what to do I could not tell; however, I resolved not to lose my corn, if possible, though I should watch it night and day. In the first place, I went among it to see what damage was already done, and found they had spoiled a good deal of it; but that as it was yet too green for them, the loss was not so great but that the remainder was likely to be a good crop if it could be saved.

I stayed by it to load my gun, and then coming away, I could easily see the thieves sitting upon all the trees about me, as if they only waited till I was gone away, and the event proved it to be so; for as I walked off, as if I was gone, I was no sooner out of their sight than they dropped down one by one into the corn again. I was so provoked, that I could not have patience to stay till more came on, knowing that every grain that they ate now was, as it might be said, a peck-loaf to me in the consequence; but coming up to the hedge, I fired again, and killed three of them. This was what I wished for; so I took them up, and served them as we serve notorious[①] thieves in England-hanged them in chains, for a terror to of them. It is impossible to imagine that this should have such an effect as it had, for the fowls[②] would not only not come at the corn, but, in short, they forsook all that part of the island, and I could never see a bird near the place as long as my scarecrows[③] hung there.

This I was very glad of, you may be sure, and about the latter end of December, which was our second harvest of the year, I reaped my corn.

I was sadly put to it for a scythe or sickle to cut it down, and all I could do was to make one, as well as I could, out of one of the broadswords[④], or cutlasses[⑤], which I saved among the arms out of the ship. However, as my first crop was but small, I had no great difficulty to cut it down; in short, I reaped it in my way, for I cut nothing off but the ears, and carried it away in a great

---

①notorious:声名狼藉的
②fowl:家禽
③scarecrow:稻草人,威吓物
④broadsword:大刀;腰刀
⑤cutlass:弯刀;短剑

basket which I had made, and so rubbed it out with my hands; and at the end of all my harvesting, I found that out of my half-peck① of seed I had near two bushels of rice, and about two bushels② and a half of barley; that is to say, by my guess, for I had no measure at that time.

However, this was a great encouragement to me, and I foresaw that, in time, it would please God to supply me with bread. And yet here I was perplexed again, for I neither knew how to grind or make meal of my corn, or indeed how to clean it and part it; nor, if made into meal, how to make bread of it; and if how to make it, yet I knew not how to bake it. These things being added to my desire of having a good quantity for store, and to secure a constant supply, I resolved not to taste any of this crop but to preserve it all for seed against the next season; and in the meantime to employ all my study and hours of working to accomplish this great work of providing myself with corn and bread.

It might be truly said, that now I worked for my bread. I believe few people have thought much upon the strange multitude of little things necessary in the providing, producing, curing, dressing, making, and finishing this one article of bread.

I, that was reduced to a mere state of nature, found this to my daily discouragement; and was made more sensible of it every hour, even after I had got the first handful of seed-corn, which, as I have said, came up unexpectedly, and indeed to a surprise.

First, I had no plough to turn up the earth—no spade or shovel to dig it. Well, this I conquered by making me a wooden spade, as I observed before; but this did my work but in a wooden manner③; and though it cost me a great many days to make it, yet, for want of iron, it not only wore out soon, but made my work the harder, and made it be performed much worse.

However, this I bore with, and was content to work it out with patience,

---

①half-peck:半配克,4夸脱
②bushel:蒲式耳
③but in a wooden manner: but in a clumsy manner 但用一个笨拙的方式

and bear with the badness of the performance. When the corn was sown, I had no harrow, but was forced to go over it myself, and drag a great heavy bough of a tree over it, to scratch it, as it may be called, rather than rake① or harrow② it.

When it was growing, and grown, I have observed already how many things I wanted to fence it, secure it, mow or reap it, cure and carry it home, thrash, part it from the chaff③, and save it. Then I wanted a mill to grind it sieves to dress it, yeast④ and salt to make it into bread, and an oven to bake it; but all these things I did without, as shall be observed; and yet the corn was an inestimable⑤ comfort and advantage to me too. All this, as I said, made everything laborious and tedious to me; but that there was no help for. Neither was my time so much loss to me, because, as I had divided it, a certain part of it was every day appointed to these works; and as I had resolved to use none of the corn for bread till I had a greater quantity by me, I had the next six months to apply myself wholly, by labour and invention, to furnish myself with utensils proper for the performing all the operations necessary for making the corn, when I had it, fit for my use.

But first I was to prepare more land, for I had now seed enough to sow above an acre of ground. Before I did this, I had a week's work at least to make me a spade, which, when it was done, was but a sorry one indeed, and very heavy, and required double labour to work with it. However, I got through that, and sowed my seed in two large flat pieces of ground, as near my house as I could find them to my mind⑥, and fenced them in with a good hedge, the stakes⑦ of which were all cut off that wood which I had set before, and knew it would grow; so that, in a year's time, I knew I should have a quick or living hedge, that would want but little repair. This work did not take me up less than

---

①rake：耙子
②harrow：耙地
③chaff：糠；谷壳
④yeast：酵母
⑤inestimable：无价的；难以估计的
⑥to my mind：to my liking 中人的意
⑦stake：桩，棍子

three months, because a great part of that time was the wet season, when I could not go abroad.

Within doors, that is when it rained and I could not go out, I found employment in the following occupations—always observing, that all the while I was at work I diverted① myself with talking to my parrot, and teaching him to speak; and I quickly taught him to know his own name, and at last to speak it out pretty loud, "Poll", which was the first word I ever heard spoken in the island by any mouth but my own. This, therefore, was not my work, but an assistance to my work; for now, as I said, I had a great employment upon my hands, as follows: I had long studied to make, by some means or other, some earthen vessels, which, indeed, I wanted sorely, but knew not where to come at them. However, considering the heat of the climate, I did not doubt but if I could find out any clay, I might make some pots that might, being dried in the sun, be hard enough and strong enough to bear handling, and to hold anything that was dry, and required to be kept so; and as this was necessary in the preparing corn, meal, &c., which was the thing I was doing, I resolved to make some as large as I could, and fit only to stand like jars, to hold what should be put into them.

It would make the reader pity me, or rather laugh at me, to tell how many awkward ways I took to raise this paste; what odd, misshapen, ugly things I made; how many of them fell in and how many fell out, the clay not being stiff enough to bear its own weight; how many cracked by the over-violent heat of the sun, being set out too hastily; and how many fell in pieces with only removing, as well before as after they were dried; and, in a word, how, after having laboured hard to find the clay—to dig it, to temper it, to bring it home, and work it—I could not make above two large earthen ugly things (I cannot call them jars) in about two months' labour.

However, as the sun baked these two very dry and hard, I lifted them very gently up, and set them down again in two great wicker② baskets, which I had

---

①divert:转移
②wicker:柳条

made on purpose for them, that they might not break; and as between the pot and the basket there was a little room to spare, I stuffed it full of the rice and barley straw; and these two pots being to stand always dry I thought would hold my dry corn, and perhaps the meal, when the corn was bruised.

Though I miscarried so much in my design for large pots, yet I made several smaller things with better success; such as little round pots, flat dishes, pitchers, and pipkins, and any things my hand turned to; and the heat of the sun baked them quite hard.

But all this would not answer my end, which was to get an earthen pot to hold what was liquid, and bear the fire, which none of these could do. It happened after some time, making a pretty large fire for cooking my meat, when I went to put it out after I had done with it, I found a broken piece of one of my earthenware vessels in the fire, burnt as hard as a stone, and red as a tile. I was agreeably surprised to see it, and said to myself, that certainly they might be made to burn whole, if they would burn broken.

This set me to study how to order my fire, so as to make it burn some pots. I had no notion of a kiln, such as the potters burn in, or of glazing them with lead, though I had some lead to do it with; but I placed three large pipkins① and two or three pots in a pile, one upon another, and placed my firewood all round it, with a great heap of embers② under them. I plied the fire with fresh fuel round the outside and upon the top, till I saw the pots in the inside red-hot③ quite through, and observed that they did not crack at all. When I saw them clear④ red, I let them stand in that heat about five or six hours, till I found one of them, though it did not crack, did melt or run; for the sand which was mixed with the clay melted by the violence of the heat, and would have run into glass if I had gone on; so I slacked my fire gradually till the pots began to abate of the red colour; and watching them all night, that I might not let the fire abate too

---

①pipkin：小瓦罐；小汲桶
②embers：余烬
③red-hot：热狗
④clear：completely 完全地

fast, in the morning I had three very good (I will not say handsome) pipkins, and two other earthen pots, as hard burnt as could be desired, and one of them perfectly glazed with the running of the sand.

After this experiment, I need not say that I wanted no sort of earthenware for my use; but I must needs say as to the shapes of them, they were very indifferent①, as any one may suppose, when I had no way of making them but as the children make dirt pies, or as a woman would make pies that never learned to raise paste.

No joy at a thing of so mean a nature was ever equal to mine, when I found I had made an earthen pot that would bear the fire; and I had hardly patience to stay till they were cold before I set one on the fire again with some water in it to boil me some meat, which it did admirably well; and with a piece of a kid I made some very good broth, though I wanted oatmeal, and several other ingredients requisite to make it as good as I would have had it been.

My next concern was to get me a stone mortar to stamp or beat some corn in; for as to the mill, there was no thought of arriving at that perfection of art with one pair of hands. To supply this want, I was at a great loss; for, of all the trades in the world, I was as perfectly unqualified for a stone-cutter as for any whatever; neither had I any tools to go about it with. I spent many a day to find out a great stone big enough to cut hollow, and make fit for a mortar, and could find none at all, except what was in the solid rock, and which I had no way to dig or cut out; nor indeed were the rocks in the island of hardness sufficient, but were all of a sandy, crumbling② stone, which neither would bear the weight of a heavy pestle, nor would break the corn without filling it with sand. So, after a great deal of time lost in searching for a stone, I gave it over, and resolved to look out for a great block of hard wood, which I found, indeed, much easier; and getting one as big as I had strength to stir, I rounded it, and formed it on the outside with my axe and hatchet, and then with the help of fire and infinite labour, made a hollow place in it, as the Indians in Brazil make their canoes.

---

①they were very indifferent: they were not very good 他们不是很好

②crumble: 破碎，粉碎

After this, I made a great heavy pestle or beater of the wood called the iron-wood; and this I prepared and laid by against I had my next crop of corn, which I proposed to myself to grind, or rather pound into meal to make bread.

My next difficulty was to make a sieve or searce, to dress my meal, and to part it from the bran and the husk; without which I did not see it possible I could have any bread. This was a most difficult thing even to think on, for to be sure I had nothing like the necessary thing to make it—I mean fine thin canvas or stuff to searce the meal through. And here I was at a full stop for many months; nor did I really know what to do. Linen I had none left but what was mere rags; I had goat's hair, but neither knew how to weave it or spin it; and had I known how, here were no tools to work it with. All the remedy that I found for this was, that at last I did remember I had, among the seamen's clothes which were saved out of the ship, some neckcloths of calico or muslin①; and with some pieces of these I made three small sieves proper enough for the work; and thus I made shift for some years: how I did afterwards, I shall show in its place.

The baking part was the next thing to be considered, and how I should make bread when I came to have corn; for first, I had no yeast. As to that part, there was no supplying the want, so I did not concern myself much about it. But for an oven I was indeed in great pain. At length I found out an experiment for that also, which was this: I made some earthen-vessels very broad but not deep, that is to say, about two feet diameter, and not above nine inches deep. These I burned in the fire, as I had done the other, and laid them by; and when I wanted to bake, I made a great fire upon my hearth, which I had paved with some square tiles of my own baking and burning also; but I should not call them square.

When the firewood was burned pretty much into embers or live coals, I drew them forward upon this hearth, so as to cover it all over, and there I let them lie till the hearth was very hot. Then sweeping away all the embers, I set down my loaf or loaves, and whelming down the earthen pot upon them, drew the embers all round the outside of the pot, to keep in and add to the heat; and

---

①neckcloths of calico or muslin:白布或棉布领带

thus as well as in the best oven in the world, I baked my barley-loaves, and became in little time a good pastrycook① into the bargain; for I made myself several cakes and puddings of the rice; but I made no pies, neither had I anything to put into them supposing I had, except the flesh either of fowls or goats.

It need not be wondered at if all these things took me up most part of the third year of my abode here; for it is to be observed that in the intervals of these things I had my new harvest and husbandry to manage; for I reaped my corn in its season, and carried it home as well as I could, and laid it up in the ear, in my large baskets, till I had time to rub it out, for I had no floor to thrash it on, or instrument to thrash② it with.

And now, indeed, my stock of corn increasing, I really wanted to build my barns bigger; I wanted a place to lay it up in, for the increase of the corn now yielded me so much, that I had of the barley about twenty bushels, and of the rice as much or more; insomuch that now I resolved to begin to use it freely; for my bread had been quite gone a great while; also I resolved to see what quantity would be sufficient for me a whole year, and to sow but once a year.

Upon the whole, I found that the forty bushels of barley and rice were much more than I could consume in a year; so I resolved to sow just the same quantity every year that I sowed the last, in hopes that such a quantity would fully provide me with bread, & c.

Questions for Discussion

Discuss Crusoe as an embodiment of the rising middle-class virtues in the mid-18th century England.

---

①pastrycook:做西点、面包的人
②thrash:打谷;逆风浪行

Unit 2 Jonathan Swift (1667–1745)

Appreciation

The other project was, a scheme for entirely abolishing all words whatsoever; and this was urged as a great advantage in point of health, as well as brevity. For it is plain, that every word we speak is, in some degree, a diminution of our lunge by corrosion, and consequently, contributes to the shortening of our lives. An expedient was therefore offered, "that since words are only names for things, it would be more convenient for all men to carry about them such things as were necessary to express a particular business they are to discourse on." 另一项计划则是，无论什么词汇，一概废除。他们坚决主张，不论从健康的角度考虑，还是从简练的角度考虑，这一计划都大有好处，因为大家都清楚，我们每说一个词，或多或少会对肺部有所侵蚀，这样也就缩短了我们的寿命。因此他们就想出了一个补救的办法：既然词只是事物的名称，那么，大家在谈到具体事情的时候，把表示那具体事情所需的东西带在身边，不是来得更方便吗？

Jonathan Swift was born in Dublin, Ireland. And he is probably the foremost prose satirist in the English language, and is less well known for his poetry. He is also known for two styles of satire: the Horatian and Juvenalian styles.

Swift's family had several interesting literary connections: His grandmother, Elizabeth (Dryden) Swift, was the niece of Sir Erasmus Dryden, grandfather of the poet John Dryden. The same grandmother's aunt, Katherine (Throckmorton) Dryden, was the first cousin of Elizabeth, wife of Sir Walter Raleigh. His great-great grandmother, Margaret (Godwin) Swift, was the sister of Francis Godwin, author of *The Man in the Moone* which influenced parts of Swift's *Gulliver's Travels*. His uncle, Thomas Swift, married a daughter of the poet and playwright Sir William Davenant, a godson of William Shakespeare.

Brief Introduction

Gulliver's Travels contains four parts; each of them deals with one particular voyage of the hero and his extraordinary adventures on some remote island.

The third part, which is often considered to be the least interesting, deals with a series of the hero's adventures at several places. The first place that Gulliver gets to is the floating island of Laputa. Gulliver finds out here the king and the noble persons are a group of absent-minded philosophers and astronomers who care for nothing but mathematics and music and who speak always in mathematical terms of lines and circles. They often do useless research work, for example a scientist makes researches on how to get sunlight from cucumbers. Another scientist is studying how to construct a house by first building the room and then laying the base. Through these descriptions, Swift satirizes the scientists who keep themselves aloof from practical life.

Selected Reading

Gulliver's Travels

Part III. A VOYAGE TO LAPUTA, BALNIBARBI, LUGGNAGG, GLUBBDUBDRIB, AND JAPAN.

Chapter 5

The author permitted to see the grand academy of Lagado①. The academy largely described. The arts where in the professors employ themselves.

This academy is not an entire single building, but a continuation of several houses on both sides of a street, which growing waste, was purchased and applied to that use.

I was received very kindly by the warden, and went for many days to the academy. Every room has in it one or more projectors; and I believe I could not be in fewer than five hundred rooms.

The first man I saw was of a meagre aspect, with sooty hands and face, his hair and beard long, ragged, and singed in several places. His clothes, shirt,

---

①Lagado: Lagado is the capital of the nation Balnibarbi, which is ruled by a tyrannical king from a flying island called Laputa. Lagado is on the ground below Laputa, and also has access to Laputa at any given time to proceed in an attack or defense

and skin, were all of the same colour. He has been eight years upon a project for extracting sunbeams out of cucumbers, which were to be put in phials hermetically sealed①, and let out to warm the air in raw inclement summers. He told me, he did not doubt, that, in eight years more, he should be able to supply the governor's gardens with sunshine, at a reasonable rate: but he complained that his stock was low, and entreated me "to give him something as an encouragement to ingenuity, especially since this had been a very dear season for cucumbers." I made him a small present, for my lord had furnished me with money on purpose, because he knew their practice of begging from all who go to see them.

I went into another chamber, but was ready to hasten back, being almost overcome with a horrible stink. My conductor pressed me forward, conjuring me in a whisper "to give no offence, which would be highly resented;" and therefore I durst not so much as stop my nose. The projector of this cell was the most ancient student of the academy; his face and beard were of a pale yellow; his hands and clothes daubed over with filth. When I was presented to him, he gave me a close embrace, a compliment I could well have excused. His employment, from his first coming into the academy, was an operation to reduce human excrement to its original food, by separating the several parts, removing the tincture which it receives from the gall②, making the odour③ exhale, and scumming off the saliva. He had a weekly allowance, from the society, of a vessel filled with human ordure, about the bigness of a Bristol barrel.

I saw another at work to calcine④ ice into gunpowder; who likewise showed me a treatise he had written concerning the malleability⑤ of fire, which he intended to publish.

---

① hermetically sealed: completely sealed, especially against the escape or entry of air 密封的
② gall: 胆汁
③ odour: 气味
④ calcine: 煅烧
⑤ malleability: 可塑性

There was a most ingenious architect, who had contrived a new method for building houses, by beginning at the roof, and working downward to the foundation; which he justified to me, by the like practice of those two prudent insects, the bee and the spider.

There was a man born blind, who had several apprentices in his own condition: their employment was to mix colours for painters, which their master taught them to distinguish by feeling and smelling. It was indeed my misfortune to find them at that time not very perfect in their lessons, and the professor himself happened to be generally mistaken. This artist is much encouraged and esteemed by the whole fraternity.

In another apartment I was highly pleased with a projector who had found a device of ploughing the ground with hogs, to save the charges of ploughs, cattle, and labour. The method is this: in an acre of ground you bury, at six inches distance and eight deep, a quantity of acorns, dates, chestnuts, and other mast or vegetables, whereof these animals are fondest; then you drive six hundred or more of them into the field, where, in a few days, they will root up the whole ground in search of their food, and make it fit for sowing, at the same time manuring it with their dung: it is true, upon experiment, they found the charge and trouble very great, and they had little or no crop. However it is not doubted, that this invention may be capable of great improvement.

I went into another room, where the walls and ceiling were all hung round with cobwebs, except a narrow passage for the artist to go in and out. At my entrance, he called aloud to me, "not to disturb his webs." He lamented "the fatal mistake the world had been so long in, of using silkworms, while we had such plenty of domestic insects who infinitely excelled the former, because they understood how to weave, as well as spin." And he proposed further, "that by employing spiders, the charge of dyeing silks should be wholly saved;" whereof I was fully convinced, when he showed me a vast number of flies most beautifully coloured, wherewith he fed his spiders, assuring us "that the webs would take a tincture from them; and as he had them of all hues, he hoped to fit everybody's fancy, as soon as he could find proper food for the flies, of certain gums, oils, and other glutinous① matter, to give a strength and consistence to the threads."

There was an astronomer, who had undertaken to place a sun-dial upon the great weathercock on the town-house, by adjusting the annual and diurnal motions of the earth and sun, so as to answer and coincide with all accidental turnings of the wind.

I was complaining of a small fit of the colic, upon which my conductor led me into a room where a great physician resided, who was famous for curing that disease, by contrary operations from the same instrument. He had a large pair of bellows②, with a long slender muzzle of ivory: this he conveyed eight inches up the anus, and drawing in the wind, he affirmed he could make the guts as lank as a dried bladder. But when the disease was more stubborn and violent, he let in the muzzle while the bellows were full of wind, which he discharged into the body of the patient; then withdrew the instrument to replenish it, clapping his thumb strongly against the orifice③ of then fundament; and this being repeated three or four times, the adventitious④ wind would rush out, bringing the noxious⑤ along with it, (like water put into a pump) and the patient recovered. I saw him try both experiments upon a dog, but could not discern any effect from the former. After the latter the animal was ready to burst, and made so violent a discharge as was very offensive to me and my companion. The dog died on the spot, and we left the doctor endeavouring to recover him, by the same operation.

I visited many other apartments, but shall not trouble my reader with all the curiosities I observed, being studious of brevity.

I had hitherto seen only one side of the academy, the other being appropriated to the advancers of speculative learning, of whom I shall say

---

①glutinous：有黏性的
②bellows：风箱
③orifice：口、孔
④adventitious：偶然的
⑤noxious：毒

something, when I have mentioned one illustrious person more, who is called among them "the universal artist". He told us, "he had been thirty years employing his thoughts for the improvement of human life." He had two large rooms full of wonderful curiosities, and fifty men at work. Some were condensing air into a dry tangible substance, by extracting the nitre①, and letting the aqueous② or fluid particles percolate③; others softening marble, for pillows and pin-cushions; others petrifying the hoofs of a living horse, to preserve them from foundering. The artist himself was at that time busy upon two great designs; the first, to sow land with chaff④, wherein he affirmed the true seminal virtue to be contained, as he demonstrated by several experiments, which I was not skilful enough to comprehend. The other was, by a certain composition of gums, minerals, and vegetables, outwardly applied, to prevent the growth of wool upon two young lambs; and he hoped, in a reasonable time to propagate the breed of naked sheep, all over the kingdom.

We crossed a walk to the other part of the academy, where, as I have already said, the projectors in speculative learning resided.

The first professor I saw, was in a very large room, with forty pupils about him. After salutation, observing me to look earnestly upon a frame, which took up the greatest part of both the length and breadth of the room, he said, "Perhaps I might wonder to see him employed in a project for improving speculative knowledge, by practical and mechanical operations. But the world would soon be sensible of its usefulness; and he flattered himself, that a more noble, exalted thought never sprang in any other man's head. Every one knew how laborious⑤ the usual method is of attaining to arts and sciences; whereas, by his contrivance, the most ignorant person, at a reasonable charge, and with a little bodily labour, might write books in philosophy, poetry, politics, laws,

---

①nitre：硝
②aqueous：水
③percolate：过滤
④chaff：糠
⑤laborious：费力的

mathematics, and theology, without the least assistance from genius or study." He then led me to the frame, about the sides, whereof all his pupils stood in ranks. It was twenty feet square, placed in the middle of the room. The superfices was composed of several bits of wood, about the bigness of a die, but some larger than others. They were all linked together by slender wires. These bits of wood were covered, on every square, with paper pasted on them; and on these papers were written all the words of their language, in their several moods, tenses, and declensions; but without any order. The professor then desired me, "to observe; for he was going to set his engine at work." The pupils, at his command, took each of them hold of an iron handle, whereof there were forty fixed round the edges of the frame; and giving them a sudden turn, the whole disposition of the words was entirely changed. He then commanded six-and-thirty of the lads, to read the several lines softly, as they appeared upon the frame; and where they found three or four words together that might make part of a sentence, they dictated to the four remaining boys, who were scribes. This work was repeated three or four times, and at every turn, the engine was so contrived, that the words shifted into new places, as the square bits of wood moved upside down.

Six hours a day the young students were employed in this labour; and the professor showed me several volumes in large folio, already collected, of broken sentences, which he intended to piece together, and out of those rich materials, to give the world a complete body of all arts and sciences; which, however, might be still improved, and much expedited, if the public would raise a fund for making and employing five hundred such frames in Lagado, and oblige the managers to contribute in common their several collections.

He assured me "that this invention had employed all his thoughts from his youth; that he had emptied the whole vocabulary into his frame, and made the strictest computation of the general proportion there is in books between the numbers of particles, nouns, and verbs, and other parts of speech."

I made my humblest acknowledgment to this illustrious person, for his great communicativeness; and promised, "if ever I had the good fortune to return to my native country, that I would do him justice, as the sole inventor of this wonderful machine;" the form and contrivance of which I desired leave to delineate on paper, as in the figure here annexed. I told him, "although it were the custom of our learned in Europe to steal inventions from each other, who had thereby at least this advantage, that it became a controversy which was the right owner; yet I would take such caution, that he should have the honour entire, without a rival."

We next went to the school of languages, where three professors sat in consultation upon improving that of their own country.

The first project was, to shorten discourse, by cutting polysyllables[①] into one, and leaving out verbs and participles, because, in reality, all things imaginable are but norms.

The other project was, a scheme for entirely abolishing all words whatsoever; and this was urged as a great advantage in point of health, as well as brevity. For it is plain, that every word we speak is, in some degree, a diminution of our lunge by corrosion, and, consequently, contributes to the shortening of our lives. An expedient was therefore offered, "that since words are only names for things, it would be more convenient for all men to carry about them such things as were necessary to express a particular business they are to discourse on." And this invention would certainly have taken place, to the great ease as well as health of the subject, if the women, in conjunction with the vulgar and illiterate, had not threatened to raise a rebellion unless they might be allowed the liberty to speak with their tongues, after the manner of their forefathers; such constant irreconcilable enemies to science are the common people. However, many of the most learned and wise adhere to the new scheme of expressing themselves by things; which has only this inconvenience attending it, that if a man's business be very great, and of various kinds, he must be obliged, in proportion, to carry a greater bundle of things upon his back, unless he can afford one or two strong servants to attend him. I have often beheld two of those sages almost sinking under the weight of their

---

①polysyllables：多音节词

packs, like pedlars① among us, who, when they met in the street, would lay down their loads, open their sacks, and hold conversation for an hour together; then put up their implements, help each other to resume their burdens, and take their leave.

But for short conversations, a man may carry implements in his pockets, and under his arms, enough to supply him; and in his house, he cannot be at a loss. Therefore the room where company meet who practise this art, is full of all things, ready at hand, requisite to furnish matter for this kind of artificial converse.

Another great advantage proposed by this invention was, that it would serve as a universal language, to be understood in all civilised nations, whose goods and utensils are generally of the same kind, or nearly resembling, so that their uses might easily be comprehended. And thus ambassadors would be qualified to treat with foreign princes, or ministers of state, to whose tongues they were utter strangers.

I was at the mathematical school, where the master taught his pupils after a method scarce imaginable to us in Europe. The proposition, and demonstration, were fairly written on a thin wafer, with ink composed of a cephalic② tincture③. This, the student was to swallow upon a fasting stomach, and for three days following, eat nothing but bread and water. As the wafer digested, the tincture mounted to his brain, bearing the proposition along with it. But the success has not hitherto been answerable, partly by some error in the quantum or composition, and partly by the perverseness of lads, to whom this bolus④ is so nauseous, that they generally steal aside, and discharge it upwards, before it can operate; neither have they been yet persuaded to use so long an abstinence, as the prescription requires.

---

①pedlars：商贩
②cephalic：头
③tincture：浸染、药酒
④bolus：药丸、小球

Questions for Discussion

Analyze *Gulliver's Travels* to illustrate the use of satire in the third part.

Unit 3　William Blake (1757 – 1827)

Appreciation

  To see a World in a Grain of Sand，一沙一世界，
  And a Heaven in a Wild Flower，一花一天堂。
  Hold Infinity in the palm of your hand，无限掌中置，
  And Eternity in an hour. 刹那成永恒。

Auguries of innocence

Songs of Innocence

  William Blake was a Pre-Romanticist or forerunner of the romantic poetry of the 19th century, the most extraordinary literary genius of his age.

  Blake was the son of a London tradesman. In his childhood, he was a strange and imaginative child. He never went to school but learned to read and write at home. He was poet, painter, and engraver, who created a unique form of illustrated verse; his poetry, inspired by mystical vision, is among the most original, lyric, and prophetic in the language.

  Blake was the most independent and the most original of all the romantic poets of the 18th century, showing contempt for the rule of reason, and treasuring the individual's imagination. His lyrics display all the characteristics of the romantic spirit (natural sentiment and individual originality). Blake's most popular poems have always been *Songs of Innocence* (1789). These lyrics—fresh, direct observations—are notable for their eloquence. In 1794, disillusioned with the possibility of human perfection, Blake issued *Songs of Experience*, employing the same lyric style and much of the same subject matter as in *Songs of Innocence*. Blake wrote his poem *The Tiger* in plain and direct language.

  His poems often carry the lyric beauty with immense compression of meaning. He tends to present his view in visual images rather that abstract ideas. Symbolism in wide range is also a distinctive feature of his poetry. His poems were full of romantic spirit, imagery symbolism and revolutionary spirit. He influenced the Romantic poets with recurring themes of good and evil, heaven and hell, knowledge and innocence, and external reality versus inner imagination. He paved the way for the romantic movement of the 19th century. He was not really understood by his peers, but the 20th century readers appreciate the greatness he achieved in his varied fields of interest.

Brief Introduction

After the French Revolution broke out, the English government felt so alarmed as to strengthen the suppression of democratic activities in England. London, the English capital appeared quite different from before. It was filled with gloom, terror and misery.

The speaker wanders through the streets of London and comments on his observations. He sees despair in the faces of the people he meets and hears fear and repression in their voices. The woeful cry of the chimney sweeper stands as a chastisement to the Church, and the blood of a soldier stains the outer walls of the monarch's residence. The nighttime holds nothing more promising: the cursing of prostitutes corrupts the newborn infant and sullies the "Marriage hearse".

William Blake's *London* is a poem about a society that is troubled by the mistakes of the generation before. Blake uses the rhetorical components of imagery, alliteration, and word choice to illustrate the meaning of the poem. Blake creates complexity by using his rhetorical skills, which in turn opens up the poem for personal interpretation. The rhythm pattern is iambic tetrameter, trochaic tetrameter and the rhyme scheme is abab, cdcd, efef, dgdg. Repetition is Anvil music.

Selected Reading

London

<blockquote>
I wander thro'① each charter'd street,
Near where the charter'd② Thames does flow.
</blockquote>

---

①thro': through

②charter'd: given liberty of freedom, but also taken over as private property 被霸占的街道，当时伦敦的街道均被有钱人所霸占

And mark in every face I meet
Marks of weakness, marks of woe.

In every cry of every Man,
In every Infant's cry of fear,
In every voice: in every ban①
The mind-forg'd manacles I hear

How the Chimney-sweeper's cry②
Every blackening Church appalls,
And the hapless Soldier's sigh③
Runs in blood down Palace walls.

But most thro' midnight streets I hear
How the youthful Harlot's curse
Blasts the new-born Infant's tear④
And blights with plagues the Marriage hearse⑤.

---

①ban: a prohibition, also possibly a marriage ban-notice of intended matrimony 本节中诗人连用 5 个 every 以强调伦敦城中无论男女老幼，都不能幸免被蹂躏的命运

②How the Chimney-sweeper's cry/Every blackening Church appalls: How the chimney sweepers'cry appalls every blackening Church. Chimney-sweeper's cry: 扫烟囱孩子的哭声，当时，有许多穷孩子以扫烟囱为生。blackening Church: 被熏黑的教堂。这里诗人采用了借代的手法，意指黑心的僧人

③the hapless Soldier's sigh/ Runs in blood down Palace walls: Palace 指的是政府所在的宫殿。In blood: in the form of blood。18 世纪的英国政府派遣成千上万的士兵到国外为扩张英国势力而战，许多伤兵回国后沦为乞丐，流落街头。他们的哀号仿佛在以鲜血和生命向政府抗议

④tear: the harlot infects the parents with venereal disease, and thus the infant is inflicted with prenatal blindness 新生儿的父母感染疾病，垂直遗传给婴儿，导致他生下来就失明

⑤hearse: the marriage coach becomes a funeral hearse. 诗人把 marriage 和 hearse 连在一起，使人想起妇女由于生活所迫沦为妓女的悲惨命运。对于这些备受凌辱的妇女来说，婚姻对于她们毫无幸福可言。因此，婚车一如灵柩

Questions for Discussion

1. What is the theme of *London*?
2. Analyze the following words in *London*: mark, five every, blackning Church, Palace, marriage hearse. How do these words help the writer to strengthen the theme?
3. What is the most striking formal feature of *London*? What role does it play?
4. How do you understand "Chartered Street" and "Chartered Thames"? What does the speaker see when he wanders? What is the atmosphere in London? Pay attention to the repetition of the word. What role does it serve?
5. What kind of figures of speech are used in this quatrain? Analyze "Chimney-sweeper's cry appalls every blackning Church" and "the hapless Soldier's sigh runs down Palace walls in blood".

Unit 4 Robert Burns (1759 – 1796)

Appreciation

Till a' the seas gang dry, my dear, 纵使大海干涸水流尽,
And the rocks melt wi' the sun; 太阳将岩石烧作灰尘,
I will luve thee still, my dear, 亲爱的, 我永远爱你,
While the sands o' life shall run. 只要我一息犹存。

Born on January 25, 1759, in Alloway, Scotland, to William and Agnes Brown Burnes, Robert Burns followed his father's example by becoming a tenant farmer. As a poet he recorded and celebrated aspects of farm life, regional experience, traditional culture, class culture and distinctions, and religious practice and belief in such a way as to transcend the particularities of his inspiration, becoming finally the national poet of Scotland.

Brief Introduction

A Red, Red rose has been regarded as one of the best love poems. It is ballad and also a popular love song in reality. The poem contains about 100 words merely. It is very short and brief, but it has presented a pure-hearted and impressive love story for us. It is about a couple of lovers: the hero is going to leave his lover for a while, and the content is the oath he wants to express to his lover. The writer uses many precise and simple words to speak out his true and unchangeable love to his lover. It can make readers feel the deep and strong affection.

Selected Reading

A Red, Red Rose

O, my Luve's① like a red, red rose
That's newly sprung in June;
O, my Luve's like the melodie②,
That's sweetly play'd③ in tune.

As fair art④ thou⑤, my bonnie⑥ lass⑦,
So deep in luve am I;
And I will luve thee still, my dear,

---

①Luve：苏格兰方言 = ove，注意大写 L，表达了"重要"和"唯一"的内涵
②melodie：来自法语，是 19、20 世纪法国从德国的抒情歌曲学来的，它是带伴奏的艺术歌曲。19 世纪的 melodie 一般用严肃抒情诗做歌词，由钢琴伴奏的独唱演员演唱。Melodie 的特点是诗歌与音乐的完美统一。因此，melodie 准确来说不是"乐曲""曲调"，而是"歌曲"
③play'd：played，诗歌用字
④art：are，古英语，第二人称系动词
⑤thou：you，古英语，第二人称主格
⑥bonnie：苏格兰方言，健康的，美丽的，可爱的，可人的
⑦lass：年轻未婚女子，姑娘；多数用于非正式对少女的称呼；因与 lassie 有关，所以也有女性恋人的意思

Till a'① the seas gang dry.

Till a' the seas gang② dry, my dear,
And the rocks melt wi'③ the sun;
I will luve thee④ still, my dear,
While the sands o'⑤ life shall run.

And fare – thee – weel⑥, my only Luve!
And fare – thee – weel, a while!
And I will come again, my Luve,
Tho'⑦ 'twere⑧ ten thousand mile!

Questions for Discussion

A Valediction: *Forbidding Mourning* and *A Red*, *Red Rose* are two love poems, but they are completely different. Choose your favorite one and make an analysis on it.

Terms

1. Satire
2. Neoclassicism
3. Fiction
4. Sentimentalism

---

①a': all, 诗歌语言
②gang: go, 苏格兰方言
③wi': with, 诗歌语言
④thee: you, 古英语, 第二人称宾格
⑤o': of, 诗歌语言
⑥fare – thee – weel: (bid) farewell (to) thee, 诗歌语言
⑦tho': though, 诗歌语言
⑧'twere: it were (起到省略一个音节的作用), 诗歌语言

Chapter 5

Romanticism in English Literature

I. Historical Background

The French Revolution was a period of far-reaching social and political upheaval in France that lasted from 1789 until 1799, and was partially carried forward by Napoleon during the later expansion of the French Empire. The conflict between the old and the new class and the anger and desire brought by enlightenment catalyzed this Revolution. On July 14, 1789, the Parisian people stormed the Bastille, which marked the outbreak of the French Revolution and its influence soon swept all over Europe. Inspired by liberal and radical ideas, the Revolution profoundly altered the course of modern history, triggering the global decline of absolute monarchies while replacing them with republics and liberal democracies.

The French Revolution had a major impact on Europe and the New World, which gave a great stimulus to the growth of modern nationalism, and all social contradictions in England sharpened, too. People of the lower classes and the progressive intellectuals hoped to realize "liberty, equality and fraternity" in England. Britain saw minority support but the majority, and especially the elite, strongly opposed the French Revolution.

I. Literature Background

Romanticism rose and grew under the impetus of the Industrial Revolution and French Revolution which was an especially important influence on the political thinking of many of the Romantic poets. Though Romanticism was a revolt against aristocratic social and political norms of the Age of Enlightenment, it as well was a reaction against the scientific rationalization of nature.

At the turn of the 18th and 19th century romanticism appeared in England as a new trend in literature. The Romantic period was one of major social change in England because of the depopulation of the countryside and the rapid development of overcrowded industrial cities. In 1798 William Wordsworth and Samuel Taylor Coleridge published *Lyrical Ballads* which marked the beginning of the Romantic Age. It is an age of romantic enthusiasm, an age of poetry and an age for women novelists. In 1832, the last romantic writer Walter Scott died, so in that year, the Romantic Age came to an end.

Romanticism is an international artistic literary, intellectual and philosophical movement originated in Europe toward the end of the 18th century and in most areas was at its peak in the approximate period from 1800 to 1850.

1. Contrast With Neoclassicism

The Romanticists paid great attention to the spiritual and emotional life of man. The stylistic keynote of Romanticism is intensity, and its watchword is "imagination": remembered childhood, unrequited love, and the exiled hero were constant themes. Romantics had a new intuition for the primal power of the wild landscape, the spiritual correspondence between Man and Nature, and the aesthetic principle of "organic" form. Characteristics of Romanticism Imagination were worship of nature, symbolism and myth, simplicity and humanity, spontaneity.

Romanticism constitutes a change of direction from attention to the outer world of social civilization to the inner world of the human spirit. In essence it designates a literary and philosophical theory which tends to see the individual as the very center of all life and all experience. It also places the individual at the center of art, making literature most valuable as an expression of this or her unique feelings, particular attitudes and valuing its accuracy in portraying the individual's experiences.

2. Two Schools of Romantic Poets

Lake poets

The elder generation represented by Wordsworth, Coleridge and Southey were known as Lake Poets because they lived and knew one another in the last few years of the 18th century in the district of the great lakes in Northwestern England. The former two published *The Lyrical Ballads* together in 1798, while all three of them had radical inclinations in their youth but later turned conservative and received pensions and poet laureateships from the aristocracy. They sang the beautiful nature and their poems were simple, pure and fresh.

Active romanticists

Younger generation represented by Byron, Shelley and Keats, firm supporters of the French Revolution, expressed the aspiration of the labouring classes and set themselves against the bourgeois society and the ruling class, as they bore a deep hatred for the wicked exploiters and oppressors and had an intensive love for liberty. They are referred to as Satanic Poets by Robert Southey for their violent imagination and rebellious spirit. Their poems were full of fighting spirit and political consciousness.

3. Types of Poetry

In terms of content

Lyrical Poems: Songs 韵文   odes 颂诗   Elegy 挽诗
Narrative Poems: Epics (heroic poems) 史诗   Ballads 民谣
Dramatic Poems: usu. in dialogue; in blank verse

In terms of meter

Metrical Poems 格律诗: regular rhyme; regular rhythm; definite number of lines
Free Verse 自由诗: irregular rhyme and rhythm; irregular number of lines
Blank Verse 无韵诗: without rhyme; with rhythm

Unit 1   William Wordsworth (1770 – 1850)

Appreciation

They flash upon that inward eye 花儿闪现在我脑海(心灵)中
Which is the bliss of solitude; 那独处时分特有的奇享
And then my heart with pleasure fills, 我的心于是也漾满欢愉,
And dances with the daffodils. 伴着水仙花翩然起舞。

On April 7, 1770, William Wordsworth was born in Cockermouth, Cumbria,

England. Equally important in the poetic life of Wordsworth was his 1795 meeting with the poet, Samuel Taylor Coleridge. It was with Coleridge that Wordsworth published the famous *Lyrical Ballads* in 1798. And the poems themselves are some of the most influential in Western literature.

Wordsworth's most famous work, *The Prelude* (1850), is considered by many to be the crowning achievement of English romanticism. The poem, revised numerous times, chronicles the spiritual life of the poet and marks the birth of a new genre of poetry.

Brief Introduction

Writing Bachground: A visit to Ullswate 阿尔斯沃特湖畔 by Dorothy Wordsworth, from The Grasmere Journal—Thursday 15 April, 1802.

I Wandered Lonely as a Cloud is a poem about nature. The poem can be divided into two parts: the scenery and lyrical. With his pure and poetic language, Wordsworth brings us into a beautiful world where there are daffodils, trees and breeze. We follow the poet at every turn of his feelings. We share his sadness when he *wandered lonely as a cloud* and his delight the moment his heart "with pleasure fills". We come to realize the great power of nature that may influence our life deeply as revealed in the poem.

Through describing a scene of joyful daffodils recollected in memory, the poet hopes to illustrate his theory of poetic inspiration—"spontaneous overflow of powerful feelings, which originates in emotion recollected in tranquility". *I Wandered Lonely as a Cloud* becomes one of the best examples of the Romantic idea of nature.

Selected Reading

I Wandered Lonely as a Cloud

I wandered lonely as a cloud
That floats on high[①] o'er vales[②] and hills,
When all at once I saw a crowd,

---

①on high: in the sky, 在空中
②vales: 谷；溪谷

A host, of golden daffodils①;
Beside the lake, beneath the trees,
Fluttering② and dancing in the breeze.

Continuous as the stars that shine
And twinkle on the milky way,
They stretched in never-ending line
Along the margin of a bay:
Ten thousand saw I at a glance,
Tossing③ their heads in sprightly④ dance.

The waves beside them danced; but they
Out-did the sparkling⑤ waves in glee⑥:
A poet could not but be gay,
In such a jocund company:
I gazed—and gazed—but little thought
What wealth the show to me had brought:

For oft, when on my couch I lie
In vacant⑦ or in pensive⑧ mood,
They flash upon that inward eye⑨

---

①daffodils：水仙花
②Fluttering：飘动
③Tossing：使……上下摇动
④sprightly：活泼的；愉快的
⑤sparkling：闪闪发光的
⑥glee：快乐
⑦vacant：空虚的；空的
⑧pensive：沉思的，忧郁的
⑨inward eye：the soul, 指心灵

Which is the bliss① of solitude②;
And then my heart with pleasure fills,
And dances with the daffodils.

Questions for Discussion

1. Try to interpret the meaning of the title *I Wandered Lonely as a Cloud* and the theme.
2. Analyze the figure of speech in *I Wandered Lonely as a Cloud*.
3. What is the poem about?
   Appreciation of poetry in the three areas _____, _____, _____.
   The poem can be divided into two parts: _____ and _____.
   This poem with a strong color _____.
4. Explain "that inward eye".
5. Make an analysis on *I Wandered Lonely as a Cloud*.

Unit 2 Samuel Taylor Coleridge (1772 – 1834)

Appreciation

At length did cross an Albatross,终于飞来了一头信天翁,
Thorough the fog it came;它穿过海上弥漫的云雾,
As if it had been a Christian soul,仿佛它也是一个基督徒,
We hailed it in God's name.我们以上帝的名义向它欢呼。

Samuel Taylor Coleridge, a leader of the British Romantic movement, was born on October 21, 1772, in Devonshire, England. In 1798 Coleridge and Wordsworth collaborated on a joint volume of poetry entitled *Lyrical Ballads*. The collection is

---

①bliss：极乐；天赐的福
②solitude：孤独；隐居

considered the first great work of the Romantic school of poetry and contains Coleridge's famous poem, *The Rime of the Ancient Mariner*. Main Works: *Christabel* (1816), Kubla Khan (1816), Biographia Literaria (1817). He died in London on July 25,1834.

Brief Introduction

An Ancient Mariner, unnaturally old and skinny, with deeply-tanned skin and a "glittering eye", stops a Wedding Guest who is on his way to a wedding reception with two companions. He tries to resist the Ancient Mariner, who compels him to sit and listen to his woeful tale. The Ancient Mariner tells his tale, largely interrupted save for the sounds from the wedding reception and the Wedding Guest's fearsome interjections.

The Ancient Mariner tells the Wedding Guest that he wanders from country to country, and has a special instinct that tells him to whom he must tell his story. After he tells it, he is temporarily relieved of his agony. The Ancient Mariner tells the Wedding Guest that better than any merriment is the company of others in prayer. He says that the best way to become close with God is to respect all of his creatures, because he loves them all. Then he vanishes. Instead of joining the wedding reception, the Wedding Guest walks home, stunned. We are told that he awakes the next day "sadder and... wiser" for having heard the Ancient Mariner's tale.

Selected Reading

The Rime of the Ancient Mariner

Argument

How a ship having passed the line was driven by storms to the cold country towards the South Pole; and how from thence she made her course to the tropical Latitude of the Great Pacific Ocean; and of the strange things that befell; and in what manner the Ancient Mariner came back to his own country.

PART I

It is an ancient Mariner,
And he stoppeth one of three.

"By thy long grey beard and glittering eye,
Now wherefore stopp'st thou me?

The Bridegroom's doors are opened wide,
And I am next of kin;
The guests are met, the feast is set:
May'st hear the merry din."

He holds him with his skinny hand,
"There was a ship," quoth he.
"Hold off! unhand me, grey-beard loon!"
Eftsoons① his hand dropt he.

He holds him with his glittering eye—
The Wedding-Guest stood still,
And listens like a three years' child:
The Mariner hath his will②.

The Wedding-Guest sat on a stone:
He cannot choose but hear;
And thus spake③ on that ancient man,
The bright-eyed Mariner.

"The ship was cheered, the harbour cleared,
Merrily did we drop
Below the kirk④, below the hill,

---

①eftsoons: at once, 立刻
②The Mariner hath his will: the Mariner has gained the control of the will of the Wedding Guest by "his glittering eye"
③spake: 说(speak 的过去式)
④kirk: church, 教堂

Below the lighthouse top.

The Sun came up upon the left,
Out of the sea came he!
And he shone bright, and on the right
Went down into the sea.

Higher and higher every day,
Till over the mast at noon①—"
The Wedding-Guest here beat his breast,
For he heard the loud bassoon.

The bride hath paced into the hall,
Red as a rose is she;
Nodding their heads before her goes
The merry minstrelsy②.

The Wedding-Guest he beat his breast,
Yet he cannot choose but hear;
And thus spake on that ancient man,
The bright-eyed Mariner.

And now the STORM-BLAST came, and he
Was tyrannous and strong:
He struck with his o'ertaking wings,
And chased us south along.
With sloping masts and dipping prow③,

---

①Till over the mast at noon: the ship had reached the equator (the "Line"), 他的船已经到达赤道
②minstrelsy: 吟游技艺
③prow: 船首;机头

As who pursued with yell and blow
Still treads the shadow of his foe,
And forward bends his head,
The ship drove fast, loud roared the blast,
And southward aye we fled.

And now there came both mist and snow,
And it grew wondrous cold:
And ice, mast-high, came floating by,
As green as emerald①.

And through the drifts the snowy clifts
Did send a dismal② sheen③:
Nor shapes of men nor beasts we ken—
The ice was all between.

The ice was here, the ice was there,
The ice was all around:
It cracked and growled, and roared and howled,
Like noises in a swound④!

At length did cross an Albatross⑤
Thorough the fog it came;
As if it had been a Christian soul,
We hailed it in God's name.

---

①emerald：绿宝石
②dismal：凄凉的，忧郁的
③sheen：光辉
④swound: swoon，昏晕；狂喜
⑤Albatross：信天翁

It ate the food it ne'er had eat,
And round and round it flew.
The ice did split with a thunder-fit;
The helmsman① steered us through!

And a good south wind sprung up behind;
The Albatross did follow,
And every day, for food or play,
Came to the mariner's hollo!

In mist or cloud, on mast or shroud②,
It perched③ for vespers④ nine;
Whiles all the night, through fog-smoke white,
Glimmered the white Moon-shine.

"God save thee, ancient Mariner!
From the fiends, that plague thee thus! —
Why look'st thou so?"—With my cross-bow⑤
I shot the ALBATROSS.

Questions for Discussion

Analyze *The Rime of the Ancient Mariner* written by Samuel Taylor Coleridge.

---

①helmsman:舵手
②shroud: the rope supporting the mast, 绳子支持桅杆
③perch:栖息;就位
④vesper:晚祷
⑤cross-bow:弩

Chapter 5　Romanticism in English Literature

Unit 3　George Gordon Byron (1788 – 1824)

Appreciation

THE isles of Greece! the isles of Greece! 希腊群岛，美丽的希腊群岛！
Where Burning Sappho loved and sung, 火热的萨弗在这里唱过恋歌；
Where grew the arts of war and peace, 在这里，战争与和平的艺术并兴，
……
Where Delos rose and Phoebus sprung! 狄洛斯崛起，阿波罗跃出海面！
Eternal summer gilds them yet, 永恒的夏天还把海岛镀成金色，
But all, except their sun, is set. 可是除了太阳，一切已经消沉。

George Gordon Byron was born on January 22, 1788 in Aberdeen, Scotland, and inherited his family's English title at the age of ten, becoming Baron Byron of Rochdale.

He was commonly known simply as Lord Byron, was an English poet and a leading figure in the Romantic Movement. He travelled widely across Europe, especially in Italy where he lived for seven years. Later in life, Byron joined the Greek War of Independence fighting the Ottoman Empire, for which many Greeks revere him as a national hero. He died in 1824 at the young age of 36 from a fever contracted while in Missolonghi. Due to his outspoken trait in political affairs and his rocky personal life, Byron was forced to flee England and settled in Italy and began writing his masterpiece, *Don Juan*, an epic-satire novel-in-verse loosely based on a legendary hero. When he died on April 19, 1824, at the age of 36, *Don Juan* was yet to be finished, though 17 cantos had been written.

His major works include, *Childe Harold's Pilgrimage* (1812), *Prometheus* (1816), *The Lament of Tasso* (1817), *Heaven and Earth* (1821), *The Prophecy of Dante* (1819), *The Age of Bronze* (1823).

Today, Byron's *Don Juan* is considered one of the great long poems in English written since Milton's *Paradise Lost*. Modern critics generally consider it to be Byron's masterpiece. The Byronic hero, characterized by passion, talent, and rebellion, pervades Byron's work and greatly influenced the work of later Romantic poets. Byron was a British poet and a leading figure in Romanticism, and was regarded as one of the greatest European poets.

Brief Introduction

Don Juan is a satiric poem by Lord Byron, based on the legend of Don Juan. Byron himself called it an "Epic Satire". Don Juan was of noble origin, and he was amiable and charming to ladies. He loved a married woman Julia, after the affair was discovered, he was compelled to go abroad. Because of a shipwreck, Juan fell into the sea, finally reached the seashore of a Greek Isles. There Juan fell in love with Haidee, the beautiful daughter of a pirate. But her father returned and forced them to part resulting in her heart-broken death, and Juan was sold as a slave to Constantinople, but managed to escape and joined the Russian Army. Then Juan was sent back to England to perform a political mission.

The poem is in eight line iambic pentameter with the rhyme scheme ab ab ab cc—often the last rhyming couplet is used for a humor comic line or humorous bathos. This rhyme scheme is known as ottava rima, a rhyming stanza form of Italian origin, used for long poems on heroic themes which effect of ottava rima in English is often comic. The language is colloquial and conversational.

"The Isles of Greece" is the important episode of the poem, taken from Canto III of *Don Juan*. Don Juan and his adventures form the structure of the poem. In the early 19th century, Greece was under the rule of the Turks. By contrasting the freedom of ancient Greece and the present enslavement, the poet appealed to the people to fight for liberty.

Byron's true intention is to dipict a panoramic view of different types of society and employs his rich knowledge of the world and the wisdom to represent in Byronic hero attributes like rebelling, suffering exile and etc. This technique is used in the shipwreck scene with different elements, such as tragic heroism, selfishness and complete virtual comedy, which is fully justified in the love story between Juan and Haidee. The different emotions of love, enjoyment, suffering, hatred and fear build into the brilliant pictures of life. The combination of the real and ideal Don Juan form a whole story, with an immediate reponse shown in a stabilizing voic.

Chapter 5 Romanticism in English Literature

Selected Reading

The Isles of Greece

1

THE isles of Greece! the isles of Greece!
Where burning Sappho[①] loved and sung,
Where grew the arts of war and peace[②],
Where Delos[③] rose and Phoebus[④] sprung!
Eternal summer gilds them yet,
But all, except their sun, is set.

2

The Scian and the Teian muse[⑤],
The hero's harp, the lover's lute[⑥],
Have found the fame your shores refuse[⑦];
Their place of birth alone is mute
To sounds which echo further west

---

①burning Sappho：热情的萨福，是公元前 7 世纪末至 6 世纪初古希腊勒斯波斯 Lesbos 杰出的女抒情诗人，善于写情诗，其作品热情奔放，极负盛名

②the arts of war and peace：文治武功；战争与和平的艺术 arts of war：军事学

③Delos：爱琴海中的得洛斯岛，位于爱琴海西南部的希腊；相传太阳神阿波罗 Apollo 生在得洛斯，阿波罗神殿也在这里

④Phoebus：Apoll，希腊神话中的太阳神

⑤The Scian and the Teian Muse：the Scian Muse，指荷马史诗《伊利亚特》Illiad 和《奥德修纪》Odyssey 的作者；the Teian Muse，指古希腊诗人阿那克里翁；Muse，希腊神话中掌管文艺、音乐等的九位女神，专指诗神

⑥The hero's harp, the lover's lute：前者指荷马，也指荷马的史诗，抒情诗人阿那克里翁以大型乐器竖琴这里比喻创作英雄史诗作者荷马，小巧的琵琶比喻写爱情诗的阿那克里昂。英雄史诗是在比较大型的乐器竖琴 harp 伴奏下演唱的；后者是在比较小型的乐器 lute 伴奏下演唱的。爱情诗一般是比较甜美的，这里指阿那克里翁，也指他的爱情诗

⑦Have found the fame your shores refuse：荷马和阿那克里翁被希腊故土忘却了，但他们在其他地方却深受崇敬

Than your sires'"Islands of the Blest①".

3

The mountains look on Marathon—
And Marathon looks on the sea;
And musing there an hour alone,
I dream'd that Greece might yet be free
For, standing on the Persians' grave②,
I could not deem myself a slave.

4

A king sat on the rocky brow③
Which looks on sea-born Salamis④;
And ships, by thousands, lay below,
And men in nations⑤;—all were his!
He counted them at break of day—
And when the sun set, where were they?

5

And where are they? and where art thou,
My country⑥? On thy voiceless shore

---

①your sires' "Islands of the Blest":blest,blessed,极乐岛,你们祖先的宝岛。根据希腊神话,为众神所宠爱的人们死后,他们的灵魂都前往遥远的西部海域的极乐岛居住。古希腊诗人以此称现代的佛得角群岛 Cape Verde 或加那利群岛 the Canaries,在今塞内加尔以西,或加那利群岛 the Canaries 在今摩洛哥以西。宙斯(Zeus)让他所宠爱的人住在大地边缘的忘忧之岛,无人生之苦。这说明荷马和阿那克里翁的名声远扬,超出了古希腊人当时所知道的历史范围

②Persians' grave:指入侵的波斯军在马拉松战役中战死士兵葬身的坟墓

③A king sate on the rocky brow:rocky brow,悬崖。薛西斯一世率领强大的波斯舰队在希腊沿海萨拉米斯(Salamis)岛旁的海战,原以为强大的波舰队有1,200艘舰,小艇3,000艘必胜,不料被希腊海军仅300艘舰只一举全歼。据埃斯库罗斯 Aeschylus 悲剧《波斯人》,实际当时薛西斯480年9月9日坐在埃嘉勒山上 Aegaleos 目睹舰队一日内化为乌有

④Salamis:萨拉米斯,位于爱琴海萨罗尼克湾内,希腊阿帝卡州岛屿

⑤men in nations:men,soldiers,指波斯军队中从被波斯征服的亚非国家里招募的士兵

⑥And where are they? And where art thou...country:拜伦假托一位希腊人怀古讽今:由上一行的过去时态(were)变成现在时态(are),诗人从古到今的时间转折旨在调转笔锋,将听众的注意力引向当前希腊人民遭受土耳其人奴役这一现实,从古代波斯人的败绩转到被奴役的希腊

Chapter 5　Romanticism in English Literature

　　The heroic lay① is tuneless now—
　　The heroic bosom beats no more!
　　And must thy lyre, so long divine,
　　Degenerate into hands like mine②?
6
　　'Tis something, in the dearth of fame③,
　　Though link'd among a fetter'd race④,
　　To feel at least a patriot's shame,
　　Even as I sing, suffuse⑤ my face;
　　For what is left the poet here?
　　For Greeks a blush—for Greece a tear⑥.
7
　　Must we but weep o'er days more blest?
　　Must we but blush?—Our fathers bled⑦.
　　Earth! render back from out thy breast⑧
　　A remnant of our Spartan dead⑨!
　　Of the three hundred grant but three,

---

　　①The heroic lay：lay-song，英雄之歌
　　②And must thy lyre, so long divine...mine：lyre，七弦琴，古希腊人作为伴唱诗歌的乐器，此处指诗歌
　　③in the dearth of fame：dearth, lack，在这屈辱的时候缺少伟大人物和英雄壮举
　　④link'd among a fetter'd race：被锁在一个被奴役的民族之内，指希腊从1453到1829年在土耳其的统治之下
　　⑤suffuse：overspread with colour，redden 血
　　⑥For Greeks a blush—for Greece a tear：希腊的不幸催人泪下，希腊当为之羞愧
　　⑦Must we but blush?—Our fathers bled：拜伦模仿头韵体诗用but、blush、bled押头韵，句中略作停顿，造成强烈的效果
　　⑧Earth! Render back from out thy breast.—Thermopylae：公元前480年，波斯军队入侵希腊，斯巴达王莱奥尼达斯率领300名斯巴达勇士，在通往希腊东部的关隘温泉关据险固守3天，和薛西斯一世率领的波斯侵略军血战，后因希腊奸细给波斯人指路，腹背受敌，全部阵亡
　　⑨Spartan dead：指在温泉关战役中阵亡的300名斯巴达士兵。古希腊的斯巴达人以作战骁勇著称。温泉关是希腊北部和中部交界处的险要关隘，位于高山和海岸之间

· 93 ·

To make a new Thermopylae①.

8

What, silent still, and silent all?
Ah! no; the voices of the dead
Sound like a distant torrent's fall,
And answer, "Let one living head,
But one arise, —we come, we come!"
'Tis but the living who are dumb.

9

In vain—in vain: strike other chords②;
Fill high the cup of Samian wine③!
Leave battles to the Turkish hordes,
And shed the blood of Scio's vine④!
Hark! rising to the ignoble call⑤—
How answers each bold bacchanal⑥!

10

You have the Pyrrhic dance⑦ as yet,

---

①Thermopylae：得摩比利或温泉关；此处指著名的温泉关战役，因附近有两个硫黄温泉而得名

②strike other chords：弹奏别的曲调吧，即歌唱与抗争无关的其他主题

③Samian wine：萨摩斯岛 Samos 所产的酒；萨摩斯是爱琴海中距小亚细亚大陆最近的希腊岛屿，盛产葡萄，以葡萄酒闻名

④Leave battles to the Turkish hordes, vine：hordes 游牧部落。Scio's vine 希奥（意）以出产葡萄、橙子和柠檬著称。当时希腊人受"蛮人"hordes 的奴役，只饮葡萄之血即葡萄酒。诗人讽刺土耳其蛮人，旨在刺激希腊人起来斗争

⑤the ignoble call：ignoble, dishonourable,不光彩的号召

⑥bold Bacchanal：勇敢的酒徒，酒神巴克斯的崇拜者，意含讽刺；Bacchanal 来源于Bacchus，希腊神话中的酒神

⑦Pyrrhic dance：在希腊的节日里流行这种舞蹈，以急速的笛子伴奏，舞者做各种进攻和防守状。是古希腊伊庇鲁斯国王皮瑞克发明并以其名字命名的模拟战斗的一种战舞，舞步轻快，源出于塞萨利南部多里斯 Doris，斯巴达士兵的部分训练内容，舞者身穿盔甲。这种风俗一直流传至罗马时代的后期

Where is the Pyrrhic phalanx① gone?
Of two such lessons, why forget
The nobler and the manlier one?
You have the letters Cadmus② gave—
Think ye he meant them for a slave?

11

Fill high the bowl with Samian wine!
We will not think of themes like these!
It made Anacreon's song divine③;
He served—but served Polycrates④—
A tyrant; but our masters then
Were still, at least, our countrymen.

12

The tyrant of the Chersonese⑤
Was freedom's best and bravest friend;

---

①Pyrrhic phalanx：古希腊军队的步兵方阵，一般是前后八人，由手持长矛和短剑的步兵组成。据传说这种舞蹈是以希腊西北部伊庇鲁斯（Epirus）国王皮瑞克（Pyrrhicus，公元前319－公元前272）的名字命名的，这种方阵多次击败罗马军队

②Cadmus：卡德摩斯，希腊传说中的人物，腓尼基国王阿革诺尔 Agenor 之子，建立了底比斯城 Thebes，将腓尼基字母传入希腊

③It made Anacreon's song divine：它使阿那克里昂的诗歌成为天上之曲。阿那克里昂 Anacreon 是公元前6世纪的希腊诗人，歌颂醇酒和爱情，诗风壮丽，可谓神化所主，不似人间来者。It 指 Samian wine

④Polycrates：波利克拉特斯，公元前6世纪希腊萨摩斯岛的僭主，在东爱琴海上建立霸权，他崇尚文艺，诗人阿那克里翁在波斯人入侵忒俄斯期间，曾在萨摩斯岛避居波利克拉特斯宫廷。后被波斯人钉死在十字架上

⑤the Chersonese：Tyrant，按古希腊语，指拥有绝对权利的统治者。指米太亚德（Miltiades，公元前540－公元前489），雅典统帅，公元前490年决定性的马拉松战役中以11,000兵力击败了波斯的10万大军，后来成为半岛 Chersonese 僭主：源自希腊文 Chersonesos 半岛。（poetic）半岛，此处大写，特指格拉里珀黎 Grallipoli，位于达达尼尔海峡 Dardanelles 北面

That tyrant was Miltiades①!
Oh! that the present hour would lend
Another despot of the kind②!
Such chains as his were sure to bind③.

13
Fill high the bowl with Samian wine!
On Suli's rock, and Parga's shore④,
Exists the remnant of a line
Such as the Doric mothers bore⑤;
And there, perhaps, some seed is sown,
The Heracleidan⑥ blood might own.

14
Trust not for freedom to the Franks⑦——
They have a king who buys and sells⑧:

---

①Miltiades:米太亚德,公元前480年,波斯人全面入侵阿提卡,他被任命为十大元帅之一,他鼓动希腊人奋起御敌,并在马拉松战役中击败波斯侵略军。公元前5世纪初,成为色雷斯半岛 Thracian Chersonese 今达达尼亚半岛的君主。他曾和波斯王大流士一起和锡西厄人 Scythians 作战,后脱离波斯人,逃到雅典。虽曾招致专制罪指控,但获开释

②Oh! that the present hour would lend...kind:Oh, I wish(that)。为但愿现在能有 Miltiades 这样一位君主鼓动人们起来斗争

③Such chains as his were sure to bind:such chains,锁链一定能把希腊人团结起来;用 chains 一词,说明 miltiades 既是独裁者,又有团结人民的组织才干。Bind, to unite (the Greeks)

④On Suli's rock, and Parga's shore:苏里;希腊伊庇鲁斯,今希腊西部和阿尔巴尼亚南部的山区。拜伦在《恰尔德·哈罗尔德游记》Childe Harold 中说,当地的人民正在抗击土耳其侵略军,他认为爱好自由的希腊人的后代当在那里作战。拜伦在希腊时招募500名苏里壮士参加独立军,自己出钱支付他们的军饷

⑤Such as the Doric mothers bore:Doric mothers,多利安人即斯巴达人的母亲们;多利安母亲所生的人,指斯巴达勇士。Doric of Dorians,多利安人的,指古希腊最早的居民多利安人,是古希腊人的一支,进入埃夫罗塔斯河谷,建立了斯巴达城邦,因此多利安人指斯巴达人

⑥The Heracleidan: of Hercules,传说希腊神话中的大力神赫丘利 Hercues 的后裔,此处指斯巴达人。Blood,古希腊人的血统

⑦Franks:法兰克人,一般指法国人或拉丁族人;此处泛指西欧人。地中海东部诸国和岛屿,包括叙利亚、黎巴嫩等在内的自希腊至埃及的地区的人们对西欧人的总称

⑧They have a king who buys and sells:指他们(the Franks)的国王为自己的利益而拿其他民族的利益做交易。诗人劝告希腊人不要依赖外国人为他们争得自由

In native swords and native ranks①,
The only hope of courage dwells:
But Turkish force and Latin fraud②
Would break your shield, however broad.

15

Fill high the bowl with Samian wine!
Our virgins dance beneath the shade—
I see their glorious black eyes shine;
But, gazing on each glowing maid,
My own the burning tear-drop laves③,
To think such breasts must suckle slaves.

16

Place me on Sunium's marble steep④—
Where nothing, save⑤ the waves and I,
May hear our mutual murmurs⑥ sweep:
There, swan-like, let me sing and die⑦;
A land of slaves shall ne'er be mine—
Dash down yon cup of Samian wine⑧!

---

①In native swords and native ranks：依靠自己的武装，依靠自己的队伍

②Latin fraud：指西欧人的欺诈。拜伦认为希腊人要获得自由，只能依靠自己

③My own the burning tear-drop laves：laves，washes，正常的语序是 the burning tear-drop laves my own：laves，washes，fills. My own：my own eyes

④Sunium's marbled steep：Sunium 现称 Cape Colennam，位于希腊的阿提卡南部森纽 Sunium，指雅典保护神雅典娜 Athena 之庙，位于雅典东南约 50 千米，即今天的开普柯罗尼（Cape Coloni）

⑤save：except

⑥our mutual murmurs：指诗人的哀叹和海浪的涛声似乎在相互低声对答

⑦swan-like，let me sing and die：传说天鹅总在死前歌唱。诗人被比作天鹅，如以 the Swan of Avon 喻莎士比亚，以 the Mantuan swan 喻维吉尔

⑧Dash down yon cup of Samian wine：yon（古），yongder，that. 摔碎那个盛萨摩斯美酒的杯子！传说天鹅将死时会唱起悲歌，这里暗示诗人决心像天鹅那样唱一首英勇战斗的歌

Questions for Discussion

1. Who is "Sappho" in line 2?
   Who is "Phoebus" in line 4?
   Whom does the "Scia Jian muse" refer to?
   This selection consists of two six-lined stanzas of of iambic tetr meter, with a rhyme scheme of _____.
2. What is the whole section *The Isles of Greece* about?
3. What is the theme of *The Isles of Greece*?

Unit 4 John Keats (1795 – 1821)

Appreciation

"**Beauty is truth, truth beauty**" 美即是真，真即是美
…….
Away! away! for I will fly to thee, 去吧！去吧！我要朝你飞去，
Not charioted by Bacchus and his pards 不用和酒神坐文豹的车驾
……
Was it a vision, or a waking dream? 噫，这是个幻觉，还是梦寐？
Fled is that music:—Do I wake or sleep? 那歌声去了：——我是睡？是醒？

English Romantic poet John Keats was born on October 31, 1795, in London. Having no formal education or literary training, Keats read well in Greek and Elizabethan literature, and had Homer, Spenser, Shakespeare and Milton among his literary passions. To seek a warm climate, later in life he went to Italy to improve his health. He died there on February 23, 1821, at the age of 25, and was buried in the Protestant cemetery.

Keats was known as a sensuous poet whose poetry describes the beauty of the natural world and art as the vehicle for his poetic imagination. His skill with poetic imagery and sound reproduces this sensuous experience for his readers. His poetry evolves from this love of nature and art into a deep compassion for humanity. He was one of the main figures of the second generation of Romantic poets along with Lord Byron and Percy Bysshe Shelley.

His artistic aim is to create a beautiful world of imagination as opposed to the miserable reality of truth. As the principal poets of the English Romantic movement, Keats is mainly known for such poems as *Ode on a Grecian Urn* 希腊古瓮颂, *On the Grasshopper and the Cricket* 蛐蛐与蟋蟀, *Bright Star* 闪亮的星星, *When I have Fear* 当我害怕的时候, *To Autumn* 秋颂, *On Melancholy* 忧郁颂.

His five long poems: *Endymion* 恩底弥翁, *Isabella* 伊莎贝拉, *The Pot of Basil* 芳香的草本植物, *The Eve of St. Agnes* 圣·爱格尼斯节前夕, *Lamia* 莱米亚, *Hyperion* 赫坡里昂. He is, like Shakespeare, Milton and Wordsworth, one of the indisputable great English poets. And his mighty poems will no doubt have a lasting place in the history of English literature.

Brief Introduction

A nightingale had built its nest near the house of a friend of the Keats in Hampstead in the spring of 1819. In the deep of night, under the thick branches, Clarion in bird song, the poet wrote the first 8 stanzas in one breath multiple lines of *Ode to a Nightingale*. Inspired by the bird's song, Keats composed the poem in one day.

Ode to a Nightingale describes a series of conflicts between reality and the Romantic ideal of uniting with nature. Here Keats not only expresses his rapture upon hearing the beautiful songs of the nightingale and his desire to go to the ethereal world of beauty together with the bird, but also shows his deep sympathy for and his keen understanding of human miseries in the society in which he lived.

The tone of the poem rejects the optimistic pursuit of pleasure found within Keats's earlier poems and explores the themes of nature, transience and mortality, the latter being particularly personal to Keats. Instead, the songbird is capable of living through its song, which is a fate that humans cannot expect. The poem ends with an acceptance that pleasure cannot last and that death is an inevitable part of life. The nightingale's song is the dominant image and dominant "voice" within the ode. Keats seems to write the nightingale, but in fact he uses the nightingale to express his colorful imagination.

Selected Reading

Ode to a Nightingale

My heart aches, and a drowsy① numbness pains
My sense, as though of hemlock② I had drunk,
Or emptied some dull opiate to the drains③
One minute past, and Lethe-wards④ had sunk:
'Tis not through envy of thy happy lot,
But being too happy in thine happiness, —
That thou, light-winged Dryad⑤ of the trees
    In some melodious⑥ plot
Of beechen⑦ green, and shadows numberless,
    Singest of summer in full-throated ease.

O, for a draught of vintage⑧! that hath been
Cool'd a long age in the deep-delved earth,
Tasting of Flora⑨ and the country green,

---

①drowsy: 昏昏欲睡的;沉寂的
②hemlock: 毒药
③to the drains: to the last dreg
④Lethe-wards: toward Lethe, meaning "forgetful of all things"
⑤Dryad: fairy in the woods, the nightingale
⑥melodious: 悦耳的
⑦beechen: 山毛榉制的
⑧vintage: 古老的，葡萄收获期
⑨Flora: god of flower in Roman myth Flora. Here it refers to the fragrance of flowers.

Dance, and Provencal song①, and sunburnt mirth②!
O for a beaker full of the warm South,
Full of the true, the blushful③ Hippocrene④,
With beaded bubbles winking⑤ at the brim,
And purple-stained mouth;
That I might drink, and leave the world unseen,
And with thee fade away into the forest dim:

Fade far away, dissolve, and quite forget
What thou among the leaves hast never known,
The weariness, the fever, and the fret⑥
Here, where men sit and hear each other groan;
Where palsy⑦ shakes a few, sad, last gray hairs,
Where youth grows pale, and spectre-thin, and dies;
Where but to think is to be full of sorrow
And leaden-eyed despairs,
Where Beauty cannot keep her lustrous⑧ eyes,
Or new Love pine at them⑨ beyond tomorrow.

Away! away! for I will fly to thee,

---

①Provencal song: the love lyrics of the native minstrels in Provence, France in the 12th century

②sunburnt mirth: the joy of people living in the south of Europe where people enjoy the sunshine very much

③blushful: 脸红的

④Hippocrene: the spring on Mount Helicon where Apollo and the Nine Muses reside. If someone drinks the spring he will have the inspiration for poetry, （赫利孔山上的）灵泉；诗之灵感 Here in this line, it refers to wine

⑤wink: 眨眼

⑥fret: 烦躁

⑦palsy: 麻痹

⑧lustrous: 有光泽的

⑨them: "her lustrous eyes" in line 29

Not charioted[①] by Bacchus[②] and his pards[③],
But on the viewless wings of Poesy,
Though the dull brain perplexes and retards[④]:
Already with thee! tender is the night,
And haply the Queen-Moon is on her throne,
Cluster'd around by all her starry Fays[⑤];
But here there is no light,
Save what from heaven is with the breezes blown
Through verdurous[⑥] glooms and winding mossy[⑦] ways.

I cannot see what flowers are at my feet,
Nor what soft incense hangs upon the boughs,
But, in embalmed darkness, guess each sweet
Wherewith the seasonable month endows[⑧]
The grass, the thicket, and the fruit-tree wild;
White hawthorn[⑨], and the pastoral[⑩] eglantine[⑪];
Fast fading violets cover'd up in leaves;
And mid-May's eldest child[⑫],
The coming musk-rose, full of dewy[⑬] wine,
The murmurous haunt of flies on summer eves.

---

①charioted：驾驭
②Bacchus：god of wine riding a chariot led by pards (leopards)，酒神巴克斯
③pards：伙伴
④retard：延迟
⑤Fays：fairies
⑥verdurous：碧绿的
⑦mossy：生苔的
⑧endows：赋予
⑨hawthorn：山楂；山楂树
⑩pastoral：牧歌；田园诗
⑪eglantine：野蔷薇的一种
⑫mid-May's eldest child：the flower that is earliest in blossom in May, musk-rose in line 49
⑬dewy：带露水的

Chapter 5　Romanticism in English Literature

Darkling① I listen; and, for many a time
I have been half in love with easeful Death,
Call'd him soft names in many a mused rhyme,
To take into the air my quiet breath②;
Now more than ever seems it rich to die,
To cease upon the midnight with no pain,
While thou art pouring forth thy soul abroad③
In such an ecstasy!
Still④ wouldst thou sing, and I have ears in vain—
To thy high requiem⑤ become a sod.

Thou wast⑥ not born for death, immortal Bird⑦!
No hungry generations⑧ tread thee down;
The voice I hear this passing night was heard
In ancient days by emperor and clown⑨.
Perhaps the self-same song that found a path
Through the sad heart of Ruth⑩, when, sick for home,
She stood in tears amid the alien corn⑪;

---

①darkling: in the dark 在暗处
②breath: life 生命
③abroad: out 异国
④still: always 永远
⑤requiem: 安魂曲
⑥wast: the archaic form of "were" for the second person singular, 古老的形式的"是"第二人称单数
⑦immortal Bird: the nightingale 夜莺
⑧hungry generations: meaning "the devouring time"
⑨emperor and clown: emperor and peasant, meaning "everyday"
⑩Ruth: ancestor of King David. After her husband's death in the famine, she fled with her mother-in-law to the foreign land and made a living on the remnant of wheat left in the field. Here Keats imagined that Ruth was standing in the wheat field of the foreign land missing her home
⑪corn: wheat 小麦

The same that oft-times hath
Charm'd magic casements, opening on the foam
Of perilous① seas, in faery lands② forlorn③.

Forlorn! the very word is like a bell
To toll me back from thee to my sole self!
Adieu! the fancy cannot cheat so well
As she is fam'd④ to do, deceiving elf.
Adieu! adieu! thy plaintive⑤ anthem⑥ fades
Past the near meadows, over the still stream,
Up the hill-side; and now, 'tis buried deep
In the next valley-glades:
Was it a vision, or a waking dream?
Fled is that music:—Do I wake or sleep?

Questions for Discussion

1. What are the artistic features of *Ode to a Nightingale*?
2. What is the theme of *Ode to a Nightingale*?
3. Why is the bird—Nightingale immortal?

---

①perilous:危险的
②faery lands: fairy lands 仙境
③forlorn: remote and far away 孤独的
④fam'd: famed, namely widely known
⑤plaintive:哀伤的
⑥anthem:赞美诗;圣歌

Unit 5　Percy Bysshe Shelley (1792 – 1822)

Appreciation

The trumpet of a prophecy! O, Wind, 吹起预言的号角！啊，西风，
If Winter comes, can Spring be far behind? 如果严冬已经来临，春天怎能遥远？

　　Percy Bysshe Shelley was born on August 4, 1792, at Field Place, near Horsham, Sussex, England. On July 8, 1822, shortly before his thirtieth birthday, Shelley was drowned in a storm while attempting to sail from Leghorn to La Spezia, Italy, in his schooner, the *Don Juan*.

　　Shelley is perhaps best known for such classic poems as *Ozymandias*, *Ode to the West Wind*, *To a Skylark*, *Music*, *When Soft Voices Die*, *The Cloud* and *The Masque of Anarchy*. Long poems include *Queen Mab* (1813) 麦布女王, *Alastor* 阿拉斯特, *Prometheus Unbound* (1819) 解放的普罗米修斯.

　　He was one of the major English Romantic poets and regarded by critics as among the finest lyric poets in the English language. Shelley became an idol of the next three or four generations of poets, including important Victorian and Pre-Raphaelite poets.

Brief Introduction

　　The speaker invokes the *Wild West Wind* of autumn, which scatters the dead leaves and spreads seeds so that they may be nurtured by the spring, and asks that the wind, a "destroyer and preserver", hear him. The speaker calls the wind the "dirge / of the dying year", and describes how it stirs up violent storms, and again implores it to hear him. The speaker says that the wind stirs the Mediterranean from "his summer dreams", and cleaves the Atlantic into choppy chasms, making the "sapless foliage" of the ocean tremble, and asks for a third time that it hear him.

　　The speaker says that if he were a dead leaf that the wind could bear, or a cloud it could carry, or a wave it could push, or even if he were, as a boy, "the comrade" of the wind's "wandering over heaven", then he would never have needed to pray to the wind and invoke its powers. He pleads with the wind to lift him "as a wave, a leaf, a cloud!"—for though he is like the wind at heart, untamable and proud—he is now chained and bowed with the weight of his hours upon the earth.

The speaker asks the wind to "make me thy lyre", to be his own Spirit, and to drive his thoughts across the universe, "like withered leaves, to quicken a new birth". He asks the wind, by the incantation of this verse, to scatter his words among mankind, to be the "trumpet of a prophecy". Speaking both in regard to the season and in regard to the effect upon mankind that he hopes his words to have, the speaker asks: "If winter comes, can spring be far behind?"

Selected Reading

Ode to the West Wind

I

O wild West Wind, thou breath of Autumn's being①,
Thou, from whose unseen presence the leaves dead②
Are driven, like ghosts from an enchanter fleeing③,

Yellow, and black, and pale, and hectic red,
Pestilence-stricken multitudes: O thou,
Who chariotest to their dark wintry bed

The winged seeds, where they lie cold and low,
Each like a corpse within its grave, until
Thine azure sister of the Spring shall blow

Her clarion o'er the dreaming earth, and fill

---

①thou breath of Autumn's being: 你秋日生命的呼吸。being: the totality of all things that exist

②from whose unseen presence the leaves dead: the leaves (turn) dead from whose unseen presence

③like ghosts from an enchanter fleeting: like ghosts fleeting from an enchanter, 如同逃离巫师的鬼魂。enchanter: a sorcerer or magician, 巫师, 魔术师

(Driving sweet buds like flocks to feed in air)
With living hues and odours plain and hill①:

Wild Spirit, which art moving everywhere②;
Destroyer and Preserver; hear, O hear!

II

Thou on whose stream, 'mid the steep sky's commotion,
Loose clouds like Earth's decaying leaves are shed,
Shook from the tangled boughs of Heaven and Ocean③,

Angels④ of rain and lightning: there are spread
On the blue surface of thine airy surge,
Like the bright hair uplifted from the head

Of some fierce Maenad⑤, even from the dim verge
Of the horizon to the zenith's height,
The locks⑥ of the approaching storm. Thou dirge⑦

Of the dying year, to which this closing night
Will be the dome of a vast sepulchre
Vaulted with all thy congregated might

Of vapours, from whose solid atmosphere

---

①With living hues and orders plain and hill: and fill plain and hill with living hues and orders
②Wild spirit, which art moving everywhere: 这里的 spirit 指西风
③Loose clouds like earth's decaying leaves are shed, / Shook from the tangled boughs of Heaven and Ocean: 诗人把海天景色比作秋日落叶,使画面显得雄浑壮阔
④Angel: a divine messenger 报信者, 使者
⑤Maenad: 迈娜德, 希腊神话中酒神巴克斯的女祭司, 性情狂暴乖戾, 诗人把雷雨前的乱云比作妖女的蓬发
⑥locks: 妖女的头发, 比喻暴雨来临之前纷乱的云彩
⑦dirge: a funeral hymn or lament, 哀歌, 挽歌

Black rain, and fire, and hail will burst: O hear!

III

Thou who didst① waken from his summer dreams
The blue Mediterranean, where he lay,
Lulled by the coil② of his crystalline streams,

Beside a pumice isle in Baiae's bay③,
And saw in sleep old palaces and towers
Quivering within the wave's intenser day,

All overgrown with azure moss and flowers
So sweet, the sense faints picturing them! Thou
For whose path the Atlantic's level powers

Cleave themselves into chasms, while far below
The sea-blooms and the oozy woods which wear
The sapless foliage of the ocean, know
Thy voice, and suddenly grow grey with fear,
And tremble and despoil themselves: O hear!

IV

If I were a dead leaf thou mightest bear;
If I were a swift cloud to fly with thee;
A wave to pant④ beneath thy power, and share

The impulse of thy strength, only less free
Than thou, O Uncontrollable! If even
I were as in my boyhood, and could be

---

①didst: did
②coil: disturbance; a fuss 喧闹, 骚扰, 这里指海水的拍击声
③Baiae's bay: 意大利那不勒斯附近的一个旅游胜地, 古罗马国王在此建了许多行宫
④pant: to breathe rapidly in short gasps, 喘气, 急促地呼吸

The comrade of thy wanderings over Heaven,
As then, when to outstrip thy skiey speed
Scarce seemed a vision; I would ne'er have striven

As thus with thee in prayer in my sore need.
Oh! lift me as a wave, a leaf, a cloud!
I fall upon the thorns of life! I bleed!

A heavy weight of hours has chained and bowed
One too like thee: tameless, and swift, and proud.

V

Make me thy lyre, even as the forest is①:
What if my leaves are falling like its own②!
The tumult of thy mighty harmonies③

Will take from both④ a deep, autumnal tone,
Sweet though in sadness. Be thou, Spirit fierce,
My spirit! Be thou me, impetuous one!

Drive my dead thoughts over the universe
Like withered leaves to quicken a new birth!
And, by the incantation of this verse,
Scatter, as from an unextinguished hearth
Ashes and sparks, my words among mankind!
Be through my lips to unawakened Earth

---

①even as the forest is: just as the forest is (thy lyre)
②like its own: like the forest's own (leaves)
③thy mighty harmonies: the sound of the west wind
④both: the poet himself and the forest

The trumpet of a prophecy①! O Wind,
If Winter comes, can Spring be far behind?

Questions for Discussion

1. What is the image of West Wind?
2. Please analyze the form of *Ode to the West Wind*.
3. Please analyze the theme of *Ode to the West Wind*.

Unit 6　Jane Austen (1775－1817)

Appreciation

　　It is a truth universally acknowledged, that a single man in possession of a good fortune, must be in want of a wife. 凡是有钱的单身汉，总想娶位太太，这已经成了一条举世公认的真理。

　　Jane Austen was born on December 16, 1775, at Steventon in Hampshire, where her father was a rector. She was the second daughter and seventh child in a family of eight. The household was lively and bookish. The family also enjoyed writing and performing plays for evening entertainment. Jane Austen began writing when she was still a little girl. In 1801 the family moved to Bath and after the death of her father in 1805, to Southampton, settling in 1809 with her mother and sisters in a house in Chawton, Hampshire, provided by her brother Edward (1768－1852). Jane Austen never married. She died quietly at Winchester in 1817 and was buried in the cathedral there. Between 1795 and 1798 she worked on three novels. The first to be published was *Sense and Sensibility*. The writing of *First Impressions* got under way and it eventually turned out to be her most famous work *Pride and Prejudice*, but *Northanger Abbey*, a skit on the contemporary Gothic novel.

---

①The trumpet of a prophecy: the clarion call for a new times. prophecy, 预言

Jane Austen's novels deal mainly with middle-class families, set usually in rural communities, though occasionally in a town, for example, Bath. Her plots hinge mostly on the development of a love affair leading to the heroine's marriage. Her penetrating observation of human behavior results in insights that transcend period.

Jane Austen is one of the realistic novelists. She drew vivid and realistic pictures of everyday life of the country society in her novels, whose main concern is about human beings in their personal relations, human beings with their families and neighbors. Stories of love and marriage provide the framework for all her novels and in them women are always taken as the major characters. Describing individuals coping with ordinary life and social pressures, she explores the centres of human experience, with a sharp, satiric wit to expose the follies, hypocrisies, and false truths of the world.

Although Jane Austen was a contemporary of the great Romantics, her novels retain a certain Regency classicism and detachment, keeping always a sense of proportion. She is successful in the employment of irony and frequent use of witty and delightful dialogues.

Jane Austen was an English novelist whose works of romantic fiction, set among the landed gentry, earned her a place as one of the most widely read writers in English literature. Her realism, biting irony and social commentary have gained her historical importance among scholars and critics.

Brief Introduction

Pride and Prejudice tells a story which centers on a series of misunderstandings between Elizabeth and Darcy. Elizabeth is a lively young middle-class woman who has a satirical temperament whereas Darcy, born in a wealthy upper-class family, is an unconsciously arrogant young man. He first offends Elizabeth with his haughty contempt for the "inferiority of her connections" and the "want of propriety" apparently displayed by her son-in-law hunting mother, officer-chasing younger sisters and kind but indolent and cynical father. On account of this, Elizabeth makes up her mind not to care about Darcy at all. However, Darcy reluctantly finds himself a suitor of Elizabeth. As he proposes to Elizabeth, he can't help showing his pride for his own status. What is more, he thinks that he is lowering himself and this he communicates to Elizabeth. Elizabeth, in return, develops a strong dislike for and prejudice against Darcy and rejects Darcy's proposal. Then the two part each other. Later, Darcy writes a letter explaining his past conducts to Elizabeth and frees himself from Elizabeth's charges against him. After a series of events, reconciliation of the two comes. As Darcy renews his proposal to Elizabeth, he realizes that it was his pride that made him arrogant and insensitive. Elizabeth, in turn, accepts his offer with the knowledge that her prejudice caused her to mistake his real character. When they join their hands together, they find happiness and a better understanding of each other.

The preoccupation with socially advantageous marriage in the 19th century England society manifests itself here, because in claiming that a single man in possession of a good fortune must be in want of a wife, the narrator reveals that the reverse is also true: a single woman, whose socially prescribed options are quite limited, is in (perhaps desperate) want of a husband.

Selected Reading

Pride and Prejudice

Chapter 1

It is a truth universally acknowledged, that a single man in possession of a good fortune must be in want of a wife.

However little known the feelings or views of such a man may be on his first entering a neighbourhood, this truth is so well fixed in the minds of the surrounding families, that he is considered as the rightful property of some one or other of their daughters.

"My dear Mr. Bennet," said his lady to him one day, "have you heard that Netherfield Park① is let at last?"

Mr. Bennet replied that he had not.

---

①Netherfield Park: the name of an estate in the neighborhood where the Bennets lived

"But it is," returned she; "for Mrs. Long① has just been here, and she told me all about it."

Mr. Bennet made no answer.

"Do not you want to know who has taken it?" cried his wife impatiently.

"You want to tell me, and I have no objection to hearing it."

This was invitation enough.

"Why, my dear, you must know, Mrs. Long says that Netherfield is taken by a young man of large fortune from the north of England; that he came down on Monday in a chaise and four② to see the place, and was so much delighted with it that he agreed with Mr. Morris③ immediately; that he is to take possession before Michaelmas④, and some of his servants are to be in the house by the end of next week."

"What is his name?"

"Bingley."

"Is he married or single?"

"Oh! single, my dear, to be sure! A single man of large fortune; four or five thousand a year. What a fine thing for our girls!"

"How so? How can it affect them?"

"My dear Mr. Bennet," replied his wife, "how can you be so tiresome! You must know that I am thinking of his marrying one of them."

"Is that his design in settling here?"

"Design! nonsense, how can you talk so! But it is very likely that he may fall in love with one of them, and therefore you must visit him as soon as he comes."

"I see no occasion for that. You and the girls may go, or you may send them by themselves, which perhaps will be still better; for, as you are as

---

①Mrs. Long: a neighbor of the Bennets
②a chaise and four: a carriage drawn by four horses, 一辆四轮马车
③Mr. Morris: the man who owns the Netherfield Park
④Michaelmas: a church festival in honor of the archangel Michael. The day is set on September 29, 米迦勒节(宗教节日)

handsome as any of them, Mr. Bingley might like you the best of the party."

"My dear, you flatter me. I certainly have had my share of beauty, but I do not pretend to be any thing extraordinary now. When a woman has five grown up daughters, she ought to give over thinking of her own beauty."

"In such cases, a woman has not often much beauty to think of."

"But, my dear, you must indeed go and see Mr. Bingley when he comes into the neighbourhood."

"It is more than I engage for, I assure you."

"But consider your daughters. Only think what an establishment it would be for one of them. Sir William and Lady Lucas① are determined to go, merely on that account, for in general, you know they visit no new comers. Indeed you must go, for it will be impossible for us to visit him, if you do not."

"You are over-scrupulous, surely. I dare say Mr. Bingley will be very glad to see you; and I will send a few lines by you to assure him of my hearty consent to his marrying which ever he chuses of the girls; though I must throw in a good word for my little Lizzy②."

"I desire you will do no such thing. Lizzy is not a bit better than the others; and I am sure she is not half so handsome as Jane③, nor half so good humoured as Lydia④. But you are always giving her the preference."

"They have none of them much to recommend them," replied he; "they are all silly and ignorant like other girls; but Lizzy has something more of quickness than her sisters."

"Mr. Bennet, how can you abuse your own children in such way? You take delight in vexing me. You have no compassion on my poor nerves."

"You mistake me, my dear. I have a high respect for your nerves. They are my old friends. I have heard you mention them with consideration these twenty years at least."

---

①Sir William and Lady Lucas: a couple, neighbor of the Bennets
②Lizzy: the second daughter of the Bennets
③Jane: the eldest daughter of the Bennets
④Lydia: the youngest daughter of the Bennets

"Ah! You do not know what I suffer."

"But I hope you will get over it, and live to see many young men of four thousand a year come into the neighbourhood."

"It will be no use to us if twenty such should come, since you will not visit them."

"Depend upon it, my dear, that when there are twenty I will visit them all."

Mr. Bennet was so odd a mixture of quick parts[①], sarcastic humour, reserve, and caprice, that the experience of three and twenty years had been insufficient to make his wife understand his character. Her mind was less difficult to develope. She was a woman of mean understanding, little information, and uncertain temper. When she was discontented, she fancied herself nervous. The business of her life was to get her daughters married; its solace was visiting and news.

Questions for Discussion

1. Analyze the opening sentence: "It is a truth universally acknowledged that a single man in possession of a good fortune must be in want of a wife."
2. Make an analysis of the title *Pride and Prejudice*.
3. What are the special features of the novel?
4. What is the theme of the novel?
5. How many major couples have you found in this novel?
6. What's your attitude towards marriage?

Terms

1. Romanticism
2. Ode
3. Lyric

---

①quick parts: wit, 智慧

4. Terza rima
5. Image
6. Imagery
7. Byronic hero
8. Round character

Chapter 6

19th-Century English Literature

I. Historical Background

The Victorian Age

The mid-and-late 19th century is generally known as the Victorian age, controlled by the rule of Queen Victoria. This is a period of dramatic change leading England to the summit of development as a powerful nation. The rising bourgeoisie were getting political importance as well as wealth. England became the world's workshop and London the world's bank. London became the center of Western civilization.

Literacy increased as the masses started to be educated and started to think for themselves. This stage had got ready for the coming of the Golden Age of the English novel. Along with other forms of literature, they displayed a mirror of the Victorian society and a powerful weapon of its criticism. The English critical realists of the 19th century truthfully reflect the evil of the upper class in bourgeois society as well as of the lower class. Generally speaking, Victorian literature vividly portrays the reality of the age.

II. Literature Background

The Victorian Age is one of the greatest and most creative periods in the history of English literature, standing only next to the Elizabethan Age and the Age of Romanticism.

1. Diversity in Victorian Literature

Unlike the previous two periods of Neoclassicism and Romanticism, there was no dominant literary theory in Victorian literature. Several literary trends existed side by side.

(1) Chartist literature

(2) Realistic novels, the greatest literary achievement

(3) Poetry of the "Big Three"—Alfred Tennyson, Robert Browning & Matthew Arnold

(4) Aesthetic Movement which advocated the theory of "art for art's sake"

2. Major Literary Figures

A. Novel: The novel was the dominant form in Victorian literature. It was a principal form of entertainment.

(1) The Rise of the Women Novelists

(2) Types of Novels since the 18th century: Realistic novels (picaresque novels); Romantic novels (historical novels, Gothic novels)

Charles Dickens: *Oliver Twist*, *David Copperfield*

William Thackeray: *The Snobs of England*, *Vanity Fair*

Gorge Eliot: *The Mill on the Floss*

Charlotte Brontë: *Jane Eyre*

Emily Brontë: *Wuthering Heights*

Thomas Hardy: *Tess of the D'Urbervilles*, *Jude the Obscure*

B. Poetry:

In many ways, Victorian poetry is a continuation of the Romantic poetry of the previous age. Dramatic monologue is the great achievement of Victorian poetry, originally a soliloquy in drama. Here it refers to a narrative poem in which one character speaks to one or more imaginary listeners. Alfred Tennyson poet laureate & the spokesman of the age. He voices the doubt and the faith, the grief and the joy of English people in an age of fast social change.

(1) Alfred Tennyson: *In Memoriam*, *Idylls of the King*

(2) Robert Browning: *The King and the Book*

(3) Elizabeth Barrett Browning

C. Drama: *Aestheticism & art for art's sake*

Oscar Wilde: *The Picture of Dorian Gray*, *The Importance of Being Earnest*

Chapter 6   19th-Century English Literature

Unit 1   Charles Dickens (1812 – 1870)

Appreciation

It was the best of times, it was the worst of times, it was the age of wisdom, it was the age of foolishness, it was the epoch of belief, it was the epoch of incredulity, it was the season of Light, it was the season of Darkness, it was the spring of hope, it was the winter of despair... 这里最好的时代,也是最坏的时代;是智慧时代,也是愚蠢的时代;是信仰的时代,也是怀疑的时代;是光明的季节,也是黑暗的季节;是充满希望的春天,也是令人绝望的冬天。

Charles Dickens, the greatest author of 15 novels, volumes of stories, travel books, sketches and essays, was the greatest representative of English realism. He was especially famous for the vivid comic characterizatio and his powerful social criticism. His works were created during the Victorian age.

Charles Dickens was born in February, 1812 at Landport, a district of Portsmouth. His father was a hardworking but imprudent clerk, who later showed his character as Mr. Micawber in *David Copperfield*. In 1850, Dickens published *David Copperfield*, a semi-autobiographical novel that was the author's own favorite. Then it was followed by three novels: *Hard Times* (1854), *Little Dorrit* (1857), and *A Tale of Two Cities* (1859). The next one, *Great Expectations* (1861) was meant to be his best and successful work. His influence on the development of the European novel was enormous, and his power has greatly lighted world literature.

Brief Introduction

It tells the story of the development of a young man's moral values in the process of his life—from childhood in the provinces to gentleman's status in London. Similar to Dickens' memories of his own childhood, in his early years the young Pip seems to have no power to stand against injustice or to ever realize his dreams for a better and rich life. However, as he grows into a technical worker and then an educated young man, he reaches an important realization: grand schemes and dreams are never what they first seem to be. Pip himself is not always honest, and careful readers can catch him in several obvious contradictions between his truth and imagination.

Selected Reading

Great Expectations

Chapter 39

I was three-and-twenty years of age. Not another word had I heard to enlighten me on the subject of my expectations, and my twenty-third birthday was a week gone. We had left Barnard's Inn more than a year, and lived in the Temple. Our chambers were in Garden-court, down by the river.

Mr. Pocket① and I had for some time parted company② as to our original relations, though we continued on the best terms. Notwithstanding③ my inability to settle to anything—which I hope arose out of the restless and incomplete tenure on which I held my means—I had a taste for reading, and read regularly so many hours a day. That matter of Herbert's④ was still progressing, and everything with me was as I have brought it down to the close of the last preceding chapter.

Business had taken Herbert on a journey to Marseilles 马赛. I was alone, and had a dull sense of being alone⑤. Dispirited and anxious, long hoping that tomorrow or next week would clear my way⑥, and long disappointed, I sadly missed the cheerful face and ready response of my friend.

---

①Mr. Pocket：文中指匹普的监护人
②parted company：解除关系
③notwithstanding：尽管，虽然
④That matter of Herbert's：与赫伯特有关系，赫伯特是匹普童年的伙伴
⑤a dull sense of being alone：文中指感到孤苦伶仃，索然无趣
⑥clear my way：文中指事件等开始明朗起来

It was wretched weather①; stormy and wet, stormy and wet; and mud, mud, mud, deep in all the streets. Day after day, a vast heavy veil had been driving over London from the East, and it drove still, as if in the East there were an eternity② of cloud and wind. So furious had been the gusts, that high buildings in town had had the lead stripped off their roofs; and in the country, trees had been torn up, and sails of windmills carried away; and gloomy accounts③ had come in from the coast, of shipwreck and death. Violent blasts of rain had accompanied these rages of wind④, and the day just closed as I sat down to read had been the worst of all.

Alterations⑤ have been made in that part of the Temple since that time. And it has not now so lonely a character as it had then, nor is it so exposed to the river. We lived at the top of the last house, and the wind rushing up the river shook the house that night, like discharges of cannon, or breakings of a sea. When the rain came with it and dashed against the windows, I thought, raising my eyes to them as they rocked, that I might have fancied myself in a storm-beaten lighthouse. Occasionally, the smoke came rolling down the chimney as though it could not bear to go out into such a night; and when I set the doors open and looked down the staircase, the staircase lamps were blown out; and when I shaded my face with my hands and looked through the black windows (opening them, ever so little, was out of the question in the teeth of⑥ such wind and rain) I saw that the lamps in the court were blown out, and that the lamps on the bridges and the shore were shuddering, and that the coal fires in barges on the river were being carried away before the wind like red-hot splashes in the rain⑦.

I read with my watch upon the table, purposing to close my book at eleven

---

① wretched weather：糟糕透顶的天气
② eternity：永恒的风云
③ gloomy accounts：令人扫兴的事情
④ violent blasts of rain had accompanied these rages of wind：风雨交加
⑤ alteration：变化
⑥ in the teeth of：顶着狂风暴雨
⑦ like red-hot splashes in the rain：像一阵阵红热的雨点

o'clock. As I shut it, Saint Paul's, and all the many church-clocks in the City①—some leading, some accompanying, some following—struck that hour. The sound was curiously flawed by the wind; and I was listening, and thinking how the wind assailed and tore it, when I heard a footstep on the stair.

What nervous folly made me start, and awfully connect it with the footstep of my dead sister, matters not. It was past in a moment, and I listened again, and heard the footstep stumble in coming on. Remembering then that the staircase-lights were blown out, I took up my reading-lamp and went out to the stair-head. Whoever was below had stopped on seeing my lamp, for all was quiet.

"There is some one down there, is there not?" I called out, looking down.

"Yes," said a voice from the darkness beneath.

"What floor do you want?"

"The top. Mr. Pip."

"That is my name.—There is nothing the matter?"

"Nothing the matter," returned the voice. And the man came on.

I stood with my lamp held out over the stair-rail, and he came slowly within its light. It was a shaded lamp, to shine upon a book, and its circle of light was very contracted②; so that he was in it for a mere instant, and then out of it. In the instant, I had seen a face that was strange to me, looking up with an incomprehensible air of being touched and pleased by the sight of me.

Moving the lamp as the man moved, I made out that he was substantially dressed, but roughly; like a voyager by sea. That he had long iron-grey hair. That his age was about sixty. That he was a muscular man, strong on his legs, and that he was browned and hardened by exposure to weather③. As he ascended the last stair or two, and the light of my lamp included us both, I saw, with a stupid kind of amazement, that he was holding out both his hands to me.

---

①the City: 伦敦的市中心
②its circle of light was very contracted: 灯光照射的范围有限
③exposure to weather: 饱经风霜

"Pray① what is your business?" I asked him.

"My business?" he repeated, pausing. "Ah! Yes. I will explain my business, by your leave."

"Do you wish to come in?"

"Yes," he replied; "I wish to come in, Master."

I had asked him the question inhospitably enough, for I resented the sort of bright and gratified recognition that still shone in his face. I resented it, because it seemed to imply that he expected me to respond to it. But I took him into the room I had just left, and, having set the lamp on the table, asked him as civilly as I could② to explain himself.

He looked about him with the strangest air—an air of wondering pleasure, as if he had some part in the things he admired—and he pulled off a rough outer coat, and his hat. Then, I saw that his head was furrowed③ and bald, and that the long iron-grey hair grew only on its sides. But I saw nothing that in the least explained him. On the contrary, I saw him next moment once more holding out both his hands to me.

"What do you mean?" said I, half suspecting him to be mad.

He stopped in his looking at me, and slowly rubbed his right hand over his head. "It's disappointing to a man," he said, in a coarse broken voice, "after having looked forward so distant, and come so far; but you're not to blame for that—neither on us is to blame for that. I'll speak in half a minute. Give me half a minute, please."

He sat down on a chair that stood before the fire, and covered his forehead with his large brown veinous hands. I looked at him attentively then, and recoiled④ a little from him; but I did not know him.

"There's no one nigh⑤," said he, looking over his shoulder; "is there?"

---

① pray：请问
② as civilly as I could：我尽量客气地
③ furrowe：深深的皱纹
④ recoile：退缩
⑤ nigh：near

"Why do you, a stranger coming into my rooms at this time of the night, ask that question?" said I.

"You're a game one①," he returned, shaking his head at me with a deliberate affection, at once most unintelligible and most exasperating; "I'm glad you've grown up a game one! But don't catch hold of me. You'd be sorry afterwards to have done it."

I relinquished the intention he had detected, for I knew him! Even yet I could not recall a single feature, but I knew him! If the wind and the rain had driven away the intervening year, had scattered all the intervening objects, had swept us to the churchyard where we first stood face to face on such different levels, I could not have known my convict more distinctly than I knew him now, as he sat in the chair before the fire. No need to take a file from his pocket and show it to me; no need to take the handkerchief from his neck and twist it round his head; no need to hug himself with both his arms, and take a shivering turn across the room, looking back at me for recognition. I knew him before he gave me one of those aids, though, a moment before, I had not been conscious of remotely suspecting his identity.

He came back to where I stood, and again held out both his hands. Not knowing what to do for, in my astonishment I had lost my self-possession—I reluctantly gave him my hands. He grasped them heartily, raised them to his lips, kissed them, and still held them.

"You acted noble, my boy," said he. "Noble, Pip! And I have never forgot it!"

At a change in his manner as if he were even going to embrace me, I laid a hand upon his breast and put him away.

"Stay!" said I. "Keep off! If you are grateful to me for what I did when I was a little child, I hope you have shown your gratitude by mending your way of life②. If you have come here to thank me, it was not necessary. Still, however, you have found me out, there must be something good in the feeling that has brought you

---

①a game one: 这里指匹普长得英俊、潇洒
②mending your way of life: 你改过自新了

here, and I will not repulse① you; but surely you must understand that I...?"

My attention was so attracted by the singularity② of his fixed look at me that the words died away on my tongue.

"You were saying," he observed, when we had confronted one another in silence, "that surely I must understand. What, surely must I understand?"

"That I cannot wish to renew that chance intercourse with you of long ago, under these different circumstances. I am glad to believe you have repented and recovered yourself. I am glad to tell you so. I am glad that, thinking I deserve to be thanked, you have come to thank me. But our ways are different ways, none the less. You are wet, and you look weary. Will you drink something before you go?"

He had replaced his neckerchief loosely, and had stood, keenly observant of me, biting a long end of it. "I think," he answered, still with the end at his mouth and still observant of me, "that I will drink (I thank you) afore I go."

There was a tray ready on a side-table. I brought it to the table near the fire, and asked him what he would have? He touched one of the bottles without looking at it or speaking, and I made him some hot rum and water③. I tried to keep my hand steady while I did so, but his look at me as he leaned back in his chair with the long draggled end of his neckerchief between his teeth—evidently forgotten—made my hand very difficult to master. When at last I put the glass to him, I saw with amazement that his eyes were full of tears.

Up to this time I had remained standing, not to disguise that I wished him gone. But I was softened by the softened aspect of the man, and felt a touch of reproach④. "I hope," said I, hurriedly putting something into a glass for myself, and drawing a chair to the table, "that you will not think spoke harshly to you just now. I had no intention of doing it, and I am sorry for it if I did. I wish you well, and happy!"

---

①repulse：驳斥,拒绝
②singularity：奇特,奇怪,异常
③rum and water：兑水的朗姆酒
④a touch of reproach：良心上的责备

Questions for Discussion

1. What role does social class play in *Great Expectations*?
2. What lessons does Pip learn from his experience as a wealthy gentleman?
3. How is the theme of social class central to the novel?

Unit 2   The Brontë Sisters

Appreciation

Do you think I am an automaton? a machine without feelings? …… Do you think, because I am poor, obscure, plain, and little, I am soulless and heartless? You think wrong! I have as much soul as you, and full as much heart! And if God had gifted me with some beauty and much wealth, I should have made it as hard for you to leave me, as it is now for me to leave you. I am not talking to you now through the medium of custom, conventionalities, nor even of mortal flesh; it is my spirit that addresses your spirit; just as if both had passed through the grave, and we stood at God's feet, equal, as we are! 你以为我是一架机器？——一架没有感情的机器？难道就因为我一贫如洗、默默无闻、长相平庸、个子瘦小，就没有灵魂，没有心肠了？——你不是想错了吗？——我的心灵跟你一样丰富，我的心胸跟你一样充实！要是上帝赐予我一点姿色和充足的财富，我会使你同我现在一样难分难舍，我不是根据习俗、常规，甚至也不是血肉之躯同你说话，而是我的灵魂同你的灵魂在对话，就仿佛我们两人穿过坟墓，站在上帝脚下，彼此平等——本来就如此！"

There were two great woman novelists during the Victorian age. They were the Brontë sisters, Charlotte (1816 – 1855) and Emily (1818 – 1848). They were born in Yorkshire. In 1820 the family moved to Haworth, a remote and gloomy village on the Yorkshire moors. During the following years, they had a great deal of freedom to explore the surrounding countryside. Their younger sister, Ann Brontë (1820 – 1849) was also a novelist with two works. None of the Brontë sisters enjoyed a long life span and all died young. Charlotte and Emily, together with their two elder sisters, were sent to a charity school with bad food and poor living conditions, where they were cruelly treated. Their two elder sisters did not survive under the hardship and died of health failure. Charlotte and Emily were removed from the school to start a basic knowledge learning at home. Formal schooling was not much in their youth, but wide reading and home education seemed to give freedom to their imagination.

In 1846, a small volume was published with the title of *Poems* under the pennames of Currer, Ellis and Acton Bell. In 1847, Charlotte's *Jane Eyre*, Emily's *Wuthering Heights* and Anne's *Agnes Grey* were all published. However, in 1848, Emily died and Charlotte died in 1855.

Charlotte Brontë is best known for her novel *Jane Eyre*, which tells the story of an orphaned girl who falls in love with a married man.

Emily Brontë is now best remembered for her only novel *Wuthering Heights*, a classic of English literature. Initially criticized for its violent nature, this story of uncompromising passion gained recognition as an astute look at the nature of romantic love.

Anne Brontë: *Agnes Grey* (1847)
The Tenant of Wildfell Hall (1848)怀德菲尔庄园的房客

Although their literary output was relatively small, the Brontë sisters are noted for writing works that transcend Victorian conventions.

Brief Introduction

Jane Eyre lives a tragic life when she is a little child. After her parents' death, she becomes a poor orphan. And her wicked aunt Mrs. Reed adopts her on account of the last will of Jane's uncle. The woman obviously dislikes and looks down upon Jane, and also treats her badly. She is employed to be a governess who teaches a French girl Adele in Thornfield, and the host is called Mr. Rochester. Jane's kindness and faithfulness deeply attracts Mr. Rochester, who soon falls in love with her. Strangely, during the days when they're busy in preparing for the wedding, she finds that Mr. Rochester has been in a marriage with a mad woman called Bertha. After a series of events, Jane suddenly realizes who her true love is. It's Mr. Rochester. Jane returns to Thornfield only to find the manor ruined by a big fire. In the end, to Jane's joy, she finds her lover again and they hold each other's hands forever and live a happy life.

Selected Reading

Jane Eyre

Chapter 23

The vehemence[①] of emotion, stirred[②] by grief and love within me, was claiming mastery, and struggling for full sway, and asserting a right to predominate[③], to overcome, to live, rise, and reign at last: yes, and to speak.

"I grieve to leave Thornfield[④]: I love Thornfield: I love it, because I have lived in it a full and delightful life, momentarily at least. I have not been trampled[⑤] on. I have not been petrified[⑥]. I have not been buried with inferior minds, and excluded from every glimpse of communion with what is bright and energetic and high. I have talked, face to face, with what I reverence[⑦], with what I delight in, with an original, a vigorous, an expanded mind. I have known you, Mr. Rochester; and it strikes me with terror and anguish[⑧] to feel I absolutely must be torn from you forever. I see the necessity of departure; and it is like looking on the necessity of death."

"Where do you see the necessity?" he asked suddenly.

"Where? You, sir, have placed it before me."

"In what shape?"

"In the shape of Miss Ingram; a noble and beautiful woman, your bride."

"My bride! What bride? I have no bride!"

---

① vehemence：愤怒
② stir：使奋起；唤起
③ predominate：占支配地位
④ Thornfield：桑菲尔德
⑤ trample：践踏；蹂躏
⑥ petrify：吓呆，使麻木
⑦ reverence：尊敬
⑧ anguish：痛苦；苦恼

"But you will have."

"Yes; I will! I will!" He set his teeth.

"Then I must go: you have said it yourself."

"No: you must stay! I swear it—and the oath shall be kept."

"I tell you I must go!" I retorted, roused to something like passion. "Do you think I can stay to become nothing to you? Do you think I am an automaton①? A machine without feelings? And can bear to have my morsel of bread snatched from my lips, and my drop of living water dashed from my cup? Do you think, because I am poor, obscure, plain, and little, I am soulless and heartless? You think wrong! I have as much soul as you, and full as much heart! And if God had gifted me with some beauty and much wealth, I should have made it as hard for you to leave me, as it is now for me to leave you. I am not talking to you now through the medium of custom, conventionalities, nor even of mortal flesh; it is my spirit that addresses your spirit; just as if both had passed through the grave, and we stood at God's feet, equal, as we are!"

"As we are!" repeated Mr. Rochester "so," he added, enclosing me in his arms, gathering me to his breast, pressing his lips on my lips:

"so, Jane!"

"Yes, so, sir," I rejoined: "and yet not so; for you are a married man—or as good as a married man, and wed to one inferior to you—to one with whom you have no sympathy whom I do not believe you truly love; for I have seen and heard you sneer at her. I would scorn such a union: therefore I am better than you let me go!"

"Where, Jane? To Ireland?"

"Yes to Ireland. I have spoken my mind, and can go anywhere now."

"Jane, be still; don't struggle so, like a wild frantic② bird that is rending its own plumage③ in its desperation."

---

①automaton：机器人
②frantic：发疯似的；发狂的
③plumage：羽毛

"I am no bird; and no net ensnares① me; I am a free human being with an independent will, which I now exert to leave you."

Another effort set me at liberty, and I stood erect before him.

"And your will shall decide your destiny," he said: "I offer you my hand, my heart, and a share of all my possessions."

"You play a farce, which I merely laugh at."

"I ask you to pass through life at my side—to be my second self, and best earthly companion."

"For that fate you have already made your choice, and must abide by② it."

"Jane, be still a few moments, you are over-excited, I will be still too."

A waft of wind came sweeping down the laurel③—walk and trembled through the boughs④ of the chestnut. It wandered away-away—to an indefinite distance—it died. The nightingale's song was then the only voice of the hour, in listening to it, I again wept. Mr. Rochester sat quiet, looking at me gently and seriously. Some time passed before he spoke; he at last said—

"Come to my side, Jane, and let us explain and understand one another."

"I will never again come to your side: I am torn away now, and cannot return."

"But, Jane, I summon you as my wife: it is you only I intend to marry."

I was silent: I thought he mocked me.

"Come, Jane—come hither."

"Your bride stands between us."

He rose, and with a stride reached me.

"My bride is here," he said, again drawing me to him, "because my equal is here, and my likeness. Jane, will you marry me?"

Still I did not answer, and still I writhed myself from his grasp: for I was still

---

①ensnare：诱捕，使入陷阱
②abide by：遵守……；依从……
③laurel：月桂树
④bough：大树枝

incredulous①.

"Do you doubt me, Jane?"

"Entirely."

"You have no faith in me?"

"Not a whit."

"Am I a liar in your eyes?" he asked passionately. "Little sceptic②, you shall be convinced. What love have I for Miss Ingram? None, and that you know. What love has she for me? None, as I have taken pains to prove: I caused a rumour to reach her that my fortune was not a third of what was supposed, and after that I presented myself to see the result; it was coldness both from her and her mother. I would not—I could not—marry Miss Ingram. You you strange, you almost unearthly thing! I love as my own flesh. You poor and obscure, and small and plain as you are—I entreat to accept me as a husband."

"What, me!" I ejaculated③, beginning in his earnestness—and especially in his incivility④—to credit his sincerity: "me who have not a friend in the world but you—if you are my friend; not a shilling but what you have given me?"

"You, Jane, I must have you for my own—entirely my own. Will you be mine? Say yes, quickly."

"Mr. Rochester, let me look at your face: turn to the moonlight."

"Why?"

"Because I want to read your countenance-turn!"

"There! you will find it scarcely more legible than a crumpled, scratched page. Read on: only make haste, for I suffer."

His face was very much agitated and very much flushed, and there were strong workings in the features, and strange gleams in the eyes.

"Oh, Jane, you torture me!" he exclaimed. "With that searching and yet faithful and generous look, you torture me!"

---

①incredulous：怀疑的
②sceptic：怀疑论者
③ejaculate：突然说出
④incivility：非礼

"How can I do that? If you are true, and your offer real, my only feelings to you must be gratitude and devotion—they cannot torture."

"Gratitude!" he ejaculated; and added wildly "Jane, accept me quickly. Say, Edward give me my name—Edward—I will marry you."

"Are you in earnest? Do you truly love me? Do you sincerely wish me to be your wife?"

"I do; and if an oath is necessary to satisfy you, I swear it."

"Then, sir, I will marry you."

"Edward—my little wife!"

"Dear Edward!"

"Come to me—come to me entirely now," said he; and added, in his deepest tone, speaking in my ear as his cheek was laid on mine, "Make my happiness—I will make yours."

"God pardon me!" he subjoined①; "and man meddle② not with me: I have her, and will hold her."

"There is no one to meddle, sir. I have no kindred③ to interfere."

"No—that is the best of it," he said. And if I had loved him less I should have thought his accent and look of exultation④ savage⑤; but, sitting by him, roused from the nightmare of parting—called to the paradise of union—I thought only of the bliss given me to drink in so abundant a flow. Again and again he said, "Are you happy, Jane?"

And again and again I answered, "Yes," After which he murmured, "It will atone—it will atone. Have I not found her friendless, and cold, and comfortless? Will I not guard, and cherish, and solace⑥ her? Is there not love in my heart, and constancy in my resolves? It will expiate at God's tribunal⑦. I

---

①subjoin: 增补，附加
②meddle: 插手
③kindred: 亲属
④exultation: 狂喜
⑤savage: 未开化的；野蛮的
⑥solace: 慰藉
⑦tribunal: 裁决

know my Maker sanctions what I do.

For the world's judgment—I wash my hands thereof. For man's opinion—I defy it."

But what had befallen① the night? The moon was not yet set, and we were all in shadow: I could scarcely see my master's face, near as I was. And what ailed the chestnut tree? It writhed② and groaned; while wind roared in the laurel walk, and came sweeping over us.

"We must go in," said Mr. Rochester, "the weather changes. I could have sat with thee till morning, Jane."

"And so," thought I, "could I with you." I should have said so, perhaps, but a livid③, vivid spark leapt out of a cloud at which I was looking, and there was a crack, a crash, and a close rattling peal; and I thought only of hiding my dazzled④ eyes against Mr. Rochester's shoulder.

The rain rushed down. He hurried me up the walk, through the grounds, and into the house; but we were quite wet before we could pass the threshold⑤. He was taking off my shawl⑥ in the hall, and shaking the water out of my loosened hair, when Mrs. Fairfax emerged from her room. I did not observe her at first, nor did Mr. Rochester. The lamp was lit. The dock was on the stroke of twelve.

"Hasten to take off your wet things," said he; "and before you go, good-night-good-night, my darling!"

He kissed me repeatedly. When I looked up, on leaving his arms, there stood the widow, pale, grave, and amazed. I only smiled at her, and ran upstairs. "Explanation will do for another time," thought I. Still, when I reached my chamber, I felt a pang at the idea she should even temporarily

---

①befall：发生，降临
②writhe：扭动，翻滚
③livid：乌青色的
④dazzled：使目眩，使眼花
⑤threshold：门槛
⑥shawl：围巾，披肩

misconstrue what she had seen. But joy soon effaced① every other feeling; and loud as the wind blew, near and deep as the thunder crashed, fierce and frequent as the lightning gleamed, cataract②—like as the rain fell during a storm of two hours' duration, I experienced no fear and little awe. Mr. Rochester came thrice to my door in the course of it, to ask if I was safe and tranquil, and that was comfort, that was strength for anything.

Before I left my bed in the morning, little Adele came running in to tell me that the great horse-chestnut③ at the bottom of the orchard had been struck by lightning in the night, and half of it split away.

Chapter 37

Very early the next morning, I heard him up and astir, wandering from one room to another. As soon as Mary came down I heard the question: "Is Miss Eyre here?" Then: "Which room did you put her into? Was it dry? Is she up? Go and ask if she wants anything; and when she will come down."

I came down as soon as I thought there was a prospect of breakfast. Entering the room very softly, I had a view of him before he discovered my presence. It was mournful, indeed, to witness the subjugation④ of that vigorous spirit to a corporeal infirmity⑤. He sat in his chair-still, but not at rest: expectant evidently; the lines of now habitual sadness marking his strong features. His countenance reminded one of a lamp quenched, waiting to be re-lit—and alas! it was not himself that could now kindle the lustre⑥ of animated expression: he was dependent on another for that Office! I had meant to be gay and careless, but the powerlessness of the strong man touched my heart to the

---

①efface：擦掉；抹去
②cataract：大瀑布
③horse-chestnut：七叶树
④subjugation (to)：服从，屈服
⑤infirmity：虚弱
⑥lustre：光辉

quick①: still I accosted② him with what vivacity I could:

"It is a bright, sunny morning, sir," I said. "The rain is over and gone, and there is a tender shining after it: you shall have a walk soon."

I had wakened the glow: his features beamed.

"Oh, you are indeed there, my sky lark! Come to me. You are not gone: not vanished? I heard one of your kind③ an hour ago, singing high over the wood: but its song had no music for me, any more than the rising sun had rays. All the melody on earth is concentrated in my Jane's tongue to my ear (I am glad it is not naturally a silent one), all the sunshine I can feel is in her presence."

The water stood in my eyes to hear this avowal④ of his dependence: just as if a royal eagle, chained to a perch, should be forced to entreat a sparrow to become its purveyor⑤. But I would not be lachrymose⑥, I dashed off the salt drops, and busied myself with preparing breakfast.

Most of the morning was spent in the open air. I led him out of the wet and wild wood into some cheerful fields: I described to him how brilliantly green they were; how the flowers and hedges looked refreshed; how sparklingly blue was the sky. I sought a seat for him in a hidden and lovely spot, a dry stump of a tree; nor did I refuse to let him, when seated, place me on his knee. Why should I, when both he and I were happier near than apart? Pilot⑦ lay beside us, all was quiet. He broke out suddenly while clasping me in his arms:

"Cruel, cruel deserter! Oh, Jane, what did I feel when I discovered you had fled from Thornfield, and when I could nowhere find you; and, after examining your apartment, ascertained that you had no money, nor anything which could serve as an equivalent! A pearl necklace I had given you lay

---

①touched my heart to the quick：深深地触痛了我的心。quick：晦涩
②accost：走近跟某人讲话
③one of your kind：你的一个同类。文中罗切斯特将简比作云雀
④avowal：坦率承认
⑤purveyor：提供者
⑥lachrymose：爱哭的
⑦Pilot：罗切斯特先生养的狗的名字

untouched in its little casket; your trunks were left corded and locked as they had been prepared for the bridal tour. What could my darling do, I asked, left destitute① and penniless? And what did she do? Let me hear now."

Thus urged, I began the narrative of my experience for the fast year. I softened considerably what related to the three days of wandering and starvation, because to have told him all would have been to inflict unnecessary pain: the little I did say lacerated② his faithful heart deeper than I wished.

I should not have left him thus, he said, without any means of making my way: I should have told him my intention. I should have confided in him: he would never have forced me to be his mistress. Violent as he had seemed in his despair, he, in truth, loved me far too well and too tenderly to constitute himself my tyrant: he would have given me half his fortune, without demanding so much as a kiss in return, rather than I should have flung myself friendless on the wide world. I had endured, he was certain, more than I had confessed to him.

"Well, whatever my sufferings had been, they were very short," I answered: and then I proceeded to tell him how I had been received at Moor House; how I had obtained the office of schoolmistress, etc. The accession of fortune, the discovery of my relations, followed in due order. Of course, St. John Rivers' name came in frequently in the progress of my tale. When I had done, that name was immediately taken up.

"This St. John, then, is your cousin?"

"Yes."

"You have spoken of him often: do you like him?"

"He was a very good man, sir; I could not help liking him."

"A good man. Does that mean a respectable, well-conducted man of fifty? Or what does it mean?"

"St. John was only twenty-nine, sir."

---

①destitute: 匮乏的，一无所有
②lacerate: 撕裂；折磨

"'Jeune encore①,' as the French say. Is he a person of low stature, phlegmatic②, and plain? A person whose goodness consists rather in his guiltlessness of vice, than in his prowess③ in virtue?"

"He is untiringly active. Great and exalted deeds are what he lives to perform."

"But his brain? That is probably rather soft? He means well: but you shrug your shoulders to hear him talk?"

"He talks little, sir, what he does say is ever to the point. His brain is first-rate, I should think: not impressible, but vigorous."

"Is he an able man, then?"

"Truly able."

"A thoroughly educated man?"

"St. John is an accomplished and profound scholar."

"His manners, I think, you said are not to your taste? Priggish and parsonic④?"

"I never mentioned his manners; but, unless I had a very bad taste, they must suit it; they are polished, calm, and gentlemanlike."

"His appearance, I forget what description you gave of his appearance; a sort of raw curate⑤, half strangled with his white neckcloth, and stilted⑥ up on his thick-soled high-lows⑦, eh?"

"St. John dresses well. He is a handsome man: tall, fair, with blue eyes, and a Grecian profile."

(Aside.) "Damn him!" (To me.) "Did you like him, Jane?"

"Yes, Mr. Rochester, I liked him, but you asked me that before."

---

①jeune encore：还很年轻（法语）
②phlegmatic：迟钝的；冷漠的
③prowess：杰出的才能
④priggish and parsonic：古板自负，一幅牧师腔。priggish：一本正经的；parsonic：牧师似的
⑤curate：助理牧师
⑥stilt：踩高跷
⑦high-low：高帮缚带靴

I perceived, of course, the drift of my interlocutor①. Jealousy had got hold of him: she stung him; but the sting was salutary: it gave him respite② from the gnawing fang③ of melancholy. I would not, therefore, immediately charm the snake.

"Perhaps you would rather not sit any longer on my knee, Miss Eyre?" was the next somewhat unexpected observation.

"Why not, Mr. Rochester?"

"The picture you have just drawn is suggestive of a rather too overwhelming contrast. Your words have delineated very prettily a graceful Apollo: he is present to your imagination, tall, fair, blue-eyed, and with a Grecian profile. Your eyes dwell on a Vulcan④, a real blacksmith, brown, broad-shouldered: and blind and lame into the bargain."

"I never thought of it, before; but you certainly are rather like Vulcan, sir."

"Well, you can leave me, ma'am, but before you go" (and he retained me by a firmer grasp than ever), "you will be pleased just to answer me a question or two." He paused.

"What questions, Mr. Rochester?"

Then followed this cross-examination.

"St. John made you schoolmistress of Morton before he knew you were his cousin?"

"Yes."

"You would often see him? He would visit the school sometimes?"

"Daily."

"He would approve of your plans, Jane? I know they would be clever, for you are a talented creature."

"He approved of them—yes."

---

①interlocutor：对话者
②respite：暂时解脱
③fang：（毒蛇的）毒牙
④Vulcan：伏尔甘，古罗马宗教信奉的神，后成为铁匠的守护神

"He would discover many things in you he could not have expected to find? Some of your accomplishments are not ordinary."

"I don't know about that."

"You had a little cottage near the school, you say, did he ever come there to see you?"

"Now and then."

"Of an evening?"

"Once or twice."

A pause.

"How long did you reside with him and his sisters after the cousinship was discovered?"

"Five months."

"Did Rivers spend much time with the ladies of his family?"

"Yes; the back parlour was both his study and ours: he sat near the window, and we by the table."

"Did he study much?"

"A good deal."

"What?"

"Hindustani①."

"And what did you do meantime?"

"I learnt German, at first."

"Did he teach you?"

"He did not understand German."

"Did he teach you nothing?"

"A little Hindostani."

"Rivers taught you Hindostani?"

"Yes, sir."

"And his sisters also?"

"No."

"Only you?"

---

①Hindostani：印度斯坦语

"Only me."

"Did you ask to learn?"

"No."

"He wished to teach you?"

"Yes."

A second pause.

"Why did he wish it? Of what use could Hindustani be to you?"

"He intended me to go with him to India."

"Ah! Here I reach the root of the matter. He wanted you to marry him?"

"He asked me to marry him."

"That is a fiction—an impudent invention to vex me."

"I beg your pardon, it is the literal truth: he asked me more than once, and was as stiff about urging his point as ever you could be."

"Miss Eyre, I repeat it, you can leave me. How often am I to say the thing? Why do you remain pertinaciously① perched on my knee, when I have given you notice to quit?"

"Because I am comfortable there."

"No, Jane, you are not comfortable there, because your heart is not with me: it is with this cousin—this St. John. Oh, till this moment, I thought my little Jane was all mine! I had a belief she loved me even when she left me, that was an atom of sweet in much bitter. Long as we have been parted, hot tears as I have wept over our separation, I never thought that while I was mourning her, she was loving another! But it is useless grieving. Jane, leave me, go and marry Rivers."

"Shake me off, then, sir, push me away, for I'll not leave you of my own accord②."

"Jane, I ever like your tone of voice, it still renews hope, it sounds so truthful. When I hear it, it carries me back a year. I forget that you have formed a new tie. But I am not a fool—go—"

---

①pertinaciously: 固执地, 执着地

②of one's own accord: 出于自愿

"Where must I go, sir?"

"Your own way—with the husband you have chosen."

"Who is that?"

"You know—this St. John Rivers."

"He is not my husband, nor ever will be. He does not love me. I do not love him. He loves (as he can love, and that is not as you love) a beautiful young lady called Rosamond. He wanted to marry me only because he thought I should make a suitable missionary's wife, which she would not have done. He is good and great, but severe; and, for me, cold as an iceberg. He is not like you, sir: I am not happy at his side, nor near him, nor with him. He has no indulgence for me—no fondness. He sees nothing attractive in me; not even youth—only a few useful mental points. Then I must leave you, sir, to go to him?"

I shuddered involuntarily, and clung instinctively closer to my blind but beloved master. He smiled.

"What, Jane! Is this true? Is such state of matters between you and Rivers?"

"Absolutely, sir. Oh, you need not be jealous! I wanted to tease you a little to make you less sad: I thought anger would be better than grief. But if you wish me to love you, could you but see how much I do love you, you would be proud and content. All my heart is yours, sir: it belongs to you; and with you it would remain, were fate to exile the rest of me from your presence for ever."

Again, as he kissed me, painful thoughts darkened his aspect.

"My seared① vision! My crippled strength!" he murmured regretfully.

I caressed, in order to soothe him. I knew of what he was thinking, and wanted to speak for him, but dared not. As he turned aside his face a minute, I saw a tear slide from under the sealed eyelid, and trickle down the manly cheek. My heart swelled.

---

①sear：灼伤

Questions for Discussion

1. Please make an analysis of major characters Jane Eyre and Edward Rochester.
2. What do the names mean in *Jane Eyre*? Some names to consider include: Jane Eyre, Gateshead, Lowood, Thornfield, Reed, Rivers, Miss Temple, and Ferndean.

Unit 3   Thomas Hardy (1840 – 1928)

Appreciation

All waited in the growing light, their faces and hands as if they were silvered, the remainder of their figures dark, the stones glistening green-grey, the Plain still a mass of shade. 天越来越亮了，所有的人都在那儿等着，他们的脸和手都仿佛镀上了一层银灰色，而他们身体的其他部分则是黑色的，石头柱子闪耀着灰绿色的光，平原仍然是一片昏暗。

Thomas Hardy was born in a small thatched cottage near Dorchester, Dorset, on June 2, 1840. He was the last one of the greatest Victorian novelists, and was also a great poet at the turn of the 19th century.

The young Hardy had a passion for books. He had expected to have further education, but family finance situation did not support that far. Instead, he was apprenticed to a local architect at the age of 16, which forced Hardy to stay in Dorset, and provided him with the inspiration for his greatest books.

Hardy's novels were all Victorian in date. Most of them were set in Wessex, a fictional primitive and crude rural region which was Hardy's hometown he both loved and hated. These works, known as "novels of character and environment", were the most representative works. He believed in fate and attributed the tragic end of his hero or heroine to bad fortune. Therefore, he was considered to be a naturalistic writer.

Wessex Novels 威塞克斯小说

Dorset is the main background in his works, which he called Wessex—the fictional simple and beautiful though primitive rural region, threatened by the invading capitalism. The impact of scientific discoveries and modern philosophic thoughts upon man is quite obvious. Man is not the master of his destiny; he is at the mercy of indifferent forces which manipulate his behaviors and his relations to others.

Far from the Madding Crowd 远离尘嚣

The Woodlanders 林地居民

Under the Greenwood Tree 绿荫下

The Return of the Native 还乡

The Mayor of Casterbridge 卡斯特桥市长

Tess of the D'Urbervilles 德伯家的苔丝

Jude the Obscure 无名的裘德

Hardy had a deep sense of moral sympathy for England's lower classes, particularly for rural women. In 1891, Hardy published *Tess of the D'Urbervilles: A Pure Woman Faithfully Presented*. The novel, now a great classic of English literature, received mixed reviews when it first appeared, in part because it challenged the sexual morals of Hardy's day. The outcry and accusations of immortality greeted its attack on Victorian hypocrisy disgusted him. *Jude the Obscure* (1898) aroused even greater anger and Hardy stopped his writing. Most of his poems and novels reveal Hardy's love and observation of the natural world, often with symbolic effect.

Characteristics of Hardy's Novels

The underlying theme of his novels is the struggle of man against the mysterious force which rules the world, brings misfortune into man's life and predetermines his fate. This fatalism is strongly reflected in his writings. In his works, the strong elements of naturalism are combined with a tendency towards symbolism. These defects spoil the main realistic effect of his art. Hardy has a strong sense of humor and often describes nature with charm and impressiveness. He went on writing poetry and remained energetic right up to his death on January 11, 1928. He was buried in the Poets' Corner, Westminster Abbey.

Brief Introduction

Tess comes from a farmer's family, called the Durbeyfields. She has lived a poor but peaceful life. However, her father learns that they are descended from the D'Urbervilles, an ancient family once renowned in England. She meets Alec D'Urbervilles, who shows off the estate and always seduces her. Her tragic life has just begun. Despite the rumors all around, she gives birth to a child, who is called Sorrow but dies soon because of illness. For several weeks, Tess is overwhelmed by grief and sorrow. Nevertheless, without financial support, Tess has to leave home and goes to work as a dairymaid at a distant farm, where she meets Angel Claire. The two fall in love and become engaged. Then comes the wedding night, too honest to keep any secret, Tess admits about Alec D'Urbervilles and the child. She begs for forgiveness, but Angel leaves her in disgust. In the meantime, Alec D'Urbervilles, the evil person appears again. Tess stabs Alec in the heart and kills him. Then Tess and Angel Claire escape. They manage to hide for a while in a wood before they come to Stonehenge, where she is arrested. She is hanged later.

Selected Reading

Tess of the D'Urbervilles

Chapter 58

The night was strangely solemn and still. In the small hours she whispered to him the whole story of how he had walked in his sleep with her in his arms across the Froom stream①, at the imminent risk of both their lives, and laid her down in the stone coffin at the ruined abbey. He had never known of that till now.

"Why didn't you tell me next day!" he said. "It might have prevented

---

① the Froom stream: 佛鲁姆河

much misunderstanding and woe①."

"Don't think of what's past!" said she. "I am not going to think outside of now. Why should we? Who knows what tomorrow has in store?"

But it apparently had no sorrow. The morning was wet and foggy, and Clare, rightly informed that the caretaker only opened the windows on fine days, ventured to creep out of their chamber and explore the house, leaving Tess asleep. There was no food on the premises②, but there was water; and he took advantage of the fog to emerge from the mansion and fetch tea, bread, and butter, from a shop in little place two miles beyond, and also a small tin kettle and spirit-lamp③, that they might get fire without smoke. His re-entry awoke her; and they breakfasted on what he had brought.

They were indisposed to stir abroad, and the day passed; and the night following; and the next; till almost without their being aware, five days had slipped by; in absolute seclusion, not a sight or sound of a human being disturbing their peacefulness—such as it was. The changes of the weather were their only events, the birds of the New Forest their only company. By tacit consent④ they hardly once spoke of any incident of the past subsequent to their wedding-day. The gloomy intervening time seemed to sink into chaos, over which the present and prior times closed as if it never had been. Whenever he suggested that they should leave their shelter and go forwards towards Southampton or London she showed a strange unwillingness to move. "Why should we put an end to all that's sweet and lovely!" she deprecated⑤. "What must come will come." And, looking through the shutter-chink⑥: "All is trouble outside there; inside here content."

He peeped out also. It was quite true; within was affection, union, error forgiven; outside was the inexorable.

---

①woe：不幸
②premises：这里指苔丝与安吉尔在逃亡中暂时居住的一座空房子
③spirit-lamp：酒精灯
④tacit consent：默准
⑤deprecate：反对
⑥shutter-chink：百叶窗窗缝

"And—and," she said, pressing her cheek against his; "I fear that what you think of me now may not last. I do not wish to outlive your present feeling for me. I would rather not. I would rather be dead and buried when the time comes for you to despise me, so that it may never be known to me that you despised me."

"I cannot ever despise you!"

"I also hope that. But considering what my life has been I cannot see why any man should, sooner or later, be able to help despising me... How wickedly mad I was! Yet formerly I never could bear to hurt a fly or worm, and the sight of a bird in a cage used often to make me cry."

They remained yet another day. In the night the dull sky cleared; and the result was that the old caretaker at the cottage awoke early. The brilliant sunrise made her unusually brisk; she decided to open the contiguous① mansion immediately, and to air it thoroughly on such a day. Thus it occurred that having arrived and opened the lower rooms before six o'clock, she ascended to the bedchambers, and was about to turn the handle of the one wherein they lay.

At that moment she fancied she could hear the breathing of persons within. Her slipper and her antiquity had rendered her progress a noiseless one so far, and she made for instant retreat; then, deeming that her hearing might have deceived her she turned anew to the door and softly tried the handle. The lock was out of order, but a piece of furniture had been moved forward on the inside, which prevented her opening the door more than an inch or two. A stream of morning light through the shutter-chink fell upon the faces of the pair wrapped in profound slumber, Tess's lips being parted like a half-opened flower near his cheek.

The caretaker was so struck with their innocent appearance and with the elegance of Tess's gown hanging across a chair, her silk stockings beside it, the pretty parasol, and the other habits in which she had arrived because she had none else, that her first indignation at the effrontery② of tramps and vagabonds

---

① contiguous：邻近的
② effrontery：放肆

gave way to momentary sentimentality over this genteel elopement, as it seemed. She closed the door and withdrew as softly as she had come, to go and consult with her neighbors on the odd discovery.

Not more than a minute had elapsed after her withdrawal when Tess woke, and then Clare. Both had a sense that something had disturbed them, though they could not say what; and the uneasy feeling which it engendered grew stronger. As soon as he was dressed he narrowly scanned the lawn through the two or three inches of shutter-chink.

"I think we will leave at once," said he. "It is a fine day. And I cannot help fancying somebody is about the house. At any rate the woman will be sure to come today."

She passively assented, arose, clothed herself, and putting the room in order they took up the few articles that belonged to them and departed noiselessly. When they had got into the forest she turned to take a last look at the house. "Ah, happy house—good-bye!" she said. "My life can only be a question of a few weeks; why should we not have stayed there?"

"Don't say it Tess! We shall soon get out of this district altogether. We'll continue our course as we've begun it, and keep straight north. Nobody will think of looking for us there. We shall be looked for at the Wessex ports if we are sought at all. When we are in the north we will get to a port and away."

Having thus persuaded her the plan was pursued, and they kept a bee line northward. Their long repose at the manor-house① lent them walking power now; and towards mid-day they found that they were approaching the steepled city of Melchester②, which lay directly in their way. He decided to rest her in a clump of trees during the afternoon, and push onward under cover of darkness. At dusk Clare purchased food as usual, and their night march began, the boundary between Upper and Mid-Wessex being crossed about eight o'clock.

To walk across country without much regard to roads was not new to Tess, and she showed her old agility in the performance. The intercepting city,

---

①manor-house: 庄园
②the steepled city of Melchester: 尖塔之城,梅尔切斯特

ancient Melchester, they were obliged to pass through in order to take advantage of the town bridge for crossing a large river that obstructed them. It was about midnight when they went along the deserted streets, lighted fitfully by the few lamps, keeping off the pavement that it might not echo their footsteps. The graceful pile of cathedral architecture rose dimly on their left hand, but it was lost upon them now. Once out of the town they followed the turnpike-road① which after a few miles plunged across an open plain.

Though the sky was dense with cloud a diffused light from some fragment of a moon had hitherto helped them a little. But the moon had now sunk, the clouds seemed to settle almost on their heads, and the night grew as dark as a cave. However, they found their way along, keeping as much on the turf as possible that their tread might not resound which it was easy to do, there being no hedge or fence of any kind. All around was open loneliness and black solitude, over which a stiff breeze blew.

They had proceeded thus gropingly two or three miles further when on a sudden, Clare became conscious of some vast erection close in his front, rising sheer from the grass. They had almost struck themselves against it.

"What monstrous place is this?" said Angel.

"It hums," said she, "Hearken!"

He listened. The wind, playing upon the edifice, produced a booming tune, like the note of some gigantic one-stringed harp. No other sound came from it, and lifting his hand and advancing a step or two, Clare felt the vertical surface of the structure. It seemed to be of solid stone, without joint or moulding. Carrying his fingers onward he found that what he had come in contact with was a colossal rectangular pillar; by stretching out his left hand he could feel a similar one adjoining. At an indefinite height overhead something made the black sky blacker, which had the semblance of a vast architrave uniting the pillars horizontally. They carefully entered beneath and between; the surfaces echoed their soft rustle; but they seemed to be still out-of-doors. The place was roofless. Tess drew her breath fearfully, and Angel, perplexed, said

---

①turnpike-road：收费公路

"What can it be?"

Feeling sideways they encountered another tower-like pillar, square and uncompromising as the first; beyond it another, and another. The place was all doors and pillars, some connected above by continuous architraves.

"A very Temple of the Winds①." he said.

The next pillar was isolated, others, composed a trilithon②; others were prostrate, their flanks forming a causeway wide enough for a carriage; and it was soon obvious that they made up a forest of monoliths③, grouped upon the grassy expanse of the plain. The couple advanced further into this pavilion of the night, till they stood in its midst.

"It is Stonehenge④!" said Clare.

"The heathen⑤ temple, you mean?"

"Yes. Older than the centuries; older than the D'Urbervilles!... Well, what shall we do, darling? We may find shelter further on."

But Tess, really tired by this time, flung herself upon an oblong slab that lay close at hand, and was sheltered from the wind by a pillar. Owing to the action of the sun during the preceding day, the stone was warm and dry, in comforting contrast to the rough and chill grass around, which damped her skirts and shoes. "I don't want to go any further, Angel," she said stretching out her hand for his. "Can't we bide⑥ here?"

"I fear not. This spot is visible for miles by day, although it does not seem so now."

"One of my mother's people was a shepherd, now I think of it. And you used to say at Talbothays that I was a heathen. So now I am at home." He knelt down beside her outstretched form, and put his lips upon hers. "Sleepy are you dear? I think you are lying on an altar."

---

①Temple of the Winds：风神庙
②trililthon：三根连着的巨石
③monolith：独块巨石
④Stonehenge：英国南部史前巨石建筑遗址
⑤heathen：异教徒
⑥bide：停留

"I like very much to be here," she murmured. "It is so solemn and lonely—after my great happiness—with nothing but the sky above my face. It seems as if there were no folk in the world but we two. And I wish there were not—except Liza-Lu."

Clare thought she might as well rest here till it should get a little lighter, and he flung his overcoat upon her, and sat down by her side.

"Angel, if anything happens to me, will you watch over Liza-Lu for my sake?" she asked, when they had listened a long time to the wind among the pillars.

"I will."

"She is so good, and simple, and pure. Oh Angel—I wish you would marry her, if you lose me, as you will do shortly. Oh if you would!"

"If I lose you I lose all. And she is my sister-in-law."

"That's nothing, dearest. People marry sister-in-laws continually about Marlott. And Liza-Lu is so gentle and sweet, and she is growing so beautiful. Oh I could share you with her willingly when we are spirits! If you would train her and teach her, Angel, and bring her up for your own self!... She has all the best of me without the bad of me; and if she were to become yours it would almost seem as if death had not divided us.... Well—I have said it. I won't mention it again."

She ceased, and he fell into thought. In the far north-east sky, he could see between the pillars a level streak of light. The uniform concavity[①] of black cloud was lifting bodily like the lid of a pot, letting in at the earth's edge the coming day, against which the towering monoliths and trilithons began to be blackly defined.

"Did they sacrifice to God here?" asked she.

"No," said he.

"Who to?"

"I believe to the sun. That lofty stone set away by itself is in the direction of the sun, which will presently rise behind it."

"This reminds me, dear," said she. "You remember you never would

---

① concavity：凹陷处

interfere with any belief of mine before we were married? But I knew your mind all the same, and I thought as you thought—not from any reasons of my own, but because you thought so. Tell me now, Angel, do you think we shall meet again after we are dead? I want to know."

He kissed her, to avoid a reply at such a time.

"Oh, Angel—I fear that means no!" said she with a suppressed sob. "And I want so to see you again—so much, so much! What—not even you and I—Angel, who love each other so well?"

Like a greater than himself, to the critical question at the critical time he did not answer; and they were again silent. In a minute or two her breathing became more regular, her clasp of his hand relaxed, and she fell asleep. The band of silver paleness along the east horizon made even the distant parts of the Great plain appear dark and near; and the whole enormous landscape bore that impress of reserve, taciturnity①, and hesitation which is usual just before day. The eastward pillars and their architraves stood up blackly against the light, and the great flame-shaped sun-stone beyond them, and the stone of sacrifice midway. Presently the night wind died out, and the quivering little pools in the cup-like hollows of the stones lay still. At the same time something seemed to move on the verge of the dip eastward—a mere dot. It was the head of a man, approaching them from the hollow beyond the Sunstone. Clare wished they had gone onward, but in the circumstances decided to remain quiet. The figure came straight towards the circle of pillars in which they were.

He heard something behind him, the brush of feet. Turning, he saw over the prostrate columns another figure; then, before he was aware, another was at hand on the fight, under a trilithon, and another on the left. The dawn shone full on the front of the man westward, and Clare could discern from this that he was tall, and walked as if trained. They all closed in, with evident purpose. Her story, then, was true! Springing to his feet he looked around for a weapon, loose stone, means of escape, anything. By this time the nearest man was upon him.

"It's no use, sir," he said. "There are sixteen of us on the Plain, and the

---

①taciturnity: 沉默寡言

whole country is reared."

"Let her finish her sleep!" he implored in a whisper of the men, as they gathered round.

When they saw where she lay, which they had not done till then, they showed no objection; and stood watching her, as still as the pillars around. He went to the stone, and bent over her, holding one poor little hand; her breathing now was quick and small, like that of a lesser creature than a woman. All waited in the growing light, their faces and hands as if they were silvered, the remainder of their figures dark, the stones glistening green-grey, the Plain still a mass of shade. Soon the light was strong, and a ray shone upon her unconscious form, peering under her eyelids waking her.

"What is it, Angel?" she said starting up. "Have they come for me?" "Yes, dearest," he said. "They have come."

"It is as it should be!" she murmured. "Angel—I am almost glad—yes, glad! This happiness could not have lasted—it was too much—I have had enough; and now I shall not live for you to despise me."

She stood up, shook herself, and went forward, neither of the men having moved. "I am ready," she said quietly.

Questions for Discussion

1. Discuss the character of Tess. To what extent is she a helpless victim? When is she strong and when is she weak?
2. Discuss the role of landscape in the novel. How do descriptions of place match the development of the story? Does the passing of the seasons play any symbolic role?
3. The subtitle of the novel is *A Pure Woman Faithfully Portrayed*. All things considered, is Tess a pure woman? Why or Why not?
4. According to Hardy, Man is impotent before Fate, however he tries, he seldom escapes his doomed destiny. Then what causes the destruction of Tess? Is it fate, or some other force?

Terms

1. Victorian Age
2. Critical Realism
3. Realism
4. Naturalism

Chapter 7

20th-Century English Literature

I. Historical Background

The 20th century had the first global-scale war across multiple continents in World War Ⅰ and World War Ⅱ. It underwent a major shift in the way that vast numbers of people lived, as a result of changes in politics, ideology, economics, society, culture, science, technology, and medicine. Feminism demanded that women have equal rights to men. It was a century that started with horses and freighters but ended with cruise ships and the space shuttle. The 20th century saw more technological and scientific progress than all the other centuries combined since the dawn of civilization.

1. World War Ⅰ

World War Ⅰ was a global war centered in Europe that began on July 28, 1914 and lasted until November 11, 1918. The four years of the Great War was considered as the unprecedented levels of carnage and destruction. By the time World War Ⅰ ended, more than 9 million soldiers had been killed and 21 million more wounded. The Treaty of Versailles, signed in 1919, established the League of Nations and punished Germany for its aggression with reparations and the loss of territory. Tragically, the instability caused by World War Ⅰ would help make possible the rise of Nazi leader Adolf Hitler and would, only two decades later, lead to a second devastating international conflict.

World War Ⅰ had greatly influenced English literature. The catastrophic World War Ⅰ tremendously weakened the British Empire and brought about great sufferings to its people as well. Its appalling shock severely destroyed people's faith in the Victorian values; the postwar economic dislocation and spiritual disillusion produced a profound impact upon the British people, who came to see the prevalent wretchedness in capitalism.

2. World War II

World War II was a global war that lasted from 1939 to 1945. It involved the vast majority of the world's nations, eventually forming two opposing military alliances: the Allies and the Axis. It was the most widespread war in history, with more than 100 million people serving in military units from over 30 different countries. In a state of "total war", the major participants placed their entire economic, industrial, and scientific capabilities at the service of the war effort, erasing the distinction between civilian and military resources. Marked by mass deaths of civilians, including the Holocaust and the only use of nuclear weapons in warfare, it resulted in an estimated 50 million to 85 million fatalities. World War II altered the political alignment and social structure of the world. The United Nations (UN) was established to foster international co-operation and prevent future conflicts. The Soviet Union and the United States emerged as rival superpowers, setting the stage for the Cold War.

The two world wars, the most important influences on modern English literature, left their indelible marks of disillusionment and despair in many literary works of the time.

II. Literature Background

1. Historical Baclyround

Although literature in the 20th century was diversified, it reflected the political, social and scientific events of the age.

Modernism is applied to the wide range of experimental trends in the literature of the early 20th century, including symbolism, futurism, expressionism, imagism, Dadaism, and surrealism. Modernist literature is characterized chiefly by a rejection and abandonment of all literary traditions and 19th century realism.

Modernism takes the irrational philosophy and psycho-analysis as its theoretical base. The major themes of the modernist literature are the distorted, alienated and ill relationships between man and nature, man and society, man and man, man and himself. The modernist writers concentrate more on the subjective than on the objective, more on the private than on the public. They are mainly concerned with the inner being of an individual. In their writings, the past, the present, and the future are mingled together and exist at the same time in the consciousness of an individual. Its favored techniques of juxtaposition, multiple points of view, stream-of-consciousness challenge the reader to reestablish a coherence of meaning from fragmentary forms.

In the novel, vitality and interest in technical experimentation marked this period. Joseph Conrad, James Joyce, Virginia Woolf and David Herbert Lawrence were all giants of the giants. The modernist innovators were James Joyce and Virginia Woolf with the "stream of consciousness" technique and with the psychological penetration. A new view of time was developed, coupled with a deeper understanding of the consciousness. One's present was believed to be the sum of his past. Time was no longer a series of chronological moments to be presented by the novelist in sequence, but as a continuous flow in the consciousness of the individual.

The novel *Ulysses* (1922), by the expatriate Irishman James Joyce, has been called "a demonstration and summation of the entire movement", which is set during one day in Dublin, and Joyce creates parallels with Homer's epic poem *Odyssey*. Although his books were controversial because of their freedom of language and content, Joyce's revolutions in narrative form, the treatment of time, and nearly all other techniques of the novel made him a master to be studied, but only intermittently copied. Though more conventional in form, the novels of Lawrence were equally challenging to convention; he was the first to champion both the primitive and the supercivilized urges of men and women.

The 20th century was also an era of high achievements in the fields of poetry and drama. W. B. Yeats and T. S. Eliot, both Nobel Prize winners, were the two greatest British poets of this century. Together with the American poet Ezra Pound, they led a revolution in the technique of modern poetry which has prevailed to the present day. Since the 1890s, there was a revival of English drama. Several important playwrights were part of a movement known as the Irish Literary Renaissance. However, the dominant force in the early 20th century drama was George Bernard Shaw, another Irish-born playwright, who was awarded the Nobel Prize in 1925.

Chapter 7 20th-Century English Literature

Unit 1 Joseph Conrad (1857 – 1924)

Appreciation

What greatness had not floated on the ebb of that river into the mystery of an unknown earth? —The dreams of men, the seed of commonwealths, the germs of empires. 有什么样的伟大的人和事，不曾随这条河的退潮，向一个未知世界的神秘中漂浮而去啊！—人们的梦想，共和国的种子，帝国的萌芽。

Joseph Conrad was a Polish-born English novelist and writer, a dreamer, adventurer, and gentleman. He is noted for his complex narratives and formal experiments, especially in point of view and temporal shift. He is also studied for his account of imperialism, colonialism, and for his depiction of man in his inner battles with good and evil when caught in extreme conditions.

Among Conrad's best-known works are *Lord Jim* (1900) and *Heart of Darkness* (1902). In 1890, he took command of a steamship in the Belgian Congo and began to fulfill his boyhood dream of traveling to the Congo River. His experiences in the Congo came out in *Heart of Darkness*.

In Conrad's life, he was admired for his rich prose and renderings of dangerous life at sea and in exotic places. But his initial reputation as a masterful teller of adventures masked his fascination with the individual when faced with his inner battles. He has been increasingly regarded as one of the greatest English novelists.

Brief Introduction

Heart of Darkness was first published in 1902 with the story *Youth* and thereafter published separately. The story reflects the physical and psychological shock Conrad himself experienced in 1890 when he worked briefly in the Belgian Congo. The narrator, Marlow, describes a journey he took on an African river. Assigned by an ivory company to take command of a cargo boat stranded in the interior, Marlow makes his way through the treacherous forest, witnessing the brutalization of the natives by white traders and hearing tantalizing stories of a Mr. Kurtz, the company's most successful representative. He reaches Kurtz's compound in a remote outpost only to see a row of human heads mounted on poles.

Heart of Darkness in particular, provides a bridge between Victorian values and the ideals of modernism. Like its Victorian predecessors, this novel relies on traditional ideas of heroism, which are nevertheless under constant attack in a changing world and in places far from England. Like much of the best modernist literature produced in the early decades of the twentieth century, *Heart of Darkness* is as much about alienation, confusion, and profound doubt as it is about imperialism.

Selected Reading

Heart of Darkness

The "Nellie①", a cruising yawl, swung to her anchor without a flutter of the sails②, and was at rest. The flood had made, the wind was nearly calm, and being bound down the river, the only thing for us was to come to and wait for the turn of the tide.

The sea-reach of the Thames stretched before us like the beginning of an interminable waterway. In the offing the sea and the sky were welded together without a joint③, and in the luminous space the tanned sails of the barges drifting up with the tide seemed to stand still in red clusters of canvas sharply peaked④, with gleams of varnished sprits. A haze rested on the low shores that ran out to sea in vanishing flatness. The air was dark above Gravesend, and farther back still seemed condensed into a mournful gloom, brooding motionless over the biggest, and the greatest, town on earth.

The Director of Companies was our captain and our host. We four affectionately watched his back as he stood in the bows looking to seaward. On

---

①Nellie:"奈丽"号
②without a flutter of the sails:纹丝未动
③the sky were welded together without a joint:海天一色
④stand still in red clusters of canvas sharply peaked:衬着尖尖的红帆布,释放着幽光

the whole river there was nothing that looked half so nautical. He resembled a pilot, which to a seaman is trustworthiness personified. It was difficult to realize his work was not out there in the luminous estuary, but behind him, within the brooding gloom.

  Between us there was, as I have already said somewhere, the bond of the sea. Besides holding our hearts together through long periods of separation, it had the effect of making us tolerant of each other's yarns—and even convictions. The Lawyer—the best of old fellows—had, because of his many years and many virtues, the only cushion on deck, and was lying on the only rug. The Accountant had brought out already a box of dominoes①, and was toying architecturally with the bones. Marlow sat cross-legged right aft, leaning against the mizzenmast②. He had sunken cheeks, a yellow complexion, a straight back, an ascetic aspect, and, with his arms dropped, the palms of hands outwards, resembled an idol. The Director, satisfied the anchor had good hold, made his way aft and sat down amongst us. We exchanged a few words lazily. Afterwards there was silence on board the yacht. For some reason or other we did not begin that game of dominoes. We felt meditative, and fit for nothing but placid staring③. The day was ending in a serenity that had a still and exquisite brilliance. The water shone pacifically; the sky, without a speck, was a benign immensity of unstained light④; the very mist on the Essex marshes was like a gauzy and radiant fabric, hung from the wooded rises inland, and draping the low shores in diaphanous folds. Only the gloom to the west, brooding over the upper reaches, became more sombre every minute, as if angered by the approach of the sun.

  And at last, in its curved and imperceptible fall, the sun sank low, and from glowing white changed to a dull red without rays and without heat, as if about

---

 ①a box of dominoes：一盒多米诺骨牌

 ②the mizzenmast：后桅杆

 ③fit for nothing but placid staring：默然凝视着远方而无所事事

 ④without a speck, was a benign immensity of unstained light：天空纤尘不染，发着亮丽炫目的光彩

to go out suddenly, stricken to death by the touch of that gloom brooding over a crowd of men.

　　Forthwith a change came over the waters, and the serenity became less brilliant but more profound. The old river in its broad reach rested unruffled at the decline of day, after ages of good service done to the race that peopled its banks, spread out in the tranquil dignity of a waterway leading to the uttermost ends of the earth. We looked at the venerable stream not in the vivid flush① of a short day that comes and departs forever, but in the pacific yet august light of abiding memories. And indeed nothing is easier for a man who has, as the phrase goes, "followed the sea" with reverence and affection, than to evoke the great spirit of the past upon the lower reaches of the Thames. The tidal current runs to and fro in its unceasing service, crowded with memories of men and ships it had borne to the rest of home or to the battles of the sea. It had known and served all the men of whom the nation is proud, from Sir Francis Drake to Sir John Franklin②, knights all, titled and untitled—the great knights-errant of the sea. It had borne all the ships whose names are like jewels flashing in the night of time, from the "Golden Hind"③ returning with her round flanks full of treasure, to be visited by the Queen's Highness④ and thus pass out of the gigantic tale, to the "Erebus" and "Terror"⑤, bound on other conquests—and that never returned. It had known the ships and the men. They had sailed from Deptford, from Greenwich, from Erith⑥—the adventurers and the settlers; kings' ships and the ships of men on 'Change; captains, admirals, the dark "interlopers⑦" of the

―――――――――――
①the vivid flush：消逝的霞光
②from Sir Francis Drake to Sir John Franklin：从弗朗西斯·德雷克爵士到约翰·富兰克林爵士
③the "Golden Hind"："金鹿"号
④the Queen's Highness：女王
⑤the "Erebus" and "Terror"："爱勒巴斯"号和"恐怖"号
⑥sailed from Deptford, from Greenwich, from Erith：从德特福特，从格林威治，从艾瑞斯出海
⑦interlopers：闯入者

Eastern trade, and the commissioned "generals" of East India fleets①. Hunters for gold or pursuers of fame, they all had gone out on that stream, bearing the sword, and often the torch, messengers of the might within the land, bearers of a spark from the sacred fire. What greatness had not floated on the ebb of that river into the mystery of an unknown earth? —The dreams of men, the seed of commonwealths, the germs of empires②.

Questions for Discussion

> Discuss the importance of the Congo River in this narrative. Why does Marlow travel primarily by boat and seldom on land?

Unit 2   William Butler Yeats (1865 – 1839)

Appreciation

How many loved your moments of glad grace, 曾有多少人爱慕你欢畅优雅的瞬间,
And loved your beauty with love false or true. 真情或假意, 爱慕你的美丽娇艳,
But one man loved the pilgrim soul in you, 但只有一人爱你纯真的灵魂,
And loved the sorrows of your changing face. 爱你红颜老去后哀伤的脸。

William Butler Yeats was born and educated in Dublin, but spent his childhood in County Sligo. He was an Irish poet and one of the significant figures of 20th century literature. As a pillar of both the Irish and British literary establishments, in his later years of life, he served as an Irish Senator for two terms. Yeats was a driving force behind the Irish Literary Revival and, along with Lady Gregory, Edward Martyn, and others, founded the Abbey Theatre, where he served as its chief during its early years. He studied poetry in his youth and from an early age was fascinated by both Irish

---

①East India fleets: 东印度公司船队
②the seed of commonwealths, the germs of empires: 共和国的种子和帝国的萌芽

legends and the occult. His earliest volume of verse was published in 1889, and those slow-paced and lyrical poems attribute to Edmund Spenser, Percy Bysshe Shelley, and the Pre-Raphaelite poets. In the 20th century, Yeats' poetry was more physical and realistic and renounced the transcendental beliefs of his youth, though he remained preoccupied with physical and spiritual masks, as well as with cyclical theories of life. In 1923, he was awarded the Nobel Prize in Literature as the first Irishman.

Brief Introduction

It's not so hard to see *When You Are Old* is a poem to lover, showing the infinite love. Even though his well-beloved is no longer young and covered with forehead wrinkles, in his heart she is still the most beautiful. In his eyes, her beauty is eternal, and even beyond the passing of time. When recalling the wonderful old days, he is sweet. This kind of love is great and true, and the feelings have been sublimated after the test of time. She is his goddess, with love and fear. He is willing to wait for her. The love is low-key, is murmur. How evocative!

Selected Reading

When You Are Old

    When you are old and grey and full of sleep
    And nodding by the fire, take down this book[①];
    And slowly read, and dream of the soft look
    Your eyes had once, and of their shadows deep

    How many loved your moments of glad grace[②],
    And loved your beauty with love false or true[③].

---

①this book: 指写给 Maud Gonne 的诗集
②moments of glad grace: 欢畅的瞬间
③your beauty with love false or true: 假意或真心，爱慕你娇艳的容颜

But one man loved the pilgrim soul① in you,
And loved the sorrows of your changing face

And bending down beside the glowing bars②,
Murmur, a little sadly, how love fled
And paced upon the mountains overhead,
And hid his face amid a crowd of stars③.

Questions for Discussion

How could you identify the theme of this poem?

The Second Coming

Turning and turning in the widening gyre④,
The falcon⑤ cannot hear the falconer⑥;
Things fall apart; the center cannot hold;
Mere anarchy⑦ is loosed upon the world,
The blood-dimmed tide is loosed, and everywhere
The ceremony of innocence is drowned;
The best lack all conviction⑧, while the worst
Are full of passionate intensity⑨.

---

①the pilgrim soul：朝圣者般的灵魂，纯真的灵魂
②the glowing bars：闪耀的炉火旁
③a crowd of stars：群星
④the widening gyre：不断扩展的循环
⑤falcon：猎鹰
⑥falconer：训鹰者
⑦anarchy：混乱；无秩序
⑧conviction：信念
⑨intensity：强烈；强度

Surely some revelation① is at hand;
Surely the Second Coming is at hand.
The Second Coming! Hardly are those words out
When a vast image out of Spiritus Mundi②
Troubles my sight: a waste of desert sand;
A shape with lion body and the head of a man,
A gaze blank and pitiless as the sun,
Is moving its slow thighs, while all about it
Wind shadows of the indignant desert birds③.

The darkness drops again but now I know
That twenty centuries of stony sleep
Were vexed④ to nightmare by a rocking cradle,
And what rough beast, its hour come round at last,
Slouches⑤ towards Bethlehem⑥ to be born?

Questions for Discussion

1. Please analyze the image "gyre" in the first stanza.
2. What do you think of the image "the beast" in the third stanza? Please explain your idea in brief.

---

①revelation:天启,启示
②Spiritus Mundi:拉丁语,意为"world spirit",Yeats 认为宇宙的记忆是诗人或作家的灵感来源,是所有意象和象征等无意识的总和
③the indignant desert birds:愤怒的沙漠之鸟
④vexed:烦恼的,争论不休的
⑤slouche:缓慢地行走
⑥Bethlehem:伯利恒(耶路撒冷南方六英里的一个市镇,耶稣诞生地)

Unit 3 James Joyce(1882 – 1941)

Appreciation

Stephen stood at his post, gazing over the calm sea towards the headland. Sea and headland now grew dim. Pulses were beating in his eyes, veiling their sight, and he felt the fever of his cheeks. 斯蒂芬依然站在原地，目光越过风平浪静的海洋，朝那岬角望去。此刻，海面和岬角朦朦胧胧地混为一片了。他两眼的脉搏在跳动，视线模糊了，感到双颊在发热。

James Joyce was an Irish novelist and poet. He contributed to the modernist avant-garde, and is regarded as one of the most influential and important authors of the twentieth century.

Joyce is best known for *Ulysses* (1922), a landmark work in which the episodes of Homer's *Odyssey* are paralleled in an array of contrasting literary styles, perhaps most prominent among these the stream of consciousness technique he utilized. Other well-known works are the short-story collection *Dubliners* (1914), and the novels *A Portrait of the Artist as a Young Man* (1916) and *Finnegans Wake* (1939). His other writings include three books of poetry, a play, occasional journalism, and his published letters.

Joyce was born in 41 Brighton Square, Rathgar, Dublin—about half a mile from his mother's birthplace in Terenure—into a middle-class family on the way down. A brilliant student, he excelled at the Jesuit schools Clongowes and Belvedere, despite the chaotic family life imposed by his father's alcoholism and unpredictable finance. He went on to attend University College, Dublin.

In 1904, in his early twenties, Joyce emigrated permanently to continental Europe with his partner (and later wife) Nora Barnacle. They lived in Trieste, Paris, and Zurich. Though most of his adult life was spent abroad, Joyce's fictional universe centres on Dublin, and is populated largely by characters who closely resemble family members, enemies and friends from his time there. *Ulysses* in particular is set with precision in the streets and alleyways of the city. Shortly after the publication of *Ulysses*, he elucidated this preoccupation somewhat, saying, "For myself, I always write about Dublin, because if I can get to the heart of Dublin I can get to the heart of all the cities of the world. In the particular is contained the universal."

Brief Introduction

Ulysses was first serialised in parts in the American journal *The Little Review* from March 1918 to December 1920, and then published in its entirety by Sylvia Beach in February 1922, in Paris. It is considered to be one of the most important works of modernist literature, and has been called "a demonstration and summation of the entire movement". According to Declan Kiberd, "Before Joyce, no writer of fiction had so foregrounded the process of thinking."

Ulysses chronicles the peripatetic appointments and encounters of Leopold Bloom in Dublin in the course of an ordinary day, June 16, 1904. Ulysses is the Latinised name of Odysseus, the hero of Homer's epic poem *Odyssey*, and the novel establishes a series of parallels between the poem and the novel, with structural correspondences between the characters and experiences of Leopold Bloom and Odysseus, Molly Bloom and Penelope, and Stephen Dedalus and Telemachus, in addition to events and themes of the early 20th century context of modernism, Dublin, and Ireland's relationship to Britain. The novel imitates registers of centuries of English literature and is highly allusive.

Ulysses is approximately 265,000 words in length, uses a lexicon of 30,030 words (including proper names, plurals and various verb tenses), and is divided into eighteen episodes. Since publication, the book has attracted controversy and scrutiny, ranging from early obscenity trials to protracted textual "Joyce Wars". *Ulysses*' stream-of-consciousness technique, careful structuring, and experimental prose — full of puns, parodies, and allusions — as well as its rich characterisation and broad humour, made the book a highly regarded novel in the modernist pantheon. Joyce fans worldwide now celebrate June 16 as Bloomsday. In 1998, the American publishing firm Modern Library ranked *Ulysses* first on its list of the 100 best English-language novels of the 20th century.

Selected Reading

Ulysses

Chapter 1

Solemnly① he came forward and mounted② the round gunrest③. He faced about and blessed gravely thrice the tower, the surrounding land and the awaking mountains. Then, catching sight of Stephen Dedalus, he bent towards him and made rapid crosses in the air, gurgling④ in his throat and shaking his head. Stephen Dedalus, displeased and sleepy, leaned his arms on the top of the staircase and looked coldly at the shaking gurgling face that blessed him, equine in its length, and at the light untonsured⑤ hair, grained and hued like pale oak.

Buck Mulligan peeped an instant under the mirror and then covered the bowl smartly.

—Back to barracks⑥! he said sternly.

He added in a preacher's tone:

—For this, O dearly beloved, is the genuine Christine: body and soul and blood and wounds. Slow music, please.

Shut your eyes, gents. One moment. A little trouble about those white corpuscles. Silence, all.

He peered sideways up and gave a long slow whistle of call, then paused awhile in rapt attention, his even white teeth glistening here and there with gold points. Chrysostomos⑦. Two strong shrill whistles answered through the calm.

---

①solemnly:庄严地
②mounte:登上
③gunrest:炮座
④gurge:嗓子里发出的咯咯声音
⑤untonsure:未剃光
⑥barracks:营房
⑦Chrysostomos:克里索斯托

—Thanks, old chap, he cried briskly. That will do nicely. Switch off the current, will you?

He skipped off the gunrest and looked gravely at his watcher, gathering about his legs the loose folds of his gown. The plump shadowed face and sullen oval jowl recalled a prelate①, patron of arts in the middle ages. A pleasant smile broke quietly over his lips.

—The mockery of it! He said gaily. Your absurd name, an ancient Greek!

He pointed his finger in friendly jest② and went over to the parapet③, laughing to himself. Stephen Dedalus stepped up, followed him wearily halfway and sat down on the edge of the gunrest, watching him still as he propped his mirror on the parapet, dipped the brush in the bowl and lathered④ cheeks and neck.

Buck Mulligan's gay voice went on.

—My name is absurd too: Malachi Mulligan, two dactyls. But it has a Hellenic ring⑤, hasn't it? Tripping and sunny like the buck himself. We must go to Athens. Will you come if I can get the aunt to fork out twenty quid?

He laid the brush aside and, laughing with delight, cried:

—Will he come? The jejune jesuit!⑥

Ceasing, he began to shave with care.

—Tell me, Mulligan, Stephen said quietly.

—Yes, my love?

—How long is Haines going to stay in this tower?

Buck Mulligan showed a shaven cheek over his right shoulder.

—God, isn't he dreadful? He said frankly. A ponderous⑦ Saxon. He thinks

---

①prelate:中世纪作为艺术保护者的高僧
②jest:笑话
③parapet:栏杆
④lathered:肥皂沫
⑤Hellenic ring:古希腊的味道
⑥The jejune jesuit:枯燥乏味的耶稣会士
⑦ponderous:笨头笨脑

you're not a gentleman. God, these bloody English! Bursting with money and indigestion①. Because he comes from Oxford. You know, Dedalus, you have the real Oxford manner. He can't make you out. O, my name for you is the best: Kinch, the knife-blade.

He shaved warily② over his chin.

—He was raving③ all night about a black panther④, Stephen said. Where is his guncase⑤?

—A woful lunatic⑥! Mulligan said. Were you in a funk?

—I was, Stephen said with energy and growing fear. Out here in the dark with a man I don't know raving and moaning to himself about shooting a black panther. You saved men from drowning. I'm not a hero, however. If he stays on here I am off.

Buck Mulligan frowned at the lather on his razorblade. He hopped down from his perch and began to search.

His trouser pockets hastily.

—Scutter! He cried thickly.

He came over to the gunrest and, thrusting a hand into Stephen's upper pocket, said:

—Lend us a loan of your noserag⑦ to wipe my razor.

Stephen suffered him to pull out and hold up on show by its corner a dirty crumpled handkerchief.

Buck Mulligan wiped the razorblade neatly. Then, gazing over the handkerchief, he said:

—The bard's noserag! A new art colour for our Irish poets: snotgreen. You can almost taste it, can't you?

---

①indigestion：消化不良，此处指脑满肠肥的英国人
②warily：仔细地
③rave：狂言
④panther：豹
⑤guncase：枪套
⑥A woful lunatic：一个可悯可悲的疯子
⑦noserag：鼻涕布

He mounted to the parapet again and gazed out over Dublin bay, his fair oakpale hair stirring slightly.

—God! he said quietly. Isn't the sea what Algy calls it: a great sweet mother? The snotgreen sea. The scrotumtightening sea. EPI OINOPA PONTON①. Ah, Dedalus②, the Greeks! I must teach you. You must read them in the original. THALATTA! THALATTA③! She is our great sweet mother. Come and look.

Stephen stood up and went over to the parapet. Leaning on it he looked down on the water and on the mailboat clearing the harbormouth of Kingstown.

—Our mighty mother! Buck Mulligan said.

He turned abruptly④ his grey searching eyes from the sea to Stephen's face.

—The aunt thinks you killed your mother, he said. That's why she won't let me have anything to do with you.

—Someone killed her, Stephen said gloomily.

—You could have knelt down, damn it, Kinch, when your dying mother asked you, Buck Mulligan said. I'm hyperborean as much as you. But to think of your mother begging you with her last breath to kneel down and pray for her. And you refused. There is something sinister in you...

He broke off and lathered again lightly his farther cheek. A tolerant smile curled his lips.

—But a lovely mummer! He murmured to himself. Kinch, the loveliest mummer of them all!

He shaved evenly and with care, in silence, seriously.

Stephen, an elbow rested on the jagged granite⑤, leaned his palm against his brow and gazed at the fraying⑥ edge of his shiny black coat-sleeve. Pain, that was not yet the pain of love, fretted his heart. Silently, in a dream she had come to him after her death, her wasted body within its loose brown

---

①EPI OINOPA PONTON:到葡萄紫的大海上去
②Dedalus:迪达勒斯
③THALATTA:大海
④abruptly:突然
⑤the jagged granite:坑洼不平的花岗石
⑥fray:磨损

graveclothes giving off an odour① of wax and rosewood, her breath, that had bent upon him, mute, reproachful, a faint odour of wetted ashes. Across the threadbare cuff edge② he saw the sea hailed as a great sweet mother by the wellfed voice beside him. The ring of bay and skyline held a dull green mass of liquid. A bowl of white china had stood beside her deathbed holding the green sluggish bile③ which she had torn up from her rotting liver by fits of loud groaning vomiting④.

Buck Mulligan wiped again his razorblade⑤.

—Ah, poor dogsbody! he said in a kind voice. I must give you a shirt and a few noserags. How are the secondhand breeks?

—They fit well enough, Stephen answered.

Buck Mulligan attacked the hollow beneath his underlip.

—The mockery of it, he said contentedly. Secondleg they should be. God knows what poxybowsy⑥ left them off. I have a lovely pair with a hair stripe, grey. You'll look spiffing⑦ in them. I'm not joking, Kinch. You look damn well when you're dressed.

—Thanks, Stephen said. I can't wear them if they are grey.

—He can't wear them, Buck Mulligan told his face in the mirror. Etiquette⑧ is etiquette. He kills his mother but he can't wear grey trousers.

He folded his razor neatly and with stroking palps⑨ of fingers felt the smooth skin.

Stephen turned his gaze from the sea and to the plump face with its smokeblue mobile eyes.

---

①odour:气味
②threadbare cuff edge:褴褛的袖口
③green sluggish bile:暗绿色的液体
④vomite:呕吐
⑤razorblade:剃刀刃
⑥poxybowsy:酒疯子
⑦spiff:好看
⑧etiquette:礼仪
⑨palps:触须

—That fellow I was with in the Ship last night, said Buck Mulligan, says you have g. p. i. He's up in Dottyville with Connolly Norman. General paralysis of the insane!

He swept the mirror a half circle in the air to flash the tidings abroad in sunlight now radiant on the sea. His curling shaven lips laughed and the edges of his white glittering teeth. Laughter seized all his strong wellknit trunk.

—Look at yourself, he said, you dreadful bard!

Stephen bent forward and peered at the mirror held out to him, cleft by a crooked crack. Hair on end. As he and others see me. Who chose this face for me? This dogsbody to rid of vermin. It asks me too.

—I pinched it out of the skivvy's room, Buck Mulligan said. It does her all right. The aunt always keeps plainlooking servants for Malachi. Lead him not into temptation. And her name is Ursula.

Laughing again, he brought the mirror away from Stephen's peering eyes.

—The rage of Caliban① at not seeing his face in a mirror, he said. If Wilde were only alive to see you!

Drawing back and pointing, Stephen said with bitterness:

—It is a symbol of Irish art. The cracked looking-glass of a servant.

Buck Mulligan suddenly linked his arm in Stephen's and walked with him round the tower, his razor and mirror clacking② in the pocket where he had thrust them.

—It's not fair to tease you like that, Kinch, is it? He said kindly. God knows you have more spirit than any of them.

Parried③ again. He fears the lancet of my art as I fear that of his. The cold steelpen.

—Cracked looking-glass of a servant! Tell that to the oxy chap downstairs and touch him for a guinea. He's stinking with money and thinks you're not a gentleman. His old fellow made his tin by selling jalap to Zulus or some bloody

---

①Caliban:凯列班
②clack:磕碰
③parry:岔开话题

swindle or other. God, Kinch, if you and I could only work together we might do something for the island. Helleniseit. Cranly'sarm. His arm.

—And to think of your having to beg from these swine. I'm the only one that knows what you are. Why don't you trust me more? What have you up your nose against me? Is it Haines? If he makes any noise here I'll bring down Seymour and we'll give him a ragging worse than they gave Clive Kempthorpe①. Young shouts of moneyed voices in Clive Kempthorpe's rooms. Palefaces: they hold their ribs with laughter, one clasping another. O, I shall expire②! Break the news to her gently, Aubrey③! I shall die! With slit ribbons of his shirt whipping the air he hops and hobbles round the table, with trousers down at heels, chased by Ades of magdalen④ with the tailor's shears. A scared calf's face gilded with marmalade⑤. I don't want to be debagged! Don't you play the giddy⑥ ox with me!

Shouts from the open window startling evening in the quadrangle. A deaf gardener, aproned⑦, masked with Matthew Arnold's face, pushes his mower on the sombre lawn watching narrowly the dancing motes of grasshalms.

To ourselves... new paganism omphalos⑧.

—Let him stay, Stephen said. There's nothing wrong with him except at night.

—Then what is it? Buck Mulligan asked impatiently. Cough it up. I'm quite frank with you. What have you against me now?

They halted, looking towards the blunt cape of Bray Head that lay on the water like the snout⑨ of a sleeping whale. Stephen freed his arm quietly.

---

①Clive Kempthorpe：克莱夫·肯普索普
②expire：断气
③Aubrey：奥布里
④Ades of Magdalen：麦达伦学院那个手里拿着裁缝大剪刀的埃德斯
⑤marmalade：果酱
⑥giddy：头晕，惊惶
⑦aprone：穿着围裙
⑧paganism omphalos：异教教义中心
⑨snout：酣睡

—Do you wish me to tell you? He asked.

—Yes, what is it? Buck Mulligan answered. I don't remember anything.

He looked in Stephen's face as he spoke. A light wind passed his brow, fanning softly his fair uncombed hair and stirring silver points of anxiety in his eyes.

Stephen, depressed by his own voice, said:

—Do you remember the first day I went to your house after my mother's death?

Buck Mulligan frowned quickly and said:

—What? Where? I can't remember anything. I remember only ideas and sensations. Why? What happened in the name of God?

—You were making tea, Stephen said, and went across the landing to get more hot water. Your mother and some visitor came out of the drawingroom. She asked you who was in your room.

—Yes? Buck Mulligan said. What did I say? I forget.

—You said, Stephen answered, Oh, IT'S ONLY DEDALUS WHOSE MOTHER IS BEASTLY DEAD.

A flush which made him seem younger and more engaging rose to Buck Mulligan's cheek.

—Did I say that? He asked. Well? What harm is that?

He shook his constraint from him nervously.

—And what is death, he asked, your mother's or yours or my own? You saw only your mother die. I see them pop off every day in the Mater and Richmond and cut up into tripes in the dissectingroom①. It's a beastly thing and nothing else. It simply doesn't matter. You wouldn't kneel down to pray for your mother on her deathbed when she asked you. Why? Because you have the cursed jesuit② strain in you, only it's injected the wrong way. To me it's all a mockery and beastly. Her cerebral lobes are not functioning. She calls the doctor sir Peter Teazle and picks buttercups off the quilt. Humour her till it's over. You crossed her last wish in death and yet you sulk with me because I

---

①dissectingroom:解剖室
②jesuit:耶稣会

don't whinge① like some hired mute from Lalouette's. Absurd! I suppose I did say it. I didn't mean to offend the memory of your mother.

He had spoken himself into boldness. Stephen, shielding the gaping wounds which the words had left in his heart, said very coldly:

—I am not thinking of the offence to my mother.

—Of what then? Buck Mulligan asked.

—Of the offence to me, Stephen answered.

Buck Mulligan swung round on his heel. —O, an impossible person! He exclaimed.

He walked off quickly round the parapet. Stephen stood at his post, gazing over the calm sea towards the headland. Sea and headland now grew dim. Pulses were beating in his eyes, veiling their sight, and he felt the fever of his cheeks.

A voice within the tower called loudly:

—Are you up there, Mulligan?

Questions for Discussion

Chapter One introduces us to Stephen's struggle with the ins and outs of Irish identity. Please carry out an analysis.

Unit 4   Virginia Woolf (1882 – 1941)

Appreciation

A charming woman, Scrope Purvis thought her (knowing her as one does know people who live next door to one in Westminster); a touch of the bird about her, of the jay, blue-green, light, vivacious, though she was over fifty, and grown very white since her illness. 斯克洛普柏维斯认为她是一个可爱的女人(他了解她,正如你了解住在威斯敏斯特区你隔壁的人那样);她有点像只小鸟,一只樫鸟,蓝绿色,

---

①whinge:哀号,痛哭

轻盈活泼,虽然她已经年过五十,而且从生病以后变得非常苍白。

Virginia Woolf, a British writer, became one of the most innovative literary figures of the early 20th century, with novels like *Mrs. Dalloway* (1925), *Jacob's Room* (1922), *To the Lighthouse* (1927), and *The Waves* (1931). Her other works include two biographies and many important critical studies of literature and British society. Woolf's works are often linked to the development of feminist criticism, but she was also an important writer in the modernist movement. She revolutionized the novel with stream of consciousness, which allowed her to depict the inner lives of her characters in all too intimate detail. Woolf continued her experiments with fiction, particularly interested in the passage of time. In *The Waves*, she pains herself much to expand the stream-of-consciousness method, depicting characters in the context of time philosophically. The six characters represent different kinds of consciousness. Virginia Woolf is regarded as one of the greatest novelists of the 20th century for her techniques, such as interior monologues and the stream of consciousness.

Brief Introduction

Created from two short stories, *Mrs. Dalloway in Bond Street* and the unfinished *The Prime Minister*, the novel's story is about Clarissa's preparations for a party of which she is to be hostess. With the interior perspective of the novel, the story travels forwards and backcoards in time and in and out of the characters' minds to construct an image of Clarissa's life and of the inter-war social structure.

Selected Reading

Mrs. Dalloway

Mrs. Dalloway said she would buy the flowers herself.

For Lucy[①] had her work cut out for her. The doors would be taken off their hinges; Rumpelmayer's men were coming. And then, thought Clarissa

---

①Lucy:露西,达罗卫夫人家里的帮佣

Dalloway, what a morning—fresh as if issued to children on a beach.

What a lark! What a plunge! For so it had always seemed to her, when, with a little squeak① of the hinges, which she could hear now, she had burst open the French windows② and plunged at Bourton③ into the open air. How fresh, how calm, stiller than this of course, the air was in the early morning; like the flap of a wave; the kiss of a wave; chill and sharp and yet (for a girl of eighteen as she then was) solemn, feeling as she did, standing there at the open window, that something awful was about to happen; looking at the flowers, at the trees with the smoke winding off them and the rooks rising, falling; standing and looking until Peter Walsh said, "Musing④ among the vegetables?"—was that it? —"I prefer men to cauliflowers" —was that it? He must have said it at breakfast one morning when she had gone out on to the terrace—Peter Walsh. He would be back from India one of these days, June or July, she forgot which, for his letters were awfully dull; it was his sayings one remembered; his eyes his pocket-knife, his smile, his grumpiness⑤ and, when millions of things had utterly vanished—how strange it was! —a few sayings like this about cabbages.

She stiffened a little on the kerb⑥, waiting for Durtnall's van to pass. A charming woman, Scrope Purvis thought her (knowing her as one does know people who live next door to one in Westminster⑦); a touch of the bird about her, of the jay⑧, blue-green, light, vivacious⑨, though she was over fifty, and grown very white since her illness. There she perched, never seeing him, waiting to cross, very upright.

For having lived in Westminster—how many years now? over twenty, —one

---

①squeak：嘎吱嘎吱响
②French windows：法式落地窗
③Bourton：英格兰度假胜地
④muse：沉思
⑤grumpiness：坏脾气
⑥kerb：人行道
⑦Westminster：威斯敏斯特（伦敦市的一个行政区，英国议会所在地）
⑧jay：松鸭
⑨vivacious：活泼的

feels even in the midst of the traffic, or waking at night, Clarissa was positive, a particular hush, or solemnity; an indescribable pause, a suspense (but that might be her heart, affected, they said, by influenza) before Big Ben① strikes. There! Out it boomed. First a warning, musical; then the hour, irrevocable②. The leaden circles dissolved in the air. Such fools we are, she thought, crossing Victoria Street③.

Questions for Discussion

> Motifs are recurring structures, contrasts, or literary devices that can help to develop and inform the text's major themes. What are the meanings of "Big Ben" and "trees & flowers" in *Mrs. Dalloway*?

Unit 5　David Herbert Lawrence (1885 – 1930)

Appreciation

Always alone, his soul oscillated, first on the side of death, then on the side of life, doggedly. The real agony was that he had nowhere to go, nothing to do, nothing to say, and was nothing himself. 他依旧孤独地生活着，内心犹豫不决，一会儿决意要去死，一会儿又想顽强地活。真正让他痛苦的是他无处可去，无事可做，无话可说，自己不再是自己。

Born in England on September 11, 1885 in Eastwood, Nottinghamshire, David Herbert Lawrence is regarded as one of the most influential writers of the 20th century. Lawrence published many novels and poetry volumes during his lifetime, including *Sons and Lovers* and *Women in Love*, but he is best known for his infamous novel *Lady*

---

①Big Ben：大本钟
②irrevocable：不可挽回的
③Victoria Street：伦敦市中心的维多利亚大街

Chatterley's Lover. During his last years, Lawrence spent much of his time in Italy making only brief visits to England, the last in 1926. He died on March 2, 1930 at Vence in the south of France.

Lawrence was a prolific writer of poetry, novels, short stories, plays, essays, and criticism. His works are heavily autobiographical and the experiences of his early years in Nottinghamshire continued to exert a profound influence throughout his life. He had an extraordinary ability to convey a sense of specific time and place, and his writings often reflected his complex personality. Lawrence uses the terms "mental consciousness" and "blood consciousness" to distinguish between "sense" and "perception". He also wrote a number of plays, travel books such as *Etruscan Places* (1932), and volumes of literary criticism, notably *Studies in Classic American Literature* (1916).

Brief Introduction

Lawrence rewrote *sons and Lovers* four times until he was happy with it. Although before publication the work was usually entitled *Paul Morel*, Lawrence finally settled on *Sons and Lovers*. Just as the new title makes the work less focused on a central character, many of the later additions broadened the scope of the work, thereby making the work less autobiographical. While some of the editions by Garnett were on the grounds of propriety or style, others would once more narrow the emphasis back upon Paul.

Part I

The refined daughter of a "good old burgher family," Gertrude Coppard meets a rough-hewn miner, Walter Morel, at a Christmas dance and falls into a whirlwind romance characterised by physical passion. But soon after her marriage to Walter, she realises the difficulties of living off his meagre salary in a rented house. The couple fight and drift apart and Walter retreats to the pub after work each day. Gradually, Mrs. Morel's affections shift to her sons, beginning with the oldest, William.

As a boy, William is so attached to his mother that he doesn't enjoy the fair without her. As he grows older, he defends her against his father's occasional violence. Eventually, he leaves their Nottinghamshire home for a job in London, where he begins to rise up into the middle class. He is engaged, but he detests the girl's superficiality. He dies and Mrs. Morel is heartbroken, but when Paul catches pneumonia, she rediscovers her love for her second son.

Part II

Both repulsed by and drawn to his mother, Paul is afraid to leave her but wants to go out on his own, and needs to experience love. Gradually, he falls into a relationship with Miriam, a farmer's daughter who attends his church. The two take long walks and have intellectual conversations about books but Paul resists, in part because his mother disapproves. At Miriam's family's farm, Paul meets Clara Dawes, a young woman with, apparently, feminist sympathies, who has separated from her husband, Baxter.

After pressuring Miriam into a physical relationship, which he finds unsatisfying, Paul breaks with her as he grows more intimate with Clara, who is more passionate physically. But even she cannot hold him and he returns to his mother. When his mother dies soon after, he is alone.

Selected Reading

Sons and Lovers

Chapter 15

Derelict

Clara went with her husband to Sheffield, and Paul scarcely saw her again. Walter Morel seemed to have let all the trouble go over him, and there he was, crawling about on the mud of it, just the same. There was scarcely any bond between father and son, save that each felt he must not let the other go in any actual want. As there was no one to keep on the home, and as they could neither of them bear the emptiness of the house, Paul took lodgings in Nottingham, and Morel went to live with a friendly family in Bestwood.

Everything seemed to have gone smash for the young man. He could not paint. The picture he finished on the day of his mother's death—one that satisfied him—was the last thing he did. At work there was no Clara. When he came home he could not take up his brushes again. There was nothing left.

So he was always in the town at one place or another, drinking, knocking about with the men he knew. It really wearied him. He talked to barmaids①, to almost any woman, but there was that dark, strained② look in his eyes, as if he were hunting something.

Everything seemed so different, so unreal. There seemed no reason why people should go along the street, and houses pile up in the daylight. There seemed no reason why these things should occupy the space, instead of leaving it empty. His friends talked to him: he heard the sounds, and he answered. But why there should be the noise of speech he could not understand.

He was most himself when he was alone, or working hard and mechanically③ at the factory. In the latter case there was pure forgetfulness, when he lapsed④ from consciousness. But it had to come to an end. It hurt him so, that things had lost their reality. The first snowdrops came. He saw the tiny drop-pearls among the grey. They would have given him the liveliest emotion at one time. Now they were there, but they did not seem to mean anything. In a few moments they would cease to occupy that place, and just the space would be, where they had been. Tall, brilliant tram-cars ran along the street at night. It seemed almost a wonder they should trouble to rustle⑤ backwards and forwards. "Why trouble to go tilting down to Trent Bridges?" he asked of the big trams. It seemed they just as well might NOT be as be.

The realest thing was the thick darkness at night. That seemed to him whole and comprehensible and restful. He could leave himself to it. Suddenly a piece of paper started near his feet and blew along down the pavement. He stood still, rigid, with clenched fists, a flame of agony⑥ going over him. And he saw again the sick-room, his mother, her eyes. Unconsciously he had been with her, in her company. The swift hop of the paper reminded him she was gone. But he

---

①barmaids：酒吧女招待（barmaid 的名词复数）
②strain：紧张；态度不自然，勉强
③mechanically：机械地；呆板地
④lapse：倒退；丧失
⑤rustle：发出沙沙的声音
⑥agony：极大的痛苦；苦恼

had been with her. He wanted everything to stand still, so that he could be with her again.

The days passed, the weeks. But everything seemed to have fused, gone into a conglomerated① mass. He could not tell one day from another, one week from another, hardly one place from another. Nothing was distinct or distinguishable. Often he lost himself for an hour at a time, could not remember what he had done.

One evening he came home late to his lodging. The fire was burning low; everybody was in bed. He threw on some more coal, glanced at the table, and decided he wanted no supper. Then he sat down in the arm-chair. It was perfectly still. He did not know anything, yet he saw the dim smoke wavering② up the chimney. Presently two mice came out, cautiously, nibbling③ the fallen crumbs④. He watched them as it were from a long way off. The church clock struck two. Far away he could hear the sharp clinking of the trucks on the railway. No, it was not they that were far away. They were there in their places. But where was he himself?

The time passed. The two mice, careering wildly, scampered⑤ cheekily⑥ over his slippers. He had not moved a muscle. He did not want to move. He was not thinking of anything. It was easier so. There was no wrench⑦ of knowing anything. Then, from time to time, some other consciousness, working mechanically, flashed into sharp phrases.

"What am I doing?"

And out of the semi-intoxicated⑧ trance⑨ came the answer:

①conglomerate：聚结；成团
②wavering：摇摆
③nibble：啃，一点一点地咬
④crumbs：碎屑（尤指面包屑或糕饼屑）
⑤scamper：蹦蹦跳跳地跑
⑥cheekily：厚脸皮地
⑦wrench：痛苦，愁楚
⑧intoxicated：喝醉的，极其兴奋的
⑨trance：出神；恍惚

"Destroying myself."

Then a dull, live feeling, gone in an instant, told him that it was wrong. After a while, suddenly came the question:

"Why wrong?"

Again there was no answer, but a stroke of hot stubbornness inside his chest resisted his own annihilation①.

There was a sound of a heavy cart clanking down the road. Suddenly the electric light went out; there was a bruising thud② in the penny-in-the-slot meter. He did not stir, but sat gazing in front of him. Only the mice had scuttled③, and the fire glowed red in the dark room.

Then, quite mechanically and more distinctly, the conversation began again inside him.

"She's dead. What was it all for—her struggle?"

That was his despair wanting to go after her.

"You're alive."

"She's not."

"She is—in you."

Suddenly he felt tired with the burden of it.

"You've got to keep alive for her sake," said his will in him.

Something felt sulky④, as if it would not rouse⑤.

"You've got to carry forward her living, and what she had done, go on with it."

But he did not want to. He wanted to give up.

"But you can go on with your painting," said the will in him. "Or else you can beget⑥ children. They both carry on her effort."

"Painting is not living."

---

①annihilation：歼灭；灭绝
②thud：砰的一声
③scuttle：快跑，急走
④sulky：生闷气的；闷闷不乐的
⑤rouse：鼓励，鼓舞
⑥beget：成为……的父亲

"Then live. "

"Marry whom?" came the sulky question.

"As best you can. "

"Miriam?"

But he did not trust that.

He rose suddenly, went straight to bed. When he got inside his bedroom and closed the door, he stood with clenched fist.

"Mater①, my dear—" he began, with the whole force of his soul. Then he stopped. He would not say it. He would not admit that he wanted to die, to have done. He would not own that life had beaten him, or that death had beaten him. Going straight to bed, he slept at once, abandoning himself to the sleep.

So the weeks went on. Always alone, his soul oscillated②, first on the side of death, then on the side of life, doggedly③. The real agony was that he had nowhere to go, nothing to do, nothing to say, and was nothing himself. Sometimes he ran down the streets as if he were mad: sometimes he was mad; things weren't there, things were there. It made him pant. Sometimes he stood before the bar of the public-house where he called for a drink. Everything suddenly stood back away from him. He saw the face of the barmaid, the gobbling④ drinkers, his own glass on the slopped, mahogany⑤ board, in the distance. There was something between him and them. He could not get into touch. He did not want them; he did not want his drink. Turning abruptly, he went out. On the threshold⑥ he stood and looked at the lighted street. But he was not of it or in it. Something separated him. Everything went on there below those lamps, shut away from him. He could not get at them. He felt he couldn't touch the lamp-posts, not if he reached. Where could he go? There was

---

①Mater：＜英＞母亲，妈妈

②oscillate：动摇，犹豫

③doggedly：固执地，顽强地

④gobbling：狼吞虎咽地吃

⑤mahogany：桃花心木，红木

⑥threshold：门槛

nowhere to go, neither back into the inn, or forward anywhere. He felt stifled①. There was nowhere for him. The stress grew inside him; he felt he should smash.

"I mustn't," he said; and, turning blindly, he went in and drank. Sometimes the drink did him good; sometimes it made him worse. He ran down the road. For ever restless, he went here, there, everywhere. He determined to work. But when he had made six strokes, he loathed② the pencil violently, got up, and went away, hurried off to a club where he could play cards or billiards③, to a place where he could flirt④ with a barmaid who was no more to him than the brass pump-handle she drew.

He was very thin and lantern-jawed⑤. He dared not meet his own eyes in the mirror; he never looked at himself. He wanted to get away from himself, but there was nothing to get hold of.

Questions for Discussion

1. What's the main theme of *Sons and Lovers*?
2. Please analyze the relationship between Paul Morel and Miriam, and that between Paul and Clara.

Unit 6　Doris May Lessing(1919 – 2013)

Doris May Lessing was awarded the 2007 Nobel Prize in Literature. The Swedish Academy described her as "that epicist of the female experience, who with scepticism, fire and visionary power has subjected a divided civilisation to scrutiny". Lessing was

---

①stifled：窒息的
②loathe：憎恨，厌恶
③billiards：台球，弹子球
④flirt：调情，打情骂俏
⑤lantern-jawed：下巴突出的，瘦长脸的

the 11th woman and the oldest person to be awarded the Nobel Prize for Literature by the Swedish Academy in its 106-year history. In 2001, Lessing was awarded the David Cohen Prize for a lifetime's achievement in British literature. In 2008, *The Times* ranked her fifth on a list of "The 50 greatest British writers since 1945".

Lessing was a British novelist, poet, playwright, librettist, biographer and short story writer. Her novels include *The Grass is Singing*, the sequence of five novels collectively called *Children of Violence*, *The Golden Notebook*, *The Good Terrorist*, and five novels collectively known as *Canopus in Argos: Archives*.

Doris Lessing was born Doris May Tayler in Persia (now Iran) on October 22, 1919. Both of her parents were British: her father, who had been crippled in World War I, was a clerk in the Imperial Bank of Persia; her mother had been a nurse. Her family moved to Southern Africa where she spent her childhood on her father's farm in what was then Southern Rhodesia (now Zimbabwe). Doris's mother adapted to the rough life in the settlement, energetically trying to reproduce what was, in her view, a civilized, Edwardian life among savages; but her father did not, and the thousand-odd acres of bush he had bought failed to yield the promised wealth.

As a girl, Doris was educated at the Dominican Convent High School, a Roman Catholic convent all-girls school in the South Rhodesian capital of Salisbury (now Harare), the capital of South Rhodesia. She soon dropped out from the school. Lessing made herself into a self-educated intellectual. She left home at 15 and worked as a nursemaid. Lessing's early reading included Dickens, Scott, Stevenson, Kipling; later she discovered Lawrence, Stendhal, Tolstoy, Dostoevsky. Bedtime stories also nurtured her youth: her mother told them to the children and Doris herself kept her younger brother awake, spinning out tales. Doris's early years were also spent absorbing her father's bitter memories of World War I.

She started reading materials on politics and sociology and began writing. In Southern Africa, Lessing began to sell her stories to magazines. When her second marriage ended in 1949, Lessing moved to London with her young son, where she also published her first novel, *The Grass Is Singing*, and began her career as a professional writer. The book explores the complacency and shallowness of white colonial society in Southern Africa and established Lessing as a talented young novelist.

The Golden Notebook published in 1962, gained her international attention. The book is a story of fragmented post-war life told in a fragmented form. The novel concerns Anna Wulf, a writer caught in a personal and artistic crisis, who sees her life compartmentalised into various roles—woman, lover, writer, political activist. Anna eventually suffers a mental breakdown and it is only through this disintegration that she is able to discover a new "wholeness" which she writes about in the final notebook. There is no centre and all is fiction. It is a very early work of British postmodernism.

By the time of her death, she had issued more than 50 novels, some under a pseudonym.

Brief Introduction

A Woman on a Roof is a story of seven days during a June heat wave in London. One day, three men repairing the roof of an apartment building in the baking sun see a woman sunning herself on an adjoining roof, and she undoes the scarf covering her breasts. When Harry, the oldest worker, leaves to borrow a blanket to put up for shade, Stanley and the 17-year-old Tom let out wolf whistles at the woman, but she ignores them. When the three workers make their last trip to look at the woman, Stanley is so angry that he threatens to report her to the police.

Selected Reading

A Woman on a Roof

It was during the week of hot sun, that June.

Three men were at work on the roof, where the leads① got so hot they had the idea of throwing water on to cool them. But the water steamed, then sizzled②; and they make jokes about getting an egg from some woman in the flats under them, to poach③ it for their dinner. By two it was not possible to touch

---

①the leads:（英）铅皮屋顶
②sizzled：咝咝声
③poach：水煮（荷包蛋）

the guttering① they were replacing, and they speculated about what workmen did in regularly hot countries. Perhaps they should borrow kitchen gloves② with the egg? They were all a bit dizzy, not used to the heat; and they shed③ their coats and stood side by side squeezing themselves into a foot wide patch of shade against a chimney, careful to keep their feet in the thick socks and boots out of the sun. There was a fine view across several acres of roofs. Not far off a man sat in a deck chair reading the newspapers. Then they saw her, between chimneys, about fifty yards away. She lay face down on a brown blanket. They could see the top part of her: black hair, a flushed solid back, arms spread out.

"She's stark naked," said Stanley, sounding annoyed.

Harry, the oldest, a man of about forty-five, said: "Looks like it."

Young Tom, seventeen, said nothing, but he was excited and grinning.

Stanley said: "Someone'll report her if she doesn't watch out."

"She thinks no one can see," said Tom, craning his head all ways to see more.

At this point the woman, still lying prone, brought her two hands up behind her shoulders with the ends of a scarf in them, tied it behind her back, and sat up. She wore a red scarf tied around her breasts and brief red bikini pants. This being the first day of the sun she was white, flushing red. She sat smoking, and did not look up when Stanley let out a wolf whistle④. Harry said: "Small things amuse small minds," leading the way back to their part of the roof, but it was scorching⑤. Harry said: "Wait, I'm going to rig up⑥ some shade," and disappeared down the skylight⑦ into the building. Now that he'd gone, Stanley and Tom went to the farthest point they could peer at the woman. She had moved, and all they could see were two pink legs stretched on the blanket. They

---

①guttering: 檐沟
②kitchen gloves: （防烫的）棉手套
③shed: 脱掉
④wolf whistle: 挑逗口哨
⑤scorching: 灼热的
⑥rig up: 临时架起
⑦skylight: 天窗

whistled and shouted but the legs did not move. Harry came back with a blanket and shouted: "Come on, then." He sounded irritated with them. They clambered① back to him and he said to Stanley: "What about your missus②?" Stanley was newly married, about three months. Stanley said, jeering: "What about my missus?"—preserving his independence. Tom said nothing, but his mind was full of the nearly naked woman. Harry slung the blanket, which he had borrowed from a friendly woman downstairs, from the stem of a television aerial to a row of chimney-pots③ (= chimney-pot hats). This shade fell across the piece of gutter they had to replace. But the shade kept moving, they had to adjust the blanket, and not much progress was made. At last some of the heat left the roof, and they worked fast, making up for lost time. First Stanley, then Tom, made a trip to the end of the roof to see the woman. "She's on her back," Stanley said, and the older man smile tolerantly. Tom's report was that she hadn't moved, adding a jest which made Tom snicker④ but it was a lie. He wanted to keep what he had seen to himself: he had caught her in the act of rolling down the little red pants over her hips, till they were no more than a small triangle. She was on her back, fully visible, glistening with oil⑤.

Next morning, as soon as they came up, they went to look. She was already there, face down, arms spread out, naked except for the little red pants. She had turned brown in the night. Yesterday she was a scarlet-and-white woman, today she was a brown woman. Stanley let out a whistle. She lifted her head, startled, as if she'd been asleep, and looked straight over at them. The sun was in her eyes, she blinked and stared, then she dropped her head again. At this gesture of indifference, they all three, Stanley, Tom and old Harry, let out whistles and yells. Harry was doing it in parody of the younger men, making fun of them, but he was also angry. They were all angry because of her utter

---

①clamber: 爬
②missus: （伦敦方言）妻子, 太太
③chimney-pots: 烟囱管帽
④adding a jest which made Tom snicker: 加上一句俏皮话, 使 Tom 听了暗自发笑
⑤oil: 指防晒护肤油

indifference to the three men watching her.

"Bitch," said Stanley.

"She should ask us over," said Tom, snickering.

Harry recovered himself and reminded Stanley: "If she's married, her old man wouldn't like that."

"Christ," said Stanley virtuously, "if my wife lay about like that, for everyone to see, I'd soon stop her."

Harry said, smiling: "How do you know, perhaps she's sunning herself at this very moment?"

"Not a chance, not on our roof." The safety of his wife put Stanley into a good humor, and they went to work. But today it was hotter than yesterday; and several times one or the other suggested they should tell Matthew, the foreman①, and ask to leave the roof until the heat wave was over. But they didn't. There was work to be done in the basement of the big block of flats, but up here they felt free, on a different level from ordinary humanity shut in the streets or the buildings. A lot more people came out on to the roofs that day, for an hour at midday. Some married couples sat side by side in deck chairs, the women's legs stockingless and scarlet, the men in vests with reddening shoulders.

The woman stayed on her blanket, turning herself over and over. She ignored them, no matter what they did. When Harry went off to fetch more screws, Stanley said: "Come on." Her roof belonged to a different system of roofs, separated from theirs at one point by about twenty feet. It meant a scrambling climb from one level to another, edging along parapets②, clinging to chimneys, while their big boots slipped and hered slithered③, but at last they stood on a small square projecting roof looking straight down at her, close. She sat smoking, reading a book. Tom thought she looked like a poster, or a magazine cover, with the blue sky behind her and her legs stretched out. Behind

---

①foreman：工头
②parapets：(屋顶、露夕等边上的)低矮短墙
③slither：滑下

her a great crane① at work on a new building in Oxford Street② swung its black arm across roofs in a great arc. Tom imagined himself at work on the crane, adjusting the arm to swing over and pick her up and swing her back across the sky to drop her near him.

They whistled. She looked up at them, cool and remote, then went on reading. Again, they were furious. Or, rather, Stanley was. His sun-heated face was screwed into a rage as he whistled again and again, trying to make her look up. Young Tom stopped whistling. He stood beside Stanley, excited, grinning; but he felt as if he were saying to the woman: Don't associate me with him, for his grin was apologetic. Last night he had thought of the unknown woman before he slept, and she had been tender with him. This tenderness he was remembering as he shifted his feet by the jeering, whistling Stanley, and watched the indifferent, healthy brown woman a few feet off, with the gap that plunged to the street between them. Tom thought it was romantic, it was like being high on two hilltops. But there was a shout from Harry, and they clambered back. Stanley's face was hard, really angry. The boy kept looking at him and wondered why he hated the woman so much, for by now he loved her.

They played their little games with the blanket, trying to trap shade to work under; but again it was not until nearly four that they could work seriously, and they were exhausted, all three of them. They were grumbling about③ the weather by now. Stanley was in a thoroughly bad humor. When they made their routine trip to see the woman before they packed up④ for the day, she was apparently asleep, face down, her back all naked save for the scarlet triangle on her buttocks. "I've got a good mind to report her to the police," said Stanley, and Harry said: "What's eating you? What harm's she doing?"

"I tell you, if she was my wife!"

"But she isn't, is she?" Tom knew that Harry, like himself, was uneasy at

---

①crane:起重机
②Oxford Street:伦敦市中心的商业街
③grumbling about:咕哝;埋怨
④packed up:这里指收拾干活工具

Stanley's reaction. He was normally a sharp young man, quick at his work, making a lot of jokes, good company.

"Perhaps it will be cooler tomorrow," said Harry.

"But it wasn't; it was hotter, if anything, and the weather forecast said the good weather would last. As soon as they were on the roof, Harry went over to see if the woman was there, and Tom knew it was to prevent Stanley going, to put off his bad humor. Harry had grownup children, a boy the same age as Tom, and the youth trusted and looked up to him."

Harry came back and said: "She's not there."

"I bet her old man has put his foot down①," said Stanley, and Harry and Tom caught each other's eyes and smiled behind the young married man's back.

Harry suggested they should get permission to work in the basement, and they did, that day. But before packing up Stanley said: "Let's have a breath of fresh air." Again Harry and Tom smiled at each other as they followed Stanley up to the roof, Tom in the devout conviction② that he was there to protect the woman from Stanley. It was about five-thirty, and a calm, full sunlight lay over the roofs. The great crane still swung its black arm from Oxford Street to above their heads. She was not there. Then there was a flutter③ of white from behind a parapet, and she stood up, in a belted, white dressing-gown. She had been there all day, probably, but on a different patch of roof, to hide from them. Stanley did not whistle; he said nothing, but watched the woman bend to collect papers, books, cigarettes, then fold the blanket over her arm. Tom was thinking: If they weren't here, I'd go over and say... what? But he knew from his nightly dreams of her that she was kind and friendly. Perhaps she would ask him down to her flat? Perhaps... He stood watching her disappear down the skylight. As she went, Stanley let out a shrill derisive④ yell; she started, and it

---

① I bet her... his foot down: 我打赌她老头子决不容许她这样
② conviction: 深信，确信，定罪，宣告有罪
③ flutter: 摆动，鼓翼，烦扰
④ derisive: 嘲笑的，值得嘲笑的

seemed as if she nearly fell. She clutched to① save herself, they could hear things falling. She looked straight at them, angry. Harry said, facetiously②: "Better be careful on those slippery ladders, love." Tom knew he said it to save her from Stanley, but she could not know it. She vanished, frowning. Tom was full of a secret delight, because he knew her anger was for the others, not for him.

"Roll on③ some rain (hope it will rain)," said Stanley, bitter, looking at the blue evening sky.

Next day was cloudless, and they decided to finish the work in the basement.

They felt excluded, shut in the grey cement basement fitting pipes, from the holiday atmosphere of London in a heat wave. At lunchtime they came up for some air, but while the married couples, and the men in shirt-sleeves or vests, were there, she was not there, either on her usual patch of roof or where she had been yesterday. They all, even Harry, clambered about, between chimney-pots, over parapets, the hot leads stinging their fingers. There was not a sign of her. They took off their shirts and vests and exposed their chests, feeling their feet sweaty and hot. They did not mention the woman. But Tom felt alone again. Last night she had him into her flat: it was big and had fitted white carpets and a bed with a padded white leather head-board. She wore a black filmy④ negligee and her kindness to Tom thickened his throat as he remembered it. He felt she had betrayed him by not being there.

And again after work they climbed up, but still there was nothing to be seen of her. Stanley kept repeating that if it was as hot as this tomorrow he wasn't going to work and that's all there was to it. But they were all there next day. By ten the temperature was in the middle seventies⑤, and it was eighty long before

---

①clutched to: 抓, 抓住, 攥住; 握紧
②facetiously: 开玩笑地
③roll on: 但愿
④filmy: 薄薄的女式长睡袍
⑤in the middle seventies: 华氏70多度

noon. Harry went to the foreman to say it was impossible to work on the leads in that heat; but the foreman said there was nothing else he could put them on, and they'd have to. At midday they stood, silent, watching the skylight on her roof open, and then she slowly emerged in her white gown, holding a bundle of blanket. She looked at them, gravely, then went to the part of the roof where she was hidden from them. Tom was pleased. He felt she was more his when the other men couldn't see her. They had taken off their shirts and vests, but now they put them back again, for they felt the sun bruising their flesh. "She must have the hide of a rhino①," said Stanley, tugging at②(= pulling) guttering and swearing. They stopped work, and sat in the shade, moving around behind chimney stacks. A woman came to water a yellow window box③ opposite them. She was middleaged, wearing a flowered summer dress. Stanley said to her: "We need a drink more than them." She smiled and said: "Better drop down to the pub quick, it'll be closing in a minute." They exchanged pleasantries④, and she left them with a smile and a wave.

"Not like Lady Godiva⑤," said Stanley. "She can give us a bit of a chat and a smile."

"You didn't whistle at her⑥," said Tom, reproving.

"Listen to him," said Stanley, "you didn't whistle, then?"

But the boy felt as if he hadn't whistled, as if only Harry and Stanley had. He was making plans, when it was time to knock off⑦ work, to get left behind and somehow make his way over to the woman. The weather report said the hot

---

①the hide of a rhino:犀牛皮,这里是指她的皮肤经得住晒
②tugging at:使劲拉
③to water a yellow window box:给黄色窗台花箱里的花木浇水
④pleasantries:打趣的话
⑤Lady Godiva:Lady Godiva 是中世纪英国的一位贵族妇女,传说为使丈夫减免考文垂(Coventry)的苛捐杂税,她赤身裸体骑马从街上走过。裁缝 Tom 偷看了一眼,顿时遭到双目失明的报应。Peeping Tom(窥视者)由此而来。这里指在屋顶上晒日光浴的女人
⑥her:指浇花的女人
⑦knock off:(口)停工

spell was due to break①, so he had to move quickly. But there was no chance of being left. The other two decided to knock off work at four, because they were exhausted. As they went down, Tom quickly climbed a parapet and hoisted himself higher by pulling his weight up a chimney. He caught a glimpse of her lying on her back, her knees up, eyes closed, a brown woman lolling② in the sun. He slipped and clattered down, as Stanley looked for information: "She's gone down," he said. He felt as if he had protected her from Stanley, and that she must be grateful to him. He could feel the bond between the woman and himself.

Next day, they stood around on the landing below the roof, reluctant to climb up into the heat. The woman who had lent Harry the blanket came out and offered them a cup of tea. They accepted gratefully, and sat around Mrs. Pritchett's kitchen an hour or so, chatting. She was married to an airline pilot. A smart blonde, of about thirty, she had an eye for the handsome sharp-faced Stanley; and the two teased each other while Harry sat in a corner, watching, indulgent, though his expression reminded Stanley that he was married. And young Tom felt envious of Stanley's ease in badinage③; felt, too, that Stanley's getting off with Mrs. Pritchett left his romance with the woman on the roof safe and intact.

"I thought they said the heat wave'd break," said Stanley, sullen, as the time approached when they really would have to climb up into the sunlight.

"You don't like it, then?" asked Mrs. Pritchett.

"All right for some," said Stanley. "Nothing to do but lie about as if it was a beach up there. Do you ever go up?"

"Went up once," said Mrs. Pritchett. "But it's a dirty place up there, and it's too hot."

"Quite right too," said Stanley.

Then they went up, leaving the cool neat little flat and the friendly Mrs.

---

①the hot spell was due to break: 高温期快要结束
②lolling: 懒洋洋地躺着
③badinage:(法语)开玩笑,取笑逗乐

Pritchett.

As soon as they were up they saw her. The three men looked at her, resentful at her ease in this punishing sun. Then Harry said, because of the expression on Stanley's face: "Come on, we've got to pretend to work, at least."

They had to wrench another length of guttering that ran beside a parapet out of its bed, so that they could replace it. Stanley took it in his two hands, tugged, swore, stood up. "Fuck it," he said, and sat down under a chimney. He lit a cigarette. "Fuck them," he said. "What do they think we are, lizards? I've got blisters all over my hands." Then he jumped up and climbed over the roofs and stood with his back to them. He put his fingers either side of his mouth and let out a shrill whistle. Tom and Harry squatted, not looking at each other, watching him. They could just see the woman's head, the beginnings of her brown shoulders. Stanley whistled again. Then he began stamping with his feet, and whistled and yelled and screamed at the woman, his face getting scarlet. He seemed quite mad, as he stamped and whistled, while the woman did not move, she did not move a muscle.

"Barmy①," said Tom.

"Yes," said Harry, disapproving.

Suddenly the older man came to a decision. It was, Tom knew, to save some sort of scandal or real trouble over the woman. Harry stood up and began packing tools into a length of oily cloth. "Stanley," he said, commanding. At first Stanley took no notice, but Harry said: "Stanley, we're packing it in, I'll tell Matthew."

Stanley came back, cheeks mottle (marked with spots of different color), eyes glaring.

"Can't go on like this," said Harry. "It'll break in a day or so. I'm going to tell Matthew we've got sunstroke② (heatstroke caused by prolonged exposure to intensely hot sunlight 中暑, and if he doesn't like it, it's too bad." Even Harry

---

①Barmy:(俚)傻;不正常
②sunstroke:中暑

sounded aggrieved (sad)①, Tom noted. The small, competent man, the family man with his grey hair, who was never at a loss, sounded really off balance. "Come on," he said, angry. He fitted himself into the open square in the roof, and went down, watching his feet on the ladder. Then Stanley went, with not a glance at the woman. Then Tom, who, his throat beating with excitement, silently promised her on a backward glance: Wait for me, wait, I'm coming.

On the pavement Stanley said: "I'm going home." He looked white now, so perhaps he really did have sunstroke. Harry went off to find the foreman, who was at work on the plumbing② of some flats down the street. Tom slipped back, not into the building they had been working on, but the building on whose roof the woman lay. He went straight up, no one stopping him. The skylight stood open, with an iron ladder leading up. He emerged on to the roof a couple of yards from her. She sat up, pushing back hair with both hands. The scarf across her breasts bound them tight, and brown flesh bulged around it. Her legs were brown and smooth. She stared at him in silence. The boy stood grinning, foolish, claiming the tenderness he expected from her.

"What do you want?" she asked.

"I ... I came to ... make your acquaintance," he stammered, grinning, pleading with her. They looked at each other, the slight, scarlet-faced excited boy, and the serious, nearly naked woman. Then, without a word, she lay down on her brown blanket, ignoring him.

"You like the sun, do you?" he enquired of her glistening back.

Not a word. He felt panic, thinking of how she had held him in her arms, stroked his hair, brought him where he sat, lordly, in her bed, a glass of some exhilarating③ liquor he had never tasted in life. He felt that if he knelt down, stroked her shoulders, her hair, she would turn and clasp him in her arms.

He said: "The sun's all right for you, isn't it?"

She raised her head, set her chin on two small fists, "Go away," she said.

---

①aggrieved：愤愤不平
②plumbing：用测铅测
③exhilarating：提神的

He did not move. "Listen," she said, in a slow reasonable voice, where anger was kept in check, though with difficulty; looking at him, her face weary with anger, "if you get a kick① out of seeing women in bikinis, why don't you take a sixpenny bus ride to the Lido②? You'd see dozens of them, without all this mountaineering."

She hadn't understood him. He felt her unfairness pale him. He stammered③: "But I like you, I've been watching you and ..."

"Thanks," she said, and dropped her face again, turned away from him.

She lay there. He stood there. She said nothing. She had simply shut him out. He stood, saying nothing at all, for some minutes. He thought: She'll have to say something if I stay. But the minutes went past, with no sign of them in her, except in the tension of her back, her thighs, her arms—the tension of waiting for him to go.

He looked up at the sky, where the sun seemed to spin in heat; and over the roofs where he and his mates had been earlier. He could see the heat quivering where they had worked. And they expect us to work in these conditions! he thought, filled with righteous④ indignation⑤. The woman hadn't moved. A bit of hot wind blew her black hair softly; it shone, and was iridescent⑥. He remembered how he had stroked it last night.

Resentment⑦ of her at last moved him off and away down the ladder, through the building, into the street. He got drunk then, in hatred of her.

Next day when he woke the sky was grey. He looked at the wet grey and thought, vicious⑧: Well, that's fixed you, hasn't it now? That's fixed⑨ you good and proper.

①kick：（口）快感；刺激
②Lido：意大利威尼斯著名海滨浴场，这里指伦敦海德公园（HydePark）的一部分
③stammer：口吃，结巴着说出，结结巴巴地说
④righteous：正直的，正当的，正义的
⑤indignation：愤慨，义愤
⑥iridescent：彩虹色的，闪光的
⑦resentment：怨恨，愤恨
⑧vicious：恶的，不道德的，恶意的，刻毒的，堕落的，品性不端的，有错误的
⑨fixed：（口）惩罚

The three men were at work early on the cool leads, surrounded by damp drizzling① roofs where no one came to sun themselves, black roofs, slimy with rain. Because it was cool now, they would finish the job that day, if they hurried. (1963)

Questions for Discussion

1. Who are the main characters in *A Woman on a Roof* by Doris Lessing?
2. Please analyze the style and technique of *A Woman on a Roof*.
3. What is the theme for *A Woman on a Roof*?

Terms

1. Modernism
2. Stream of consciousness

---

①drizzling: 细雨的，下毛毛雨的

Reference

[1] 张伯香.英美文学选读[M].北京:外语教学与研究出版社,1999.
[2] 刘炳善.英国文学简史[M].郑州:河南人民出版社,2007.
[3] 张伯香,张文.英美文学简明教程学习指南[M].武汉:华中科技大学出版社,2015.
[4] 来安方.新编英美概况[M].郑州:河南人民出版社,2010.
[5] 刘守兰.英美名诗解读[M].上海:上海外语教育出版社,2006.
[6] 姜涛.英国文学经典教程[M].南京:东南大学出版社,2011.
[7] 刁克利.英美文学欣赏[M].北京:中国人民大学出版社,2003.
[8] 刘存波.英美文学史及作品选读[M].北京.高等教育出版社,2006.
[9] 刁克利.英国文学经典选读[M].北京:外语教学与研究出版社,2008.
[10] 王蕾,陆燕敏.英国文学选读[M].天津:天津大学出版社,2007.
[11] 刘炳善.《英国文学简史》笔记和考研真题详解[M].北京:中国石化出版社,2011.
[12] 吴伟仁.英国文学史及选读[M].北京:外语教学与研究出版社,2002.
[13] 王守仁.英国文学选读[M].北京:高等教育出版社,2002.
[13] 侯维瑞.英国文学通史[M].上海:上海外语教育出版社,1999.
[14] 陈嘉.英国文学史[M].北京:商务印书馆,1981.
[15] 李赋宁.英国中古时期文学史[M].北京:外语教学与研究出版社,2000.
[16] 王佐良,何其莘.英国文艺复兴时期文学史[M].北京:外语教学与研究出版社,2000.
[17] 吴景荣,刘意青.英国十八世纪文学史[M].北京:外语教学与研究出版社,2000.
[18] 钱青.英国十九世纪文学史[M].北京:外语教学与研究出版社,2000.
[19] 王佐良.英国二十世纪文学史[M].北京:外语教学与研究出版社,2000.
[20] 李正栓.英国文学学习指南[M].北京:清华大学出版社,2006.
[21] 张伯香.英美文学教程学习指南[M].武汉:武汉大学出版社,2006.
[22] 王佐良.英国诗歌选集[M].上海:上海译文出版社,2012.
[22] 周永启.英诗200首赏译[M].海口:海南出版社,2003.

[23]　ABRAMS M H. A glossary of literary terms [M]. Beijing:Foreign Language Teaching and Research Press, 2006.

[25]　NORTON. The Norton anthology American literature [M]. Shorter 4th ed. London:W. W. Norton & Company,1995.